The Haunted Heist

The Southern
Ghost Hunter
Mysteries
Book 3

NEW YORK TIMES BESTSELLING AUTHOR

ANGIE FOX

This is a work of fiction. Names, characters, organizations, places, events, and incidents are either products of the author's imagination or are used fictitiously.

The Haunted Heist
Copyright 2016 by Angie Fox

This edition published by arrangement with Moose Island Publishing.

Moose Island Books

First Edition

ISBN-13: 978-1-939661-35-7

More Books from Angie Fox

The Southern Ghost Hunter series
Southern Spirits
The Skeleton in the Closet
The Haunted Heist

The Accidental Demon Slayer series
The Accidental Demon Slayer
The Dangerous Book for Demon Slayers
A Tale of Two Demon Slayers
The Last of the Demon Slayers
My Big Fat Demon Slayer Wedding
Beverly Hills Demon Slayer
Night of the Living Demon Slayer

The Monster MASH series
Immortally Yours
Immortally Embraced
Immortally Ever After

Short Story Collections
A Little Night Magic
So I Married a Demon Slayer
The Real Werewives of Vampire County

Want an email when the next book comes out?
Sign up for Angie's new release alerts at
www.angiefox.com

Chapter One

I kept both hands on the soaking wet skunk in my kitchen sink while a small tsunami of water sloshed over the front of my pink sweater set and white jeans. Bath time wasn't Lucy's favorite recreational activity, and by extension it wasn't mine, either. As I readjusted my grip, she braced her back legs for a wild leap onto the counter.

"Lucy," I admonished, nudging an eggshell off her petite, velvety ear, "it wasn't my idea for you to go digging in the compost bin."

She grunted and wriggled while I slid her into a soft mound of soap bubbles and washed day-old banana off her cheeks.

My little girl loved fruit and would take it any way she could get it.

"You're almost done," I told her, rinsing the double white stripe on her back with the hand spout while she tried to eat a soap bubble.

I nearly had her calm when the spirit of my gangster housemate shimmered into view next to me. Frankie "The German" appeared in black and white, like an old movie, but I could see through him. Almost. Lucy jerked at the presence of the ghost and launched into a rolling twist that soaked me to my elbows.

"Lucille Désirée Long," I warned, regaining my grip on her.

Frankie smoothed his 1920s-style pinstripe suit and straightened his fat tie. His long face and sharp nose made him appear every bit the utterly ruthless gangster he had been when he was alive. It would have scared me if I didn't know him.

"We got company." The ghost cocked his head, and I heard the faint crunch of gravel. "A black sedan creeping down the side drive."

Strange. "I wasn't expecting anyone."

"I got this," he said, shoulders stiffening as he drew a revolver out of his coat pocket.

"Frankie, wait—"

It was eight in the morning. I doubted we were under attack.

Frankie ducked through the back wall and out onto the porch. Lucy used my split second of distraction to break for the counter. She made it halfway across before I snagged a clean towel off the kitchen island and captured her behind the toaster.

I snuggled my skunk close and towel dried her fur as I peeked out the window over the sink.

A black Mercedes parked out back. My friend Lauralee sat in the passenger seat.

Frankie holstered his gun when he saw her exit the car. I gripped my skunk a little tighter when Lauralee's uncle Reggie, the big-time banker, emerged from the driver's side.

Here I stood, drenched in skunk water, with one of the most powerful men in Sugarland about to knock on my door.

Lauralee had seen me at my worst, but Reggie was another matter. He'd never encountered me in anything more casual than a summer dress at a picnic.

I set Lucy down on the floor. Her wet fur stood out at all angles around her scrawny little body. She appeared half her usual size when wet.

"Oh my, sweetie. We've got to fix this," I told her. Not her hair or mine. Those were lost causes. But I could still put the last of the coffee on and then raid the laundry room for a dry sweater. I was on my way to dig through my laundry pile of limited options when a horrible sight stopped me in my tracks.

In all the excitement, it had quite slipped my mind that a huge black outdoor trash can occupied the space where my kitchen table used to stand. Worse, rich garden dirt filled it to the brim and provided a home for one very large, teetering, heirloom red rosebush.

How to explain… I chewed my lip as my guests started up the walk.

I certainly couldn't tell them the truth: that I'd trapped the spirit of a long-dead gangster in my house and that this was part of our attempt to free him. Lauralee might understand if I could convince her ghosts were real. But Reggie would think I'd lost my mind. He was respectable, proper. He'd come back home from Chicago to take over the oldest bank in town. And if he told another soul in Sugarland, my secret would be out before suppertime.

There simply had to be a way to handle this.

I'd hide it in the parlor.

Curling my fingers around the edge of the trash can, I pulled hard. It slid…a bit. It was heavier than I'd imagined. I gritted my teeth, wincing as my arm stretched half out of its socket while I dragged the can one foot, two feet, almost three…

"Where do you think you're going with that?" Frankie demanded.

"We have to hide…you," I said, having no time to sugarcoat it. It was either that or reveal his final resting place to my guests. Then I'd have to somehow explain that I'd mistaken Frankie's urn for a dirty old vase and dumped his ashes out into my rosebushes, grounding him on my property. And that we'd moved him inside for safekeeping. "Please step aside." I could walk through him, but it would give both of us an icy shock.

"I ain't going anywhere." He removed his white Panama hat. "Those are my ashes you're messing with." He pointed his hat at the mess. "My urn."

Heavens to Betsy, we'd left his urn nestled at the bottom of the rosebush.

I met Frankie trash-can-to-hips, eye-to-eye, trying not to let my gaze wander to the neat, round bullet hole smack dab in the middle of his pasty white forehead. He hadn't gotten it by being a nice guy. "Please, Frankie," I said, praying he had a sliver of gentleman in him, "I'm not ready to explain this to company."

"You don't got much of a choice. That can ain't budging." Frankie glided toward the back wall while I took hold of the trash can and pulled with all my might until I succeeded in tugging it into the parlor.

Except the parlor held my only piece of furniture suitable for entertaining company—a purple velvet couch I'd gotten in exchange for solving a ghostly problem.

Frankie shoved his head through the back wall and whistled. "Smokes. Get a load of that sharp suit."

"Frankie!" I protested. "You're not helping."

He didn't even bother to take his head out of the wall. "You know I can't move anything on the mortal plane."

That wasn't the point. I put my butt to the can and

pushed backward, nudging it toward an out-of-the-way corner. It slid two feet, then two more, probably leaving a mud spot on my white pants. Nobody but me could see Frankie, and if I could just get rid of the evidence…

"The big cheese is coming up the porch steps," Frankie called. "Spit-shined shoes. Ritzy watch. I like his style," he added, almost to himself. "What do you suppose he wants with you?"

My sneakers slipped on the hardwood. Dirt spilled from the top of the can. I'd barely made it past the fireplace.

"Your friend's carrying a box. They're at the door now."

No.

A knock sounded. We were out of time.

The lower branches of the rosebush flopped toward my face as I forced the can back against the wall by the antique marble fireplace in the parlor. In one smooth move, I grabbed the bedsheet from the futon and tossed it over the rosebush. "There."

"That looks worse," Frankie said.

It would have to do.

I frantically brushed dirt from my white jeans and wet sweater, and tried to pat down my hair as I hurried to answer the door. Lucy, who loved visitors, ran from the main hallway to join me. She grunted with excitement, her scraggly little body churning with each step.

Oh, to be a skunk without a mirror.

I opened the door and tried for my most carefree smile. "Good morning!"

Lauralee wore basic black jeans and a long-sleeved top. She'd tied her auburn hair into a simple ponytail. The style of the day was obviously casual, yet she took one look at me and launched into an apology. "Oh, Verity, I should have called."

"Don't say that." She was my best friend on this earth. Yes, I'd made sure we'd gotten together at her place instead of mine since I'd moved Frankie's remains—and the rosebush they surrounded—into my kitchen, but that didn't mean she should feel like she had to make an appointment to visit. "I was just giving Lucy a bath," I said, waving them inside, silently pleading for them to stay in the kitchen.

"It's my fault," Reggie said, shaking my hand warmly as he entered my home. "I surprised Lauralee and now we're surprising you." His gray-brown hair had thinned over the years, and I respected the fact that he hadn't tried to style it funny to hide that. His fine gray suit spoke of quality, as did the genteel monogram on his left shirt cuff.

Still, underneath the fancy clothing I could see the same Uncle Reggie who manned the grill at my friend's big family events. Maybe it was his blue tie with whimsical embroidered hunting dogs or the twinkle in his eye. "I dropped by Lauralee's to take her out to breakfast," he said. "She's always the one cooking and she deserves to have someone make her a good meal once in a while."

My friend beamed at the appreciation shown by her uncle and held up a small baker's box for me. "I'd just finished sugaring a batch of homemade doughnuts. I thought you might like a fresh treat." She gave an embarrassed shrug. "Sorry."

"Don't be," I said, accepting the goodies. Lauralee was a whiz in the kitchen. "It's really sweet of you. I will appreciate each and every one of them."

Meanwhile, my skunk tried to climb one of Reggie's pant legs.

"My apologies," I said, depositing the donuts on the kitchen island and going to fetch her.

"Friendly little minx, isn't she?" Reggie reached down to give my skunk a benevolent scratch between the ears. "I've heard so much about you, Lucy. Nice to finally meet you." She buried her forehead against his palm and rubbed him back, causing him to chuckle. "I'd almost forgotten how friendly everyone is down South, even the wildlife." He gave her one last pat and straightened, his eyes scanning my simple home. He made no mention of the empty rooms or the sharp outlines on the antique wallpaper where family portraits once hung, but he'd have to be blind not to notice.

Life had changed for me recently.

Lauralee eyed her uncle. "I told you Virginia Wydell went after Verity," she said, her voice chilly.

"I've made my own choices," I reminded her. I was the one who called off my wedding to the favored son of the most powerful family in three counties. His mother had just seen that I paid for it.

Lucy headed for the couch in my parlor and Reggie followed. Oh my goodness.

"How's the graphic design business going?" he asked genially, no doubt thinking he was redirecting the conversation to a better place.

"I have high hopes," I said, rushing to intercept my skunk.

My work had been in demand until my almost-mother-in-law had used her considerable influence in town to bring an end to my business.

I managed to snag Lucy, but Reggie continued on into my parlor.

"Why do wet animals always go for the couch?" he asked as he stood under the gaping hole where a centuries-old chandelier had once hung.

Reggie's gaze traveled over the used couch to the rumpled futon huddled against the opposite corner. You'd think from his pleasant demeanor that he stood in the queen's chambers. But then he spotted my sheet-draped secret.

"What have you got here?" he asked, heading straight for it.

"You don't want to—" I began.

He ripped off the sheet before I could stop him.

Lauralee gasped. "Is that one of the rosebushes from outside?"

"I can explain," I said quickly.

Only I couldn't.

Reggie tucked the sheet around the back of the bush and turned to me, the corner of his mouth quirking up. "I like it. Art should make a statement," he declared.

Lauralee touched my shoulder. "Are you all right?"

"I'm fine," I assured her.

Meanwhile her uncle took another look at the rosebush in the trash can. "Maybe you should add a trellis."

Frankie shimmered into view next to the banker. "Nobody touches it," he warned.

"It's a work in progress," I said, eyeing the gangster.

"You should display it," Reggie suggested, fingering a particularly robust bloom, "even if you're still tinkering. The flowers are pretty. So is the urn. Paint the trash can pink and the whole piece is even more feminine."

Frankie looked ready to punch him.

Reggie walked right past the gangster and lowered himself onto the couch, his arms spread over the back. "That's why I love this town. People are people. You wouldn't see a rosebush like that in Chicago."

Lauralee didn't seem convinced. "You know, Verity could really use a freelance design job," she said, joining him on the couch. "I'll bet you could hire her at the bank."

I cringed a little at her forwardness. I'd never been good at selling myself, especially to an old family friend who might not even be in need of my services.

But Reggie merely rubbed his chin. "That's not a bad idea. I'm redoing all of the bank's branding. We need brochures, advertising, everything. I'd be glad to see what you can do."

"I've worked for banks before," I said quickly, hoping he was serious.

This could save my hide. Return my business to respectability. Everybody admired the local boy who'd made good, and if he hired me, that would be like an endorsement.

"She's really talented," Lauralee said, as if putting me to work were as inevitable as the sun rising or a skunk leaping headfirst into a pile of day-old banana peels. "Nobody's given her a chance since Virginia started gunning for her."

Reggie snorted. "I'm not afraid of Virginia Wydell," he stated, as if challenging us to feel the same. "And I do need someone to" — he eyed the rosebush by my fireplace — "think outside the box."

"I can do that," I promised. My ghostly adventures had sure taught me the benefits of unconventional thinking.

Lucy wriggled out of my arms and hurried to sit at Reggie's feet like a loyal dog, as if she knew which side her bread was buttered on.

Even if I only designed a few brochures, it would pay for food. And skunk snacks. I could stop living on ramen noodles or trying to make a box of cereal and a bunch of bananas stretch out a week. I could add a few things to my rotating wardrobe of three very cute, gently used winter sweaters.

I stared in horror as my mess of a skunk reared back to jump into Reggie's lap.

"Lucy!" I grabbed her the second before she leaped.

Reggie barked out a laugh. "Look at this. Artsy and quick on her feet." He scooped Lucy out of my arms. "She's okay. I don't mind a bit of wet," he said, cradling her close. Lucy preened as he gave her a belly rub and set her back down on the floor. She nudged his ankle with her nose and rested a cheek on his shoe. "Well, we've imposed quite enough. Laura-lee and I should head to breakfast and leave you in peace." He checked his watch. "I have a meeting at ten. Come by the bank at eleven fifteen and show me what you've got."

"That sounds perfect," I told him.

He bent and gently removed Lucy from his shoe, giving her one last stroke behind the ear as he did.

"Thanks for the opportunity," I added as he crossed my parlor in long, easy strides.

"Glad to do it, Verity." He paused at the door. "We all deserve a second chance."

CHAPTER TWO

This could be my big break.

Frankie hovered in the doorway as I knelt on the hardwood floor and sorted through the finished brochures, ads, and other samples I kept in my otherwise empty upstairs bedroom. Reggie would not regret giving me this chance. I'd make sure of it.

I located my original presentation boards for Greenville Bank. While I would have normally shown Reggie my finished pieces on a computer, my broken Mac sat on the top shelf of my closet. Good thing, or I would have had to sell it. Hopefully, Reggie would rather hold the work in his own two hands. He seemed the type.

Frankie huffed. "I gotta admit I wasn't sure about that guy. But now?" He gave a low whistle. "What a break! I haven't been to the First Sugarland since I tried to rob it back in '33."

I separated the print ads from the website mockups. "I'm not taking you."

"Don't even start," he said, leveling a finger in my direction. "This is the first interesting place you've been in a month."

A sliver of guilt cut through me. Before I'd trapped him, he'd had the run of the world. Now he couldn't go anywhere unless I brought his urn along.

"I took you to the flower market last week," I offered, straightening a stack.

He opened his arms. "Why?" he pleaded, a bit impatient for my taste.

I stood with my work. "You said you wanted to see some girls with long stems."

The gangster rubbed his eyes. "That's not what I meant and you know it," he ground out as the temperature in the room dropped.

"Please don't give me a cold spot." Not while I still wore my damp sweater. I placed my presentation in the worn leather satchel I'd saved from college. "I'm trying to look normal, businesslike. I can't walk in there with your urn clanking in my purse."

If I'd been going anywhere else, I would have been glad to take him along.

Frankie had the power to show me the supernatural world. With his help, I'd been able to see and interact with some of the ghosts here in town. We'd saved my house; we'd solved a murder. Two of them, actually. We'd made some positive changes in Sugarland, not that he cared about helping anyone but himself. And I had been trying to free him. It was just that nothing had worked yet.

"You don't know what it's like." He rubbed the back of his neck. "This is like cabin fever on top of house arrest."

"We'll fix it," I promised him, slinging the bag over my shoulder. After our last adventure, everything had changed. A wise ghost had told us the secret: We needed to find the one thing Frankie loved above all else. If we buried that object with his urn and ashes, he would be free.

The gangster smirked and brushed some imaginary

lint off the sleeves of his suit jacket. "Well, it just so happens that I need to go to the bank to find what I love most."

"Amazing coincidence," I said, heading down the stairs.

"It's true," he said, completely unaffected by my attempt at sarcasm. "Me and the South Town Gang was tunneling into the vault in the basement of the First Sugarland Bank the day before I died," he said, as if he were telling me a bedtime story. "For all I know, Suds is still down there. If I could find him, he might know what happened to my favorite gun after I got shot."

"You already have a gun," I said, reaching the bottom of the stairs.

"Aha." He held up a finger. "See. That's not my favorite gun."

Sakes alive. I turned all the way around to face him. "Frankie, I can't take a gangster into a bank." It was a recipe for trouble.

Frankie sniffed and straightened his shoulders. "It's been three months. Three. And my dirt is still living in your kitchen. I know you got banged up on our last little adventure, but you're recovered now. What's it gonna take to get you to find my gun?" He stared at me as I thought. "I could have a real chance here," he added.

He said it like he believed it. "You truly think your favorite gun can set you free?"

"It's my lucky gun. I didn't go anywhere without it," he insisted. "It saved my life more than a few times, and I was holding onto it for dear life right before I died. That's love. I need to know what happened to it."

It wasn't love, it was crazy talk. I couldn't believe

I was actually going for this. But he seemed sincere, and I did want to help. "Okay," I said quickly before I could change my mind. "I'll take you to the bank." I ignored his shout of victory. And the fist pump. "You can talk to Suds." If he was even there. "You can even try to rob the place." Frankie couldn't actually touch the money anyhow. "But you cannot disturb me during my meeting."

Frankie shot me a broad grin. "Believe me, I've got bigger fish to fry."

Fine by me. Just as long as Reggie's bank wasn't on the menu.

***

I placed Frankie's urn in my brown hemp bag. Then, we headed out on Route 9 and stopped by my sister's place.

She wasn't home, but I raided her closet anyway. Melody usually wore a size smaller than me in clothes and shoes, but I managed to squeeze into a sleek, professional navy blue pencil dress and found a pair of black pumps that worked. I used her hair dryer and her curling iron, and when I slipped on the matching blazer, you couldn't even tell the dress didn't zip all the way up the back. It appeared stylish and entirely appropriate, so I considered it a victory.

Even if I couldn't quite feel my toes.

Lauralee's uncle might have overlooked my odd house and wet self, but I'd show him how well I cleaned up.

After all, in the South, lots of folks don't mind crazy, but I didn't think Bank President Reggie Thompson would want to hire it.

Frankie leaned back in the passenger seat of my

1978 avocado-green Cadillac as we cut down Main
Street and headed toward the town square.

He eyed me, his arm braced on the bench seat between us. "You sure are stoked about working for the
Man."

"My bank account has only eighty-seven dollars
and twelve cents in it." And I didn't have anything
else to sell.

Frankie dug around in his pocket and pulled out a
silver cigarette case. "Too bad gin's legal these days.
You'd make good money brewing that."

"Be serious. I'm an artist." I tightened my grip on
the steering wheel. "It's the only thing I know how
to do really well." Which meant I needed this opportunity even more. Reggie's plan to redesign all of
the bank's printed materials could provide a steady
stream of work, a respectable income.

He snapped the case closed. "You could stand to
learn some new skills," Frankie said, as if it were as
easy as that. He held a cigarette to his mouth and
struck a ghostly match. "There's decent cash to be
made in extortion, protection," he said, lighting up.

"Don't you dare smoke in my car," I said. He took a
puff. I couldn't smell the smoke at all, but it bugged
me on principle. "Roll down the window." Frankie
shot me a pained look, and I remembered he couldn't
touch anything on the physical plane. At least he had
the decency to stick his hand through the glass and let
the ghostly smoke trail outside the car.

"I'm not a criminal," I reminded him, slowing for a
group of women crossing the street to the café.

"Yet," he corrected, as if it were something to be
achieved. He took a long drag off his smoke. "I'll dig
up some whopper secrets on these shop owners. I'll
teach you how to do some nice blackmail. You can get

as creative as you like."

"Absolutely not." I turned into the main square, glad to see a few parking spots left near the front of the bank. In case he missed the memo, "I don't need your help."

He huffed, settling back in his seat. "That's not what you said the last time you got in trouble." He took another drag. "Frankie, show me this. Frankie, show me that."

"And I thank you sincerely," I told him, meaning every word. He truly had helped me in my time of need. "But I'm ready to move on and be respectable." I enjoyed making a difference when given the chance, but I also had a real life to live and I didn't intend to spend most of it on the ghostly plane.

"Fine. I don't need to be leading you around all the time," Frankie muttered, and for the first time I wondered if my sputtering career revival bothered him. It would mean spending less time with him, not relying on him. I hadn't asked the ghost for so much as a peek at the other side since our last adventure.

"Did you actually enjoy ghost hunting with me?" I teased, wondering if he'd ever admit it.

"The shoot-outs weren't bad," he muttered, his brow furrowed and his jaw ground tight. He might actually be pouting, I realized, as I homed in on a parking spot.

The First Bank of Sugarland stood near the center of the town square, as it had for the past one hundred and fourteen years.

It had been constructed at a time when society valued its craftspeople. Every door and window had been treated like a work of art, with impressive red brick facades and white limestone accents. A white cupola with an aged bronze roof crowned the historical building. After a lifetime of seeing it on an almost daily basis, it still impressed me.

"I miss some of the ghosts I met," I admitted. "I'd love to see Josephine and Matthew, but I have my life and they have their own...afterlives. It's better for all of us if I focus on the land of the living."

The gangster glanced over his shoulder to the neatly kept grassy square behind us as I eased into a parking spot in front of the bank. "So I'm supposing you don't want to know about the ghost in your backseat."

I almost rammed the curb. "That's not funny."

"Who said I'm joking?" Frankie asked, his attention drawn to the empty area behind us. "Lookie here, it's Lieutenant Brown, a son of Sugarland who defended our town from the Yankee invasion. Oh wait. Forget it. You don't care about that stuff no more."

It was difficult to say if he was teasing or not. The only thing I observed was a velvet backseat that had seen better days. And while it was tempting to meet someone new and fascinating...

The clock tower on City Hall next door began to chime eleven o'clock. That was my cue.

I shoved the car into park and cut the engine. "Let's turn over a new leaf," I said, getting out of my car.

He stayed where he was, having an animated conversation with...thin air.

Only I knew better.

And I'd almost forgotten my work samples.

"Hey," Frankie said as I gathered my portfolio from the center of the front seat. He hitched a thumb toward the empty seat behind him. "Did you know he fought at Mossy Creek? I always wanted to shoot a—" I slammed the car door.

"It doesn't matter," I told myself. I had a normal, respectable life ahead of me. With any luck, it would start at the First Sugarland Bank.

I took a deep, bracing breath, confident that I was fifteen minutes early and dressed well.

The sun shone bright, but the temperature hadn't broken forty degrees. I'd left my coat at home because let's just say the one I found at the thrift shop wasn't the kind of thing you'd wear to a business meeting or a bank or anywhere you wanted to be seen. In fact, I planned to sell it back as soon as possible.

No matter. This morning, I'd walk with confidence. I let the chilly wind hit me and focused on the good.

I had some amazing work to show the president of the bank. If this job panned out, I'd dust off my credit card, pay to fix my Mac, and get back to my old way of life.

In the meantime...I placed one foot in front of the other.

"You just walked right through the lieutenant's horse," Frankie said from behind me as I approached the three stone steps that led up to the polished mahogany doors of the bank.

"I can't feel a thing," I said, which was wonderful. When I tuned in to the ghostly plane, touching them gave me an icky feeling.

"Good, because you don't want to see what you just stepped in."

"I don't even want to see you right now," I told the ghost gliding next to me.

He cocked his head toward a stairway that led down to the basement of the bank. "Fine. I can take a hint." He eyed the thick foundation that separated us from the rooms underneath First Sugarland. "I always wondered how close the boys got to that vault in 1933."

"Why don't you go check on that?" I asked. Anything to get him out of my hair and keep my head clear.

"No sweat," he said, heading down that way. "Now I wish I had some explosives," he added, disappearing through the limestone foundation.

It wasn't my problem anymore. Nothing on the ghostly plane could touch me, I assured myself as I entered the busy bank lobby.

Chapter Three

Teller windows lined the back of the high-ceilinged room, and a carved mahogany table stood at the center, ready with deposit slips, pens, and anything else customers might need.

The place smelled like old wood and fresh popcorn, just like it had when I came here with my mom as a child. Of course, my eyes were drawn to the reception desk at the front, and the red and white striped popcorn cart parked beside it.

Today it was manned by Reggie's daughter, Em. She sighed as she piled the fluffy kernels into bags, her blond hair slicked back into a fancy twist, her diamond earrings sparkling in the light of the original brass lamp fixtures.

She turned and placed a bag of yummy-looking popcorn into a basket on her desk as I approached.

"Hi, Em. Smells great," I told her, resisting the urge to snag a treat. Maybe I'd slip one into my bag after the meeting, as a reward.

She snorted. "Three hundred calories' worth of delicious butter substitute," she said airily. She began shoveling popcorn into another bag. "Might as well tape it to your butt and skip a step."

I didn't quite know what to say to that.

On the upside, this was the most Reggie's daughter had spoken to me in years. Whenever I ran into her at Lauralee's holiday events, she usually just played on her phone.

"Well, it's nice to see you back in town," I said, trying to steer the conversation in a more positive direction. "I'm sure you'll get to meet a lot of people, working here at the bank."

She gazed at me from beneath heavy lids. "Yes. I'm the greeting peon. Mother would be so proud."

I couldn't decide if she was desperately unhappy or just a jerk. Maybe both. Either way I wouldn't hold it against her; the poor girl had been through a lot. "I was so sorry to hear about your mother's passing."

Her expression softened. "Thanks." Then her defenses snapped back into place. "She'd die all over again if she knew I was working in this backwater dump."

I felt my smile go wooden. It was one thing to have a bad couple of days or even years, but to disrespect my town? "Bless your heart," I said, stepping past her desk, determined to end this conversation on a civil note.

She gave me a quizzical look, as if she didn't quite understand this facet of Southern social manners, but I was saved from an uncomfortable exit when Reggie's voice boomed across the lobby. "Verity!" he called, as if I were a close friend. As folks said, Reggie Thompson had never met a stranger.

He shook my hand warmly. "I neglected to ask you this morning. How's your mother?"

This seemed to be the standard Sugarland greeting for anyone old enough to have been a customer at my childhood lemonade stand. "Mom's great," I told him. "She and my stepdad have their RV parked in Winter

Haven, Florida."

"Tell her I said hello and that I miss her strawberry peach pie." He grinned. "That was some extraordinary baking your mom did. Every church bake sale, I'd snap one up." He led me toward the back of the bank. "My office is this way. Come on back." He opened up a nine-foot-tall door near the teller windows. "After you."

I slowed as I admired the portraits of past bank presidents lining the hall. I'd never been back this way. "It must be wonderful to be able to come back to town and take charge of a piece of Sugarland history," I told him, my heels clicking against the original pink marble floor. "There's a steadiness to this place, a sense of tradition."

Reggie nodded. "It's good to be home."

Stan, the bank manager, eased down the narrow hallway behind us. "Excuse me," he said, stroking his mustache.

"You shaved off your beard," I said. Stan, who had graduated high school a few years ahead of me, had always been clean-shaven until last year when he'd grown a hipster beard and mustache.

Stan gave a small shrug and a conspiratorial wink. "Reggie didn't like the Fu Manchu style."

"When the Secretary of the Treasury starts wearing one, you can too," Reggie joked.

Stan glanced to the portrait of Cotton P. Cutshaw, first president of the First Bank, who sported a handlebar mustache. "Maybe I should grow one of those," Stan commented as Reggie frowned. The young manager gave a quick grin. "Maybe not. If you'll excuse me, I have to go see what security needs downstairs."

Reggie took a deep breath. "It's for his own good,"

he said, loud enough for Stan to hear. He glanced toward the lobby. "He's just stubborn, like EmmaJane."

"EmmaJane?" I asked, not quite sure whom he meant.

"My daughter," he said, leading me to the office closest to the stairway and holding the door open for me. "Her mother and I named her EmmaJane. So that's what I'm calling her now that we're home. Believe me, she's not happy about it."

"I don't imagine so." You couldn't just force a girl to change her name.

Or perhaps you could if you were Reggie.

"She'll be fine," he said, not worried in the least. His office was large, with wood-paneled walls and ornate plasterwork on the high ceiling. "EmmaJane's a good girl, but she's had it too easy." Reggie stepped around his imposing wood desk to take a seat in the tall red leather chair behind it while I tucked myself into the guest chair. Behind him loomed the tall, wood-trimmed side windows of the bank. He rested his elbows on his desk. "Her mother and I spoiled her, but that's all over now. I told her we're going back to her roots. She's going to earn her salary at this bank. No more credit cards or freeloading. She's going to work hard and live simple."

"So she wants to be a banker," I said, pulling out my work samples. "That's nice."

Reggie leaned back in his chair, the leather crackling under him. "She doesn't want to be anything."

"Ah," I said, placing my samples on the desk in front of him.

He eyed me carefully, as if he knew he was about to cross a line but planned to forge ahead anyway. "Maybe you and Lauralee can take her out sometime. Show her how to act like a nice Southern girl."

Oh my. "That's a lovely idea," I said, refusing to commit.

Truth be told, I wouldn't mind helping Em feel more comfortable in Sugarland, as long as she was willing to give our town a chance. I'd consider it a victory if she could learn to love it like I did. What I didn't like was the idea of a person as a project. It had to be her choice.

In the meantime, I showed Reggie a project of my own: the custom branding work I'd done for Greenville Bank. I also presented the more conservative brochures and overall business design I'd done for J&B Financial Advisors. By the time Reggie finished sharing his vision and we started discussing ideas for the First Bank of Sugarland, he was already nodding at every point I made.

"Yep. Still precise. Still focused." He glanced up. "Just like when you ran home and got me a nickel when you didn't have exact change at your grandma's peach stand."

I paused over my designs. "You remember that?"

"I remember everything." He leaned forward as if to share a secret. "I'm good because I pay attention to the people I surround myself with. I don't waste time, either, so I'll put it to you plain. I've got five big projects coming up and I'll hire you for every one of them if you can handle the workload. It'll be more than full time to start."

My brain flooded with a big, loud yes as the relief of a hundred hours of worry rolled off my shoulders. I was back in business. I could buy groceries. Coffee. Heat the house to seventy degrees.

I felt lighter. I stood taller. This meant…everything. I wanted to hug him. "Thank you so much," I said, grinning so wide it almost hurt.

"You're asking too little as an hourly, though." His eyes darted to a place over my head. "Lauralee is making the same mistake with her catering. Kills me that she won't fix that." His attention returned to me. "But I can do something about you. You need to be asking fifty percent more from each of your clients."

My one client. "Well, you see, I'm still trying to attract business—"

"Do it," he said, brooking no argument, "because that's what I'm going to pay you and I don't like to be overcharged."

"Okay," I said, appreciating his generosity, but not crazy about being told how to run my business.

Reggie seemed to read my mood. "Don't worry, Verity. You'll get that and more once everybody sees the work you're going to do for me." He clasped his hands together on the desk between us. "Never undervalue your time or what you do. It's the biggest mistake people make in business and in life."

"You do have a point." Reggie didn't get to where he was in life by being timid. Still, I wasn't a high-powered banker. I was quite happy as a small-town designer. This kind of assignment was so much more than I'd ever expected, and I'd be lying if I said I wasn't scared.

I took a deep breath to slow my racing heart. At least I wasn't chasing down ghosts anymore. This should be safe and predictable. It was banking, for goodness' sake. Any and all excitement would come from my marketing campaign. I could handle this. I pulled my notebook out of my bag. "Then let's agree to some due dates and deliverables. I can send you a cost estimate this afternoon."

The door to Reggie's office clicked open and a woman poked her head in. Her hair swung at cheek-level in a crisp, dark bob. "Sorry to break in on you, Reg."

"Carla," he said, greeting her enthusiastically, "get in here and meet my brilliant new marketing guru." Reggie leaned his elbows on the desk. "Verity here reminds me of you when you were first starting out." He grinned. "I've managed Carla's career from the time she was an intern at East Chicago Mortgage. Now she's my vice president."

"I'd love to talk in a sec," she said to me, more crisp than rude, "but, Reggie, they need you downstairs." She cringed, glancing at me as if she wished I wasn't present to hear what she had to say next. "It's happening. For real this time."

Reggie stood. "Right now?"

She nodded. "Jeb reported it less than a minute ago. Stan says if you hurry down, you can hear it for yourself."

"Great," he said, skirting around his desk. "Give me five minutes, Verity. My head guard has been claiming this bank is haunted. I told him to call me if something actually happened."

I tried to smile and failed. Whatever was going on down there, I had a feeling it had to do with my gangster buddy. Please don't let him be doing something crazy. I smoothed my skirt.

Carla noticed my discomfort as Reggie left. "It's a historic building. There are plenty of other explanations for the noise," she assured me.

"Naturally," I said, although I didn't believe that for a second.

She folded her hands in front of her slim-fitting, black sheath dress. "All the same, we would appreciate it if you didn't spread the ghost story around town."

"Your secret is safe with me," I assured her, quietly

and efficiently adjusting my bag on the floor, making sure Frankie's urn was safely hidden. "Ghost sightings are a regular occurrence in the South." Especially for me.

"All those old Southern belles and Civil War soldiers?" she teased. "Up in Chicago, we probably had gangsters."

I wasn't even going to touch that one.

Stan paused in the open doorway behind her. "It's freezing cold down there. And you're not going to believe the—"

She held up a finger to me and drew Stan out into the hall.

Frankie was never coming to work with me again. Even if he hadn't started the problem, he was exactly the type to make it worse. What had I been thinking, taking him to a bank? Especially the one he'd been trying to rob when he died?

"...in the vault," I heard Stan murmur.

Ah, yes. The vault—where my ghost buddy went as soon as I let him out of my sight.

I reached for my bag on the floor. I could just leave. Then Frankie would have to go with me.

Of course, then I'd be crazy Verity walking out on Reggie while no one was looking.

I turned back toward the desk. Darn it. I wouldn't put it past Frankie to help one of his old buddies pull off a heist in the middle of my business meeting.

Reggie had given me a second chance, and in return, I'd given him a full paranormal experience downstairs.

Calm down. I blew out a breath and waited for one long minute. Then another. Maybe it would be all right. Maybe—

A loud metallic scrape echoed from the basement.

I had to go. I'd tell Carla…something.

I walked out into the hall to catch her, but Stan and Carla were nowhere to be seen. The corridor and the steps leading down to the underground level stood empty.

Okay. I smoothed my sweaty palms on the skirt of my dress as I forced myself to walk slowly back to my seat. I straightened my stack of work samples. Everything would be fine. Reggie would return soon. Knowing him, he'd enjoy telling the story.

A bloodcurdling scream echoed from the floor below. A live woman's scream, and she sounded desperate.

My samples scattered as I raced out of the room and down the narrow staircase, into the marble-walled basement of the bank. To the left, near the bottom of the stairs, the immense bank vault door yawned open on its hinges.

Stan stood just beyond it, gaping. I passed him and found a panicked Carla leaning over the prone body of Reggie Thompson. "Call the ambulance! Call the ambulance!" she wailed. My stomach lurched. It was too late for an ambulance. There was no helping the banker now.

He wore a look of horror, his eyes wide open, blood pooling around his torso. He'd been shot in the heart. His right cheek had a bloody X slashed into it. And he seemed to be staring straight at me.

Chapter Four

Oh, God. Not again.

A silver-haired security guard walked up behind us. Jeb had worked at the bank for as long as I remembered. "I called the paramedics." He rested a hand on his gun belt. "Won't do any good." His mouth turned down, the heavy set of his jowls deepening. "Reggie's gone."

Carla went rigid.

"Let's hope for the best," I fudged, in a vain attempt to protect her, as if I could change what had happened.

Calmly, and with a stoicism I hadn't known I possessed, I kept my breathing steady and ignored the gut-deep urge to beat feet out of there. I tried not to look at Reggie's prone form or at Carla's narrow, shaking shoulders.

My impulse to run wasn't just part of my distress at finding Reggie this way. The air was at least ten degrees cooler inside the old bank vault, and an unsettling desperation drummed like a heartbeat. No doubt the space was haunted. With what, I had no idea.

Steel sheeting and modern fluorescent lights stretched over the ceiling. Ornate bronze safety-deposit boxes lined the walls to either side, and directly

ahead stood a modern steel safe that took up the entire back wall. There were no dark corners, no creepy
shadows. Even so, this place felt more wrong every
second I spent inside of it.

"Did any of you see what happened?" I asked. We
were standing in the spot where a murderer had
struck minutes before. He couldn't have gone far.

"I know what I see now," Jeb said, eyeing me. "We
got four people downstairs and one dead body."

"You can't be sure it's only four of us," I said, ignoring his insinuation.

He stood in the rounded entryway, blocking us in.
"Pretty dang sure. I've been watching both doors
this entire time. Nobody else has come in. Nobody's
slipped out. What are you doing down here anyway?" he asked, with an almost accusatory tone.

Wasn't it obvious? "I heard someone scream."

Stan drew a hand over his face. "She was upstairs
with Reggie right before…"

Carla retreated toward me and I realized the wide
pool of blood had seeped farther across the pink
marble floor.

I took her by the arm. "Let's get out of here."

Jeb kept a keen eye on us, but he let us out of the
vault. The air warmed the second we passed the
bronze security bars and the thick round door.

"Did anyone hear the shot?" Stan asked the group.

"The vault door was closed. I found Reggie like that
when I opened it," Carla stammered.

"It's soundproof," Stan said, shoving his hands into
his pockets.

"So no one would have heard the gunshot," I concluded.

We stared at each other uncomfortably.

The guard hardened, his attention settling on the security camera posted over the vault door. "Son of a—"

"There's no red light," Carla breathed out.

"It was working when I got here this morning," Jeb insisted.

Carla reached for it. "There's a burn mark on the wall."

Jeb stopped her. "Don't. That's evidence."

"And you're saying you never took your eyes off the vault door," Carla said, her trembling voice going hard, "but the security camera blew and you didn't notice."

The guard stood woodenly. "I might have had a momentary lapse."

She drew a sharp breath. "You were outside smoking again, weren't you?"

For the first time, Jeb appeared flustered. "I stood right outside that door," he vowed. "That door's my post, and I didn't leave it. Nobody got past me. The entire time he was in that vault—"

Stan leaned close to the guard as he murmured, "Jeb, I need to head upstairs and have the tellers close down the bank for the day."

"The police can do that," Jeb ordered. "They'll be here soon. In the meantime, we need to stay put."

Just then, a slow, eerie scrape echoed from the floor of the vault.

My breath caught in my throat.

Jeb flinched before crossing his arms over his chest, as if determined to wait it out.

"I heard the same sound upstairs," I said, moving toward the glass doors that led outside. I didn't like the idea of being trapped with whatever was making that noise.

Stan shivered. "That was the ghost in the vault," he said, as if it were fact.

"Ghosts." Carla's voice hitched. She took a deep breath and let it out. "Do you realize how ridiculous that sounds?"

Jeb eyed her. "I've been hearing odd noises since I took this job in 1973, but I gotta say, in all that time I never heard nothing like the sounds coming out of that vault since Reggie blew into town."

Carla shook her head. "Please don't talk about Reggie that way."

"What kind of noise?" I pressed.

"Digging," Stan said, his gaze darting to the open vault. "Under the floor. That's what it sounds like to me, at least." He shifted uncomfortably. "Only there's at least four feet of concrete under that marble floor. No man alive could dig through that."

Jeb exchanged a glance with Stan. "Reggie believed us when we told him about the noises, but he wanted to check it out for himself. He was in there with the door shut for five minutes, maybe. Not long enough to be dangerous."

"I don't understand," I told them.

"The vault is airtight," Stan said. "Safe for a little while, but you have to watch it."

"Reggie seemed fine," Jeb insisted. "I went back over to stand by my post at the glass doors, and when Carla went to check on him" — his voice choked up — "she found him shot through the heart."

Poor Reggie. "So nobody saw anyone go in with him?"

"Where were you?" Stan asked Carla.

She stiffened. "After we finished talking, I went down to check on Reggie. He was fine, so I stepped around the corner, into one of the privacy booths, to make a phone call." She glanced back at the small hallway at the rear left side of the lobby, toward the

narrow row of old wood cells that had always reminded me of the professor's offices in the old part
of campus at college. "I wanted to be close by in case
Reggie needed me." She notched her chin up at Stan.
"What about you?"

He appeared uncomfortable as all eyes turned to
him. "Upstairs. Working." He fidgeted with his tie.
"Ask Marcie. I changed out her drawer."

"Well, if none of us are responsible, then there's
somebody else down here," Carla said, lowering her
voice as the group drew closer. "I didn't see anyone in
the privacy booths. All the doors were open."

We all turned toward the only other hiding place — a
small alcove on the right side of the lobby. The cutout
area housed a bronze drinking fountain at the back.
The ladies' and men's room doors stood opposite
each other.

Stan gave the security guard a curt nod.

Someone could be in there. Armed and dangerous.

"I'll check it out," Jeb said, drawing his gun.

He entered the men's room. I didn't know if I wanted him to find a killer or not.

Jeb emerged a short time later. His forehead shone
with perspiration. "Nothing in that one," he said.

He entered the second room and we barely had time
to brace ourselves before we heard a scream.

On instinct, I grabbed hold of the nearest person,
which happened to be Carla. She went stiff at first,
then grabbed me right back.

Moments later, Jeb emerged clutching the elbow of a
flustered Em.

I straightened and let go of Carla, suddenly feeling
rather foolish. "Em? What are you doing down here?"

"Hiding out," Jeb said grimly.

She shook him off. "Hiding where, you dolt? You

just dragged me out of the ladies' room. Wait until I tell my father." She straightened her jacket and did a quick check of her earrings. "What are you all doing standing around?"

"Oh, Em —" I began, not sure how to deliver the news.

"This is ridiculous," she interrupted, adjusting her purse over her shoulder. "I'm going out to lunch."

"There's been an accident," Carla said, instinctively glancing back toward the vault and Reggie's prone body inside.

Em followed Carla's gaze, her face falling when she saw her father's prone form.

She rushed to the open vault before anyone could stop her and let out a cry when she saw all of him.

I hurried for Em, who stood inside the rounded doorway, her hands touching over her mouth as if she were praying.

"Oh, my God," she stammered, unable to look away. Her purse dropped from her shoulder. "I — Dad is dead." I touched her on the arm and shivered at the chill clinging to her. "What does that mean? Where am I going to live?" she asked, focused on the grue-some scene in front of her. "What do I do now?"

The wail of sirens sounded outside. "The police are here," Stan called.

"It's going to be okay," I said, wrapping an arm around Em's shoulder and gathering her purse. "Step outside and wait with us."

I guided her to a small reception area by the door and helped her into one of the wingback chairs.

Em sat motionless, staring at the floor.

Jeb stood away from the group and eyed us as if he expected one of us to make a move in the time it took for the police to enter the building. I understood his caution. One of the four people with whom I was now locked downstairs was most likely an armed killer.

And only the killer knew exactly what had happened.

Unless my ghost friend had seen any of this. I searched the lobby, but caught no sign of Frankie.

Two police officers rushed down the main stairway. "Open the side entrance," they ordered.

Jeb propped open the doors to the outside.

Seconds later, paramedics pushed through, followed by Homicide Detective Pete Marshall.

The detective—who also happened to be the bane of my existence—wore a suit coat, a white shirt with what appeared to be a coffee stain, and a hard expression. "Stan." He nodded. "Jeb," he added, matter-of-fact as he followed the paramedics toward the vault. "And you," he said, eyes narrowing at me, his voice lingering in the downstairs lobby as he entered the vault.

Chapter Five

Maybe I wasn't the homicide detective's favorite person, but I didn't appreciate the withering look he gave me, as if I were something he'd have to scrape off the bottom of his shoe. No doubt he'd have plenty of questions for me, starting with the reason for my presence at Sugarland's only two murders in recent history.

This was becoming a bit of a bad habit.

Heavens. I didn't know what to make of this place or this crime or any of it.

It was time for the handsome officer Ellis Wydell to run interference for me. Only he hadn't arrived at the scene with the others. I strained to see past the three officers who entered with Marshall, hoping Ellis would walk through the door next. Not that these were the best circumstances to reunite with my almost, sort of, we were still figuring it out, boyfriend.

Instead, a young officer with a military haircut approached us. I recognized him as one of Lauralee's regulars at the diner. His name tag read Duranja. "You were all here during the time of death?" he confirmed.

Em drew a lock of hair behind her ear. "I have no idea," she said, broken.

"She was," Stan said, confirming it for her. "We

found her hiding out in the bathroom."

Em didn't move, but her features went hard.

"I was upstairs," I answered, with a nod to Carla. "I ran down when I heard her scream."

He looked to Reggie's right-hand woman. "And you screamed because?"

Carla stared him down. "I found...Reggie."

Stan gripped the back of the couch with both hands. "I was heading down when Carla screamed," he said woodenly.

"No," I countered. "I was in Reggie's office with the door open. Stan would have had to pass me to get down here, and if he was heading down the stairs when Carla screamed, I would have been right behind him. He was already downstairs when I got here."

"You gotta be kidding me," Stan protested. "Why would you say that? You think I killed him?"

"No." Maybe. "I'm only trying to understand what happened."

Duranja motioned to the officer standing outside the open vault door. "Tom, head to the top of the stairs. Make sure nobody else comes down here."

He ordered a second officer to make sure there was no one else present downstairs.

"Miss," he said, motioning to Reggie's daughter, "please come with me. The rest of you, have a seat," he ordered, motioning to the reception area. "Stay here and remain quiet. We'll need to question each of you."

Duranja led Em to the row of privacy booths that people used to view their safety-deposit boxes, the same ones that Jeb had checked. A fourth officer took up position outside the glass doors. I secured a place on the couch next to Jeb. Carla and Stan took the wingback chairs.

I crossed my legs and clasped both hands around my knee, feeling a twinge in my left shoulder. I ignored it and looked out at the crisp, winter morning, willing Ellis to walk through those doors.

Yes, I was fully aware that the entire police force couldn't be in one place, and of course he didn't realize I'd been caught up in yet another murder. But you'd think since he'd been so instrumental in solving the last killing, they'd want him on the scene this time as well.

Stan leaned forward, planting his elbows on his knees, refusing to look at me, as if I'd—well, I had sort of blown a hole in his alibi. "I wonder what they'll find in there," he murmured, glancing at the vault.

Jeb leaned forward. "I bet they find nothing. Crazy as it sounds, I'd wager cash money the ghost did it."

"That's ridiculous," Carla said to Jeb. "I can tell you what happened. You weren't paying attention and somebody snuck in and ambushed him."

"Who would attack Reggie?" I pressed. "He didn't have any enemies here that I know of. Did someone follow him down from Chicago?"

Carla blinked hard as she considered the question. "No. I can't think of anyone who would want to hurt Reg. He was one of those people that everyone liked."

Stan glanced at the hallway where the officer had disappeared. "Carla, you said yourself it felt freezing in that vault."

"I noticed it immediately," I admitted.

Just then, Marshall emerged from the vault. His ruddy nose had gone pink from the cold and his small dark eyes swept over us, taking in every detail of our small group. "You." He pointed at me. "No talking." He approached the group as I slunk back. "All of you, come with me." He motioned us toward the hallway near the back of the lobby, the one that held the privacy booths.

"I want each of you to take a room of your own and stay in there. My men will approach you one at a time for your statements."

I could see more officers coming down the steps. I hoped Ellis was among them. Marshall held me back as the rest of the group filed into the privacy rooms. "Miss Long, why are you at every scene of trouble in this town?"

"I'm unlucky, I suppose," I said, erring on the side of truth.

He sniffed in agreement. The detective considered me a pain in his behind, which was fine because I felt the same way about him. "Go find a room and wait for questioning."

I did so reluctantly, knowing that if Ellis arrived now, he'd have no way of knowing which one was mine.

We could hear Em's muffled shouts behind the closed door to the first booth. Carla took the next one, then Stan, and finally Jeb. The wood lining the hallway and the interiors of the small rooms reminded me of the walls in Reggie's office. I took the fifth and final booth in the row. It was old and small, with a built-in wood desk on the left wall, a single chair, and a frosted window that would make it impossible to see out the door.

Turned out, it was already occupied.

I gasped as I came face-to-chest with Frankie.

"What?" He straightened his tie as I stumbled back. "You act like you ain't never seen a ghost before."

"I'm a little jumpy right now," I admitted. It hadn't been the best morning.

"You see the dead guy in the vault?" he asked, as if we were making chitchat.

"Dead as in murdered or as in ghost?" I prodded, closing the door behind me. It was a shame when that was a logical question.

Frankie took it as par for the course. "The bloody banker," he said, hovering way too close in the small space.

"That's my client," I said, trying to keep my voice down.

"Was your client," Frankie said pragmatically. Then he winced in a rare moment of sympathy. "Hey, sorry about that."

The shadow of a police officer darkened the frosted glass window of the privacy booth.

"Never mind that," I whispered to him. "Did you see who killed Reggie?"

"Me?" the gangster asked, removing his Panama hat. "Nah." He scratched his head and with a flourish, replaced his hat. "The place was dead when I got down here." A smile played on the corner of one lip. "So me and the boys headed upstairs. Got a little caught up with a leggy teller named Sue."

He needed to focus. "Did you see who shorted out the security camera?"

"Nah." He shrugged. "It's not like it takes that much energy to do it," he added defensively. "We just didn't feel like it."

"So a ghost could do that?" I clarified. "This is important."

"Of course," he said, floating through the desk attached to the wall. "But my buddies and I didn't do it this morning."

"I heard something under the floor that sounded supernatural. Are you sure you didn't make any noise down here?"

He straightened his tie. "You can trust me."

That was debatable. "Can you ask your friends?"

"Aw, no. I see where this is going," he said, as if I'd planned this. As if I'd wanted it. "You said you were getting out of the ghost-talking business. You want to be an artist instead."

That didn't seem to be working out. "Earlier, I had the feeling you wanted a protégée," I told him.

He shook his head. "You're not talking about hanging out or robbing or stealing. You always want to try to save the world, and you don't think of the consequences."

"Oh, like justice, truth, fairness?" I mused.

"All pain and no gain." He held out his hands. "I'm trying to save my skin," he said, inspecting his silvery glowing limbs. "What's left of it." He dropped the cute act. "Look, the more I do this for you, the harder it is to get my energy back. I wouldn't mind it for the occasional robbery or blackmail." He drifted away from me, to the back right corner of the booth. "I need to know it's gonna be worth it."

I felt a twinge of guilt. "We're a team, right? You help me see things. I help you find your gun."

"No," he huffed. "You're trying to even a score that has nothing to do with you," he added. "You want to jump in headfirst and solve another murder. This is a guy you barely even knew."

That was where he had it wrong. "Reggie was Lauralee's uncle and I've known him my entire life. Besides, I'm not solving anything. I just want to find some clues to share with the police." It wasn't like we could ask Reggie. People didn't return in spirit form right away. Many never came back at all.

"Fine." Frankie poked his head through the door

next to mine. "Some cop is questioning the bank manager," he said. "That guy could use a few lessons in
putting on a game face."

"I don't mean spying on the police." And Stan
should be nervous. He'd lied about how long he was
downstairs. I was sure of it.

"Now that I helped you," Frankie continued as if
he hadn't heard me, "what have you actually done to
help me find what I need? You haul my urn around
like an afterthought." He stiffened. "Where is my urn,
by the way? Do you have it safe with you, or did you
leave my only mortal remains behind in some dead
guy's office?"

"I messed up," I admitted, ignoring his triumphant
look. He was right, I needed to do more. And it had
been a mistake to leave Frankie's urn behind. If we
lost the last bit of ashes it contained, I wouldn't be
able to take Frankie off my property anymore. "I'll fix
it," I promised. "But right now, I need your help."

He crossed his arms over his chest and seemed to
enjoy looking down at me, if only because he was
hovering two feet off the ground. "So what you're
saying is when I ask you to do me a solid, you're gonna do it. No more of this when you can, in your spare
time, after you're done browsing the flower shop."

"Hey," I said, holding up a finger. "I already said I
was sorry for that."

"I can't even complain to my buddies," he said with
a sniff. "They'd all laugh."

"Speaking of your buddies," I said, taking a seat on
the desk built into the wall, "were any of them down
here this morning?" I admit my change of topics
wasn't that crafty, but I had to ask. They might have
seen something we'd missed.

Frankie was hardly amused, but he did come

down off the wall. He took his time, running a finger through the wooden chair between us. "The South Town boys who haunt this spot stay upstairs mostly." He shrugged. "I can see why: cash and dames." I could almost hear one of his buddies hooting and hollering, based on Frankie's widening grin alone. "But the dead banker?" he asked, growing serious. "Yeah. You only need to look at his body to know who did that."

"Truly?" It would be great if Frankie had the inside track. With his help, maybe we could solve this murder mystery before anybody else got hurt. And I'd feel a lot better if I could bring some peace to poor Em. "Who?"

He paused. "Promise first."

Oh, Lordy. "Promise what?" I'd already done a lot for him. A prime portion of my rose garden was growing out of a trash can in my living room for his benefit.

He pursed his lips. "I want you to help me find my favorite gun."

"Done." I could do that.

I hoped.

He grinned. "Your killer is none other than Handsome Henry," he said, "ace hit man for the South Town Gang."

My hope deflated. "You've got to be kidding me." I couldn't tell the police that.

He leaned closer. "I'm serious, doll. The shot through the heart and the slashed cheek is Handsome Henry's calling card. He also would have known to blow the camera." An unseen presence must have said something because Frankie turned and smirked at the air. "I know. Henry is still around, working. How swell."

"That's impossible," I said, to Frankie and anybody else who might be listening. Nobody was going to hire a dead hit man to kill a live banker. Besides, "I thought everybody in your gang was killed."

Frankie's cheeks darkened at my complete lack of tact. "I was one of the first to go. Maybe some of them got out after me."

I hated to bring up Frankie's death. So did he. With a twinge of guilt, I scooted off the desk. "I'm sorry if that came out wrong." But still, we needed to reason this out. "If Handsome Henry is still alive, he'd have to be more than a hundred years old."

The gangster crossed his arms over his chest. "It ain't that hard to pull a trigger. Especially when you've done it a lot."

"But how would an old man get in and out of the bank without being seen?" And I sure didn't know of any hundred-year-old ex-gangsters in town. Unless he was a ghost. Still, he'd have to be a pretty powerful ghost to kill a man, the kind of powerful that usually signaled a poltergeist. But poltergeists left plenty of destruction in their wake, and the bank itself was un-touched. "And what reason could this ghost possibly have for going after Reggie?"

"Ah, old Handsome never needed a reason," Frankie mused, nostalgic. "The money was enough. Henry Hagar never turned down a job," he clarified.

Of the rare people who could talk to ghosts—and I was the only one I'd ever known—I had to believe there would be even fewer of us in need of a contract killer. No live person had hired Henry, I would bet on that.

There had to be another explanation. I tapped my black pump as I thought.

Some ghosts could move things on the mortal plane.

I'd seen it happen. And although I'd never experienced it, I'd seen ghosts on television leap into a living body. I stiffened. It had felt ice cold in the vault, and Carla had been freezing as she stood over Reggie. "What if Carla was possessed?"

"Ew. Yuck." He stared at me as if I'd gone off my rocker. "I ain't never heard of a ghost doing that. Do you realize how slimy you living feel?"

"I'll take your word for it." Frankie and I had touched once by accident and the results hadn't been at all pleasant. It felt like walking around in someone else's wet, cold underwear.

I paced the tiny room, making the gangster distinctly uncomfortable. "This is none of my business," I reminded myself.

I wanted to help. I did. Except the idea of getting involved again, of putting myself in Frankie's hands, of opening myself up to the other side…it scared me.

But, Reggie had been willing to stand up for me.

The people who loved him deserved peace.

I cringed. If Frankie was right and a ghost did this, then I was the only one who could discover exactly what happened.

"Do you know where Handsome Henry might be?" I asked Frankie. I supposed it wouldn't hurt to approach him.

"No you don't," Frankie warned. "Henry takes people who ask questions and he uses them for target practice."

"But—"

The door swung open and Officer Duranja stood on the other side. "Who are you talking to, Verity?"

"Myself," I said, copping the lamest excuse ever.

He shook his head like he didn't believe me. "You're lucky Marshall is already questioning the guy next to you."

Lucky indeed. But not lucky enough. Where was Ellis?

"I need to ask you some questions," the efficient officer said, crowding my space as he closed the door behind him. He handed me my purse, which I'd left in Reggie's office. "We searched it. No weapons. Just…"

An urn. I got it. "You didn't shake the urn out or wipe it down, did you?"

"No…" Duranja answered, as if he'd expected me to perhaps offer an explanation.

Not a chance.

He'd have to settle for me telling him everything I knew about Reggie's death. Except for the part about the ghost. Unfortunately, that could very well have been the most important item.

He opened his notebook. "Why were you at the bank this morning?" he began.

I answered his question, and the questions after that. I had nothing to hide.

"And what was your relationship to Reggie Thompson?"

"He was my best friend's uncle." He was also a person who had chosen to believe in me. I didn't take his kindness lightly.

"Are you aware of any person or persons who wished him harm?"

"No live ones," I said automatically.

The officer gave me a funny look.

"I'm trying to help," I assured him.

Even the people who worked with Reggie every day didn't seem to know who might be after him. More and more, it seemed like a question for the spirit world.

An ominous feeling crept over me. There was no getting around it: I had to investigate on the other side, no matter what I had to promise Frankie. I'd just have to be smart about it and make every effort count. He might not have the strength or the patience to show me everything I needed to see.

And there were still plenty of questions right here in the real world.

"Tell me what happened while the group waited for the police," Duranja pressed.

I answered all of Officer Duranja's questions quickly and completely, although we seemed to wind down our session with more questions than answers. I could sense the frustration rolling off him.

"We're done for now," he told me. "Just stay in town, and keep your phone handy in case we need to call you in for further questioning."

I slung my purse over my shoulder, glad for the clank of the urn inside. I had Frankie back at least.

"Thanks," I said, heading past the row of closed doors. Everybody else was still inside.

More police had arrived. They lingered in the lobby.

I could have left. I probably should have. But something told me it wouldn't hurt to stop by the ladies' room on the way out.

Chapter Six

The door to the ladies' room squeaked as I opened it. Tall and made from polished wood, it had to be original. A short, green-carpeted hallway led me to a lounge area as big as most modern restrooms.

It smelled old, with a hint of…spearmint.

Strange.

It was also unnaturally quiet, as if the thick walls and pipes insulated it from the commotion of the downstairs lobby.

An empty built-in phone booth stood next to a marble vanity counter that ran the length of the room to the right. At the back, a pair of worn yet comfortable-looking, pink velvet chaise lounges turned inward, toward each other, with a small glass-topped table in the middle. Gossip magazines sprawled over the table and the nearest chaise, fighting for space with wadded-up gum wrappers. Empty Evian bottles littered the floor alongside a black makeup case with a purple sleep mask flung over it.

Dollars to donuts Em had been camping out here to avoid work.

Certainly not the best way to get started on her new way of life, or at least the path Reggie had planned for her.

I looked through the magazines and the wrappers and found travel brochures, to Ecuador of all places. Beside them I found several pairs of used, disposable foam earplugs and a bag of Skinny Pop. I also learned that two of my favorite movie stars broke up. Darn. I dropped the US Magazine back onto the chaise.

Okay, so if Em had been hiding out in here in the commotion after the killer shot Reggie, she could have conceivably had her ears plugged and her eyes glued to how the Stars Are Just Like Us.

I sat on the soft, welcoming chaise—the one without the slew of magazines.

This could also be the perfect setup for a murder. She could hide out in here and wait until Reggie was alone. It wasn't as if Jeb had his eye on the ladies' room. Then, when he was out smoking, she could have killed her father and rushed back in here. If anyone asked, she could say she was reading magazines with her earplugs in.

We'd certainly believe it of her, especially if she'd been down here a lot. And it seemed like she had.

If I was right—and I sincerely hoped I wasn't—that meant the gun could still be in the bathroom.

But, surely, the officers would have looked into every nook and cranny.

Unless they hadn't had a chance yet. They were still getting her side of the story.

I stood quickly.

Where would I hide a gun in here?

Certainly not with personal possessions. But maybe…

I scurried into the bathroom beyond the lounge. Weak sconces on the walls threw more shadows than they eliminated.

I opened the door of the stall nearest the door and

checked the toilet tank. I felt a bit silly doing it, but still, this is where I would have stashed a gun. It contained nothing strange. I mustered up my courage and checked the next stall. That tank was clear as well.

The ceiling of the room appeared solid. The lone pedestal sink left nowhere to hide.

Surely, Em wouldn't have hidden anything of importance by the chairs.

I checked under the first pink chaise and found a stash of crumpled gum wrappers. Its twin yielded the same, along with a fair amount of dust. I stood, brushing off my hands. Em needed to learn to clean up after herself. I checked the makeup case and found a mishmash of lipsticks, eyeliners, and powders—all high end.

I was trying to think of where else to look when a face popped through the wall behind me.

I leapt back in surprise.

"Hey, Suds!?" Frankie barked, looking both ways, as if his buddy and I were having a little party without him.

I held a hand over my beating heart. "Frankie, you just took ten years off my life."

His brows drew together. "That's not funny. Besides, I wasn't even talking to you. What are you doing here?" he added, as if I were a crazy woman.

"Well, this is the ladies' room." In case he couldn't guess.

"Yeesh," he said, ready to pull back. Then curiosity got the best of him and he floated right in. "Somebody liked pink," he commented, checking the place out. "I'm glad you decided to stick around for a minute. I did some asking. Word has it Suds haunts downstairs only." Frankie perked up. "You hear that?"

"No," I said, straining.

The gangster crossed the lounge room and stuck his head through the wall over the makeup counter. "Suds!?" I heard him ask, his voice muffled through the wall. "Hey, you old trigger bum!" Frankie drew back, excited. "He just popped out of the floor in the men's john. Come on" — he waved me over — "you gotta meet him." Frankie walked straight through the wall.

I hesitated. Truth be told, I'd rather not venture into the men's bathroom. And I'd need Frankie's energy to see Suds anyway.

Frankie solved the second problem by blasting me with a hit of power that made my toes curl. I braced myself on the pink chaise as his energy cascaded over me in a tingling shower of otherworldly awareness that would no doubt have me seeing Suds, the spirits upstairs, and every other ghost in Sugarland.

"Frankie," I gasped. He could stand to ease up a bit.

My head felt light, my muscles and bones ached, and I gripped the tufted pink fabric. I needed to sit. I slowly lowered myself, trying to absorb everything, when Frankie's face popped out of the wall again and I nearly fell.

"This is no time to be shy," Frankie snorted.

"I understand you're eager," I said, drawing a shaking hand to my brow. I'd heard plenty about Suds. He was Frankie's best friend, his partner in crime, the guy who painted the god-awful ugly dancing scene on the side of Frankie's urn. But I felt compelled to point out an important detail. "I can't just poke my head through the wall."

Sometimes, I think Frankie forgot.

"Come around," he said.

Sure. To the men's room.

It would be lovely for the police to catch me in there.

"It's not like I ask you to meet people all the time," Frankie pointed out. "With you, I get Melody, and Ellis, and half the ghosts in the county."

"Fine," I said quickly. This was Frankie's friend and it was important to him. More than that, there was a chance that Suds could fill us in on the whereabouts of Em this morning. And Stan, and Carla. Even Reggie himself.

Not to mention Handsome Henry.

Now that I had Frankie's power, I could question Suds directly.

It was too good of an opportunity to pass up.

"I'll meet you over there," I told him.

I'd have to figure out a way to sneak into the men's room without anyone thinking it too suspicious — or strange.

Good luck with that.

I shoved myself to my feet, ignoring the weak feeling in my legs.

Be casual. I eased out of the ladies' room, quite aware that I looked worse coming out than I had going in. More police than before stood outside, talking in groups. The static from their radios echoed in the lobby.

Ellis didn't appear to be among them. As I made certain of that, I also took care to notice if anyone was watching me as I paused in front of the old brass drinking fountain before continuing across the alcove to the large polished wood door of the men's room.

I paused at the door. This was so mortifying. I'd better not get caught. It would be exceedingly difficult to explain to Detective Marshall.

I screwed up my courage and knocked gently. "Anybody in there?" I asked, in a harsh whisper.

The police hadn't noticed me. Yet.

Gah. I hesitated, not sure if I were willing to risk it. Knowing every second I debated was a chance I could be seen.

Frankie had been trying to get me to break in somewhere since I'd met him. This felt like a slippery slope.

Courage.

Frankie had been so eager for me to meet his friend. Very few things excited the gangster, besides guns and stealing and booze. It was nice to see him happy for once.

As long as I didn't get caught in here and go from witness to suspect.

I braced myself and pushed inside.

The layout mirrored the ladies' room. The lounge stood empty, save for two outdated blue leather chairs crowding a metal and glass table. I stepped forward and tripped over a brass door stopper. It made a horrific rattle as it skidded across the tile floor. I chased it down and silenced it. The last thing I needed was to draw people in here.

Heck, these were the only downstairs bathrooms. I was on borrowed time as it was.

I turned the corner and saw Frankie standing over the cowering ghost of a man. Dirt and grime streaked his tan pleated pants and chambray shirt, and a spiderweb dangled from his bowler hat. His body shook. His snub-nosed face shone with sweat and he lifted a shaking finger to point at his old, dead friend. "It's a ghost!"

"It's me, Frankie!" my buddy said, taking off his hat as if that were the issue.

"No." Suds's gray image flickered as he clawed the wall at his back.

"You're scaring him," I said to my friend.

Suds's wild eyes trained on me. "You can see him too?" Suds tried to grab my arm and I skillfully avoided his touch. "Right there." He pointed again at Frankie. His voice lowered to a croak. "He's hideous. He has a bullet hole right through his head."

Frankie drew his Panama hat low over his eyes, shooting a glare my way. "You said it was starting to become less noticeable."

I shrugged. "Maybe I'm just getting used to it."

"My friend is dead," Suds stage-whispered to me, wide-eyed. He frantically pointed a finger at his cheek. "He got shot in the face."

"Well, more like the forehead," Frankie countered.

Suds reached for me again. "We gotta get out of here."

"Hold up a minute," I said, scooting away. I hated to point out the obvious, but, "You're dead too," I added, keeping my tone as gentle as I could.

Was it possible he forgot?

"No...no..." Suds said, holding up a hand to shield himself from me of all people. "Please don't kill me. Or haunt me. Or —"

"Oh, wait," I said. He'd misunderstood. "When I said you were dead, that wasn't a threat, it was an observation."

"He came right up outa the floor," Frankie accused. "But he don't think he's a ghost."

"Patience." This was new to Suds. "I think we need to say it better."

"What do you want me to do?" Frankie huffed. "Embroider it on a pillow?"

This was ridiculous. I worked my way between Frankie and his friend. "Don't loom," I said to the gangster. "He's seriously scared of you."

Frankie backed off a bit. "I'm not looming."

"Yes, you are."

He tried to see around me. "I'm just trying to have a conversation."

Suds brought a hand to his face. "Please," he implored, wincing through his splayed fingers as if Frankie were about to strike him down. "I'm doing everything I can to avenge you."

"Frankie doesn't want vengeance," I explained to the frightened ghost.

"She don't speak for me," my jerk of a friend pointed out. He motioned for Suds to continue. "Let's hear more about this revenge you got cooking."

He yanked off his hat, crushing it in his hands. "You didn't die in vain," he said, a trickle of sweat running down his cheek. "Sure, the Chicago boys have been on our backs for the payments we shorted 'em last month, but this heist will set things right before your brother and the rest get to town. We're gonna have their money."

"My brother is dead," Frankie said, betraying no emotion.

Suds shook his head. "That don't mean the rest of the Chicago boys won't be gunning for us." He swallowed hard. "I'm almost done breaking into the vault. I'm being as quiet as I can, but it ain't easy to bust through lead sheeting and a marble floor."

"Wait. Is that you making noise in the vault?" I asked.

Frankie snapped his fingers. "If he was going to tunnel in, it'd have to be through the floor," he reasoned. "The rest of the vault is lined with iron walls a foot thick."

"How do you know this?" I pressed.

"I was on the planning committee," Frankie said

proudly.

Suds straightened, as if he realized his friend hadn't changed at all, even if he was transparent and sporting a permanent bullet hole. "I've been digging alone since yesterday," he said. "No word from the guys. No help. I got the dynamite all set up. Now I'm making the hole bigger, waiting for Lou to give the okay to blast through. He's late."

Most likely because he was dead. If Suds had been at it for as long as I thought he had, he'd spent his entire afterlife waiting for the guys to show. He had no idea that time had moved on without him.

"What date did you start?" I pressed.

"Tuesday," he answered earnestly.

"What year?"

He snorted, as if it were a silly question. "Nineteen thirty-three."

"That week started out so good," Frankie said.

"I came up for your funeral," Suds insisted. "I stayed awake two nights straight to decorate your urn."

"It's a sharp piece of work," Frankie agreed, eyeing my bag. He turned his attention back toward his friend. "Suds, I think you bit it in the tunnel."

Suds shook his head, refusing to believe it. "Of all the rotten things to say to a guy." At least he'd calmed down a touch. "I wouldn't tell you that you were dead unless I knew for sure," Suds explained, as if he spoke to a child. "And you are. You're really, really dead."

Frankie started to speak.

"Let it go," I told him.

"I'm almost through," Suds continued. "The lead sheeting is thick, but I work day and night. I could use some help." He wet his lips. "I know you're expired, Frankie, but maybe your girl here can help out."

"She does owe me one," Frankie mused.

"No." I probably couldn't get to the tunnel, if there still was one. It could have caved in by now. And even if I somehow found a decrepit tunnel underground, there was no way I was going to crawl around in it, trying to steal things. "I'm not helping you break into the First Sugarland Bank. I came here for a job, re-member? A legal job."

Frankie looked at me as if I'd stolen his prized pony. "Oh, so I help your friends, but you don't help mine."

"I'm not getting roped in by your criminal logic," I told him. "There's a difference between helping people and assisting a criminal in a bank robbery."

"That was harsh," Suds said to Frankie.

He inched closer to his friend. "You don't know half of what I put up with."

We didn't have time for this. "Look, Suds. A man was murdered this morning in the vault. Did you see anything?"

"How could I?" he asked, genuinely perplexed. "I can't go in until I get through the metal sheeting."

"You're standing on the ground level right now," I pointed out, losing patience. "You could walk out of here and stroll right into the vault. Nobody would even see you."

Suds looked down at the floor, then back at me, confused.

"Don't mess with his head," Frankie chastised me. "If Suds died trying to tunnel in from the outside and he don't think he's made it into the vault yet, then he can't go in there. It's a mental block. It happens to the best of us."

Only Suds appeared to be getting ideas. "Honestly,"

he said, sounding anything but as he rose up from the floor and gave me the once-over, "I think your wild imagination and my friend's ghostly powers are better used trying to break through the last of that lead sheeting."

I liked him better when he was scared.

"It would be fun." Frankie grinned.

"You always were a natural," Suds prodded.

"No," I said, turning to leave. I didn't want any part of it. With luck, we'd find another, saner way to figure out what was really happening in this place.

"You're just gonna walk away," Frankie accused, trailing me.

I didn't know what else he expected me to do. "I can't let a bunch of police officers find me standing in the men's room, talking to a couple of ghosts with grand delusions. I've got to get out of here."

"He's been digging for more than eighty years," Frankie pressed. "Constantly. And you can't help him snag his dream."

That was rich. "If that dream is scoring on the First Sugarland Bank, then no."

Frankie rose up and towered over me, padding his height by at least two feet. "Funny words for a dame who needed me to save her house."

"And in the process, you nearly got me killed," I pointed out.

Frankie flickered with rage. "Don't change the subject!"

"Angry ghost!" Suds launched himself off the wall and dashed straight past us and out through the closed restroom door.

I turned to my gangster buddy. "Way to go. You scared him away."

The gangster had the nerve to look offended. "Are

you saying that's my fault?" he asked, moving toward the door.

"You didn't need to get so heavy handed," I pointed out, joining him.

"It feels kind of good to be frightening," Frankie mused.

"We need to catch him." I paused at the door. Once Suds calmed down, I wanted to talk to him more about the noises in the bank and what he might have seen shortly before Reggie's death. "Make sure the coast is clear."

Frankie sighed, as if I were the problem, before he poked his head through the door. "They're busy with Carla," he said from the other side of the door.

Good. I pushed the door open and slipped out.

Chapter Seven

Sure enough, Reggie's right-hand woman stood just outside the privacy booths, arguing with a growing number of police officers.

The law enforcement presence had exploded while I'd been investigating the bathrooms. Several officers had gathered in the lobby, talking in groups. Ellis didn't appear to be among them.

"Dang it," Frankie and I both muttered.

"Do you see Suds?" I asked.

"No," Frankie groused.

Frick. "It would be hard to talk to him with all these people around, anyway."

The gangster stood next to me, scanning the lobby. "Suds was always good at lying low. If the cops are out here, he isn't."

That settled it. "I've got to get out of here," I whispered, heading for the door.

It was all too much. Reggie's death, the questioning, Frankie shoving his powers on me. It had given me a headache.

Besides that, Frankie's left foot had begun to fade away. The right one was completely gone. If we kept at this any longer, he'd start losing his shins. Lending me his power cost him energy, and I wanted him to save it for when we could make a real difference.

We'd come back when the place wasn't crawling with police and we had a chance to talk to Suds again.

I was halfway across the lobby when Em exited the area where we'd been questioned, flanked by one of the officers who had originally come in with Duranja.

She shot me a cold look as we passed, as if she knew where I'd been. I watched as he led her to the seating area in the lobby before I spoke with the officer guarding the glass doors. "Duranja said I could go."

"He told me," he said, letting me pass toward the exit that led to an outside staircase.

Frankie wasn't quite so generous. He loomed over me, his chest blocking my way. "Wait a minute. We gotta at least try to find Suds before we leave. I didn't get to ask about my missing gun."

We both had important questions to ask, but they would have to wait.

The officer at the door raised an eyebrow when I hesitated. I had to keep moving. I walked straight for Frankie, who was still blocking my path. He dodged me at the last second, and I stepped into the crisp afternoon air.

"Give it a break," I said as soon as the door closed behind me. "We'll come back after Suds has had a chance to calm down." And when police weren't all over the place. "You're not going to get anything out of him by chasing him around."

He straightened his tie. "I can't help it. It's good to see him again."

I started up the steps toward street level. "He thinks you're a ghost."

"I am a ghost. So's he."

I sighed as I took the concrete steps one by one. I didn't know how much more of this I could take.

It was more than Suds or the questioning or the death of my almost-client. This had been my big chance. Although after what had happened to poor Reggie, I supposed I needed to be grateful to be alive and well.

The sky was blue, and the sun shone bright, as if the rest of the world hadn't quite caught up to this morning's tragedy.

I was glad I didn't have to go back for a coat. And as far as my work samples went, the bank could hold onto them for now. I didn't see myself going out on many more freelance interviews, not after word of this one got out.

"Suds looked good, didn't he?" Frankie mused as he glided next to me.

"He seemed to have a lot of energy," I said, looking at the positive. "He sure yelled loud and split quickly."

"So when are we going back?" Frankie asked as we reached the top of the stairs.

"Soon." Especially if I was the only one who could pursue the Handsome Henry lead. Suds might have seen him as well. "But for now, you should probably disconnect me from the other side."

"Brace yourself," he warned.

A tingling surge jolted me as Frankie drew his power back. "That never feels good," I said on a wince.

"Yeah, I don't think we're supposed to be doing it," Frankie said.

That fact alone should have made me run far and long. Only I had important work to do, and I didn't see any other way.

I needed to learn more about this gangster hit-man theory, and what a ghost could truly do to harm a human. Frankie hadn't been able to offer me a concrete explanation when he'd brought it up. While the gangster could be enthusiastic with his opinions, he didn't always bother to check the facts.

Spectators crowded the small sidewalk that led to the front steps of the bank, where I'd entered so eagerly just a few hours ago. I saw the weekday morning McDonald's coffee crowd, police scanners in hand, along with two of my grandmother's old friends from church. And, of course, Ovis Dupre, the retired reporter who ran the Shady Oaks Extended Living Center Gazette.

"Verity Long," he called from the bottom step, his face lighting up and his voice raspy from years of cigarettes. He wore a camera around his neck and carried a notebook in his hand. "Were you present for this murder, too?" he asked, reaching for the pencil behind his ear.

"No, I wasn't," I said, hurrying past, telling him the honest truth while at the same time refusing to stick around and elaborate.

I'd always been taught to respect my elders, and Ovis was as near as you could get to an institution in this town, but he could also ask some tricky questions. I didn't feel up to his antics right now.

He started to follow me, but shuddered and dropped back when Frankie gave him a cold spot. I caught the edges of it along my spine, and it was a doozie.

"Thanks, buddy," I muttered.

The gangster glided for my car. "I don't know what you're talking about."

A dozen more casual observers peppered the parking lot and the town square beyond. My sister, Melody, stood away from the crowd, near the statue of Colonel Larimore, wearing a bright cherry red coat.

She had braided her hair into a crown on her head.

I made a beeline for her, needing a hug like I needed my next breath.

She didn't question it, just folded me into her arms.

"You're freezing," she said, hugging me tighter. "You want my coat?"

"No." I was wearing enough of her clothes already.

I let her go, not missing the concern in her eyes. "We lost half our library patrons when the police cars pulled up outside the bank," she said. "Then I saw your car out front, and you didn't leave when they cleared the lobby."

"I was inside when Reggie was murdered," I said, not bothering to sugarcoat it. This was Melody.

She let out a small gasp. "So it's true? We saw the ambulance, but..."

I nodded. "Reggie's dead." I let her absorb that for a moment. "It gets worse," I added, drawing closer. I told her about the way we'd found the body and how any one of the people I'd been with could have done it. "Frankie seems convinced it's the work of a hit man named Handsome Henry. His real name is Henry Hagar. Have you ever heard of him?"

"No," she said, glancing back at the library, "but the only research on criminals I've done has been for you. This is becoming a bad habit."

"Tell me about it," I said. Across the square, I saw Ovis gathering his courage to approach me again. Where was my spooky ghost when I needed him? "I've got to go. When you get back to the library, see what you can find about Handsome Henry and his gang record?"

The corners of her eyes wrinkled as she stared at me, trying to assess if I was serious or not. "Do you really think a hit man followed Reggie to town?"

"A most likely dead hit man," I corrected. "I know it sounds nuts."

To her credit, she didn't immediately agree. "I'll see what I can do," Melody said, nodding. "In the meantime..." She glanced over my shoulder at an approaching Ovis.

"Yeah." I cut across the square, barely missing Ovis before I slipped into my car and slammed the door. Luckily, there was nobody in the street behind me as I peeled out and made my getaway.

"You got some natural talent behind the wheel," Frankie said, approving from the passenger seat. "If you ever wanted a career in getaway—"

I clutched the wheel. "I don't want to hear about it."

"Just saying..."

Chapter Eight

I escaped toward one of the older sections of town. I refused to break the law in the way Frankie preferred, but I would bend one of my personal rules and drop in on the man I most definitely should not be seeing.

At least not in public.

"Geez, Verity," Frankie groused as we turned down Magnolia Street. "First order of business: you don't seek out the fuzz."

"Ellis must not be working today; otherwise we would have run into him at the bank. Trust me. He can help."

I'd come to depend on his ear and his support. He was a good man, with a solid moral code and a wicked sense of humor. Two things I couldn't resist.

"You want to take a cop with you to hunt down a hit man," Frankie said, as if it were the most absurd idea in the world.

"When you put it like that, my idea sounds even better," I said, as we passed mature trees and a patchwork of modest, sturdy houses that had stood since the early 1900s. Too bad I wasn't exactly subtle in my avocado-green Cadillac. This was the middle of the day, and the neighbors around here liked to talk.

Ellis and I couldn't afford to expose our budding romance to the scrutiny of the town. At least not yet. He was the brother of my ex-fiancé, and the son of the woman who would give her eyeteeth to take me down. We'd developed a sweet spot for each other on my first ghostly adventure, and if he hadn't been so danged wonderful, I would have let him go. I still might have to.

Ellis lived in a tidy bungalow with a postage-stamp front lawn. And sure enough, his police cruiser stood vigil in the side drive.

Relief washed through me as I parked out front and took the steps two at a time. I'd make it quick. This was an emergency.

I knocked on the door. "Ellis?"

No one answered. I glanced behind me, to the lace curtains fluttering in the window of the two-story across the street. I squared my shoulders and knocked again, more firmly this time. "Ellis, I need to talk to you." A sharp wind blasted me, chilling me to my toes. "There was a murder at the bank," I said, louder and more urgently than before. "Frankie thinks it could have been another gangster, a hit man. The police are there now, and—"

The door swung open and Virginia Wydell stood on the other side of the threshold.

She wore her perennially blond hair back in its usual bob, her bony figure draped in a white cashmere sweater set and beige wool trousers. Her thin lips pursed as she took in my presence on her son's front porch.

"Why, Verity Long," she drawled, "death and destruction and you at the center. Imagine that."

I schooled my features to hide my shock. "I need to see Ellis."

"My son is not your personal officer of the law," she said, her ring-clad fingers tightening on the door. "He's not your anything."

I curled my toes in my sister's overtight shoes. "I know he's home," I insisted, keeping my tone even. "I see his car."

She leaned close and rested a hand on my arm. I smelled her expensive perfume and felt the bite of her fingers as they tightened. "Don't you think you've imposed enough on this family?"

Why? Because I'd exposed some of her underhanded schemes? Even now she was fighting legal battles on a few fronts because of what I'd uncovered on my last adventure. "If you think you can make me cower, you're dead wrong."

Her eyes narrowed. "Listen closely because I'm only going to say this once, dear. You cannot hurt me, but I won't have you going after my sons. Leave Ellis alone. Now. Or I'll find out exactly what's going on with your Frankie and your gangsters and your hit man. And I'll make your life a living hell."

I pulled out of her grip, still feeling the sting of her nails on my skin. "You can't control me. Or him."

She raised a brow. "I suppose not," she said, before her voice hardened. "But in this case I don't need to. Do you really think Ellis will want you with him at our next family dinner? At Beau's big birthday party?" She smiled when I flinched. "Most of your old friends will be there — you haven't seen them since the rehearsal dinner. The smart ones stood by my son's side."

Social posturing didn't change the facts. "You know why I refused to marry Beau."

"And why you don't belong with any child of mine," she stated, as if it were fact. "Let me ask," she mused, her tone going sweet. "How did the holidays go?"

Ellis and I had gotten together for an early dinner at a restaurant two towns away. He'd spent the rest of the holiday with his family.

Even the simple things would be a battle. The special get-togethers that should bring joy would bring me pain. Virginia Wydell would make sure I had no peace so long as I associated with anyone in her family.

Her expression hardened. "I thought you learned your lesson the first time when I took you for everything you had," she drawled. "I'll do it again if you'd like. Just give me an excuse."

Her lips twisted into a faint smile as she closed the door.

I turned and walked away, and I kept going, even when I heard Ellis's voice as I opened my car door.

"Verity?" He sounded surprised and harried.

Ellis wore a flannel work shirt, jeans, and a fine dusting of plaster that would have been endearing if he hadn't appeared almost as frightened as he was confused at my sudden appearance on his front porch.

"I have to go," I said as his mother stepped onto the porch behind him, her arms crossed in front of her. I'd had a bad day and knew better than to stay for round two with Virginia. I'd come to him bruised and battered enough. And I believed her threat. She would enjoy hurting me.

He started to walk down the rest of his driveway, and I prayed he wouldn't take it personally when I sped away. In the meantime, I'd try to forget that my sweet boyfriend would rather not let anyone know we were seeing each other.

"That didn't go well," the gangster observed.

"Stop it, Frankie," I said, keeping my eyes on the road.

I'd hurt Ellis just now, but I didn't know what else to do.

Virginia was right. I'd never be a part of his family, no matter what happened between us. He'd always have to choose. I couldn't ask that of him.

My cell phone rang. The caller ID said it was Ellis.

I was putting him in an impossible position, and I was doing it to myself as well.

"You going to get that?" Frankie cringed as the phone kept ringing. The ghost didn't like electronics.

"She's probably standing right next to him," I said, letting the call go to voice mail. I wasn't ready to give up, but we definitely needed a new strategy.

I chewed my lip. Perhaps I should call him back and ask him to help me uncover a ghostly murder suspect. I could put him in harm's way. Pit him against his family. Tempt Virginia to destroy me. Engage in a hidden relationship that had no possibility of a simple, happy outcome.

Or I could just let it go. Breathe.

Ellis would understand me needing a little space from his mother.

I drove back to Route 9, toward my home and my little skunk, the two things I could count on.

Frankie eyed me. "I don't get women," he said, watching me with a mix of concern and pure bafflement.

"You don't have to," I said, continuing for home.

I parked behind my house, numb as I headed up the back porch steps. I'd neglected to lock my back door — small-town habits die hard — and I pushed it open to find my kitchen exactly as I'd left it.

A stack of work samples, the ones I'd culled from my presentation, lingered on my kitchen counter. Lauralee's donut box stood on the kitchen island. Two rejected lipsticks lined up next to it. Yes, I'd tried on all three lipsticks I owned in my preoccupation to look my best. As if it would have made a difference.

I'd started the morning so excited, and now…

At least there was one bright spot.

Lucy the skunk toddled out from her nest of blankets in the parlor, her squat body churning and her tail waving from side to side as she grunted out a greeting.

She was the most welcome sight in the world. "Did you miss me?" I asked, scooping her up.

Oh my. She'd been snug as a bug. She smelled like lemon soap and warm fur. I could feel the sleepy heat radiating off her, welcoming me home.

"She didn't miss me," Frankie remarked as Lucy gave a start and buried her face in the crook of my elbow.

I nestled her tighter. In one tragic day, everything had changed.

Reggie was gone. Em's life was forever altered, as well as Lauralee's. She'd lost her favorite uncle. And even though my experience was nothing like theirs, I'd missed out on a person whom I might have easily called a friend.

Then there was the issue of Frankie's feet. Whenever he lent me his juice, he experienced an energy drain. It made parts of him go missing until he recovered. Now both of his feet had disappeared completely.

I sighed. Technically he only had himself to blame. He'd been the one who chose to thrust his power onto me in the bathroom.

We should count ourselves lucky he was only down

two feet.

Frankie passed into the parlor and lingered by the large rubber trash can. He sifted his hands through the dirt inside, his shoulders passing through the huge, leaning rosebush that threatened to topple out.

Never mind that he couldn't actually touch any of it.

"All in all, it wasn't a bad day," he mused.

Of all the… I clutched my skunk close. "A man was killed."

"Except for that," the gangster conceded, poking around underneath the rosebush. "I have to admit, that part's kinda like old times," he added wistfully.

I stepped closer to Frankie and his project, despite Lucy's attempts to dig a burrow under my arm.

The sprawling heirloom rosebush had been my favorite before we'd dug it up and stuck it in my kitchen. Now the roots at the top of the bush had become exposed and the plant had lost some of its vigor. We really needed to plant it deeper. "What are you doing in there?"

Frankie poked his head through one of the lower branches. "Just thinking of where I should plant my gun." He gave me a long look, as if daring me to back off my promise. "Once you help me get it."

"Relax. I'm on the job," I said. "It's the only job I have."

What a depressing thought.

Lucy wriggled out of my arms and made a mad dash for the front hall. I couldn't even keep my skunk happy. Well, not with the gangster so close.

Frankie took stock of my near-empty kitchen. "I could help you open up an underground casino," he offered, with a fair dose of optimism. "You'd probably be the only one on the block."

I slipped off my heels. "I really thought today

would make a difference," I said, scooting the shoes away and taking a closer look at where the rosebush leaned precariously to one side. I tested it for steadiness and found it lacking. "What am I going to do if I can't get a job?" I asked out loud, admitting it for the first time. The bush, and my career, were both ready to keel over. I snuck a glance at Frankie. "I might not be able to make my design business work."

A thorn stabbed me and I drew back, watching the blood bubble over the pad of my thumb.

He looked at me like I was daft. "Haven't I been listing the alternatives?"

"I need to think of something legal," I specified, taking all the fun out of it for him.

I'd never wanted anything other than to own my own business, but I had to be realistic. Design wasn't paying the bills. I might be one of those people who had to give up and move on. The idea terrified me, but so did the alternative.

I had no money coming in. My only job prospect was dead.

"I don't know what I'm going to do," I told the gangster.

"You know what would make you feel better?" Frankie passed straight through the trash can with his arms outstretched in a way that, if he'd been alive, I'd have expected to become a hug. "How about we go back for my gun?"

And just like that, the moment was over.

"You could stand to be a little more sensitive," I muttered.

He shrugged. "You're not the first dame to tell me that."

I let it go. "We can't go back. Not yet. The police are still investigating. And besides, you're missing your feet."

He looked down, to the thin air after his pant cuffs ended. "I've suffered worse."

He had a point, judging from the bullet hole in his forehead. Still, I wondered if this time had been different. The energy drain didn't seem as hard on him as usual. He wasn't usually so eager to go back out again. Heck, we'd come back from adventures before with all of him gone.

"I have a question," I began.

Frankie drew back. "I'm not going into business with you as a ghost hunter."

"What?" The thought hadn't crossed my mind. Even if it would be a way to have my own business. "I don't want to hang out with you all the time." Not to mention work with him. "No. I want to know: Did you give me more power than usual back in the bank bathroom?"

I remembered it hitting me like a Mack truck, but perhaps that was only because he tossed it at me with no warning.

He shoved his hands into his pockets, as if it were a personal question. "It wasn't any different for me," he said, drawing the thought out, "except I actually wanted to do it this time."

True. He'd been eager for me to meet his friend. That could have made the difference.

"I have a feeling I would have enjoyed getting to know Suds," I said, trying to comfort him. "If he'd been up to it."

My phone rang again.

Frankie's mouth twisted as if he'd eaten something sour. "You gotta get that," he said, changing the subject.

"I hardly think now is the time," I said, withdrawing. I pulled Frankie's urn out of my bag and placed it on the counter. "It'll be Ellis again. I don't know what to say." The truth was, his mother's observations, and her threat, had shaken me. I needed to consider where we were going with this.

The ghost grinned. "Here you think I'm clueless about people."

"I understand subtleties," I informed him, removing a stack of business cards from my purse. "I read signs." In a moment of weakness, I pulled my phone out of the bag as well.

Should I call him back?

If it had been Lauralee or Melody or virtually anyone else, I wouldn't have given it a second thought. But for Ellis, I hesitated.

"Even I know you have to dial," Frankie pressed.

"Not tonight," I said, placing my phone on the counter. Ellis would want to talk about this afternoon, and I knew in my heart I wasn't ready. He'd want to fix things immediately, when pushing the issue too soon could do so much more harm than good. We had time and we trusted each other. That would have to be enough for now.

I picked up Frankie's urn and decided it should really be back on the mantle in the parlor, where it belonged. With any luck, the gangster wouldn't follow.

Ellis and I never could catch a break, even when the hospital patched us up after our last adventure. We'd held hands in the emergency room, but then his brother—my ex-fiancé—showed up. We'd been broken up for months, yet Beau proceeded to break up with me again in front of two women with food poisoning, a nurse on a caffeine high, and a kid with a broken arm.

After Beau's outburst, the staff had placed me far

from the Wydells, including Ellis, no doubt following the hospital policy on crazy families. Not that I could have visited Ellis's exam room anyway. I'd heard his mother breaking down from two closed curtains and a hallway away.

I placed Frankie's urn on the mantle, lining it up just so. I didn't know what else to do.

Ellis had let me go, not that I'd expected him to chase me or anything. In fact, I'd half hoped he wouldn't. Beau had been the type to chase me down the block, and look where that had ended up.

I headed for the hall stairs, ready to get out of my interview dress. I needed a change of clothes and a bath.

Of course, my roommate didn't take the hint. "I'm no love expert, but you should at least talk to the guy."

I halted halfway up and turned. I didn't know if he was serious or not. "Why, Frankie?" I pressed. "Why do you, of all people, care about what I do with Ellis?"

The gangster appeared thoughtful for once in his life. "Somebody's gotta look after you once I get free."

I didn't buy it, not completely. "I was fine before I met you."

He stood in the middle of the newel post. "I think you were a little sad."

For real? I turned back toward the stairs and kept climbing. "I'm not having this conversation," I said, retreating toward the bathroom. I was the social one in this relationship. It was my one and only super-power—the ability to relate to people. I didn't appre-ciate Frankie insinuating I had trouble when it came to Ellis of all people.

I wasn't avoiding my sort-of boyfriend. I just need-ed to decide how to treat us both fairly. I owed him that and more. I mean, I'd already helped to disinherit his family, publicly shamed his mother, and broken my engagement to his brother. All in the span of about six months. It was a wonder he wanted to speak to me at all.

I reached for a half-full bottle of lavender suds as I began drawing a hot bath, although at this point, I didn't think even the bubbles could save me.

We'd talk tomorrow. I'd ask him how I could help the police. I didn't have much going for me right now, but I did have this—the ability to make sure justice was done for a man who'd been nothing but good to me. I certainly wouldn't be too busy with work.

I remained in the tub until the water cooled, my thoughts churning. I wasn't usually this unsettled. Although heaven knew, Lauralee had it worse.

I called her when I got out, and Big Tom answered on the first ring.

"Verity," he said before I could even say hello. You've got to love caller ID.

"Tom," I began, "I'm so sorry about Reggie."

He let out a deep breath. "It's hard. Lauralee is at EmmaJane's house right now, spending time with her cousin."

"I can take the kids if you'd like to join her." I'd do anything I could.

"That's all right," he said gently. "EmmaJane doesn't like me much anyway. But I'll tell Lauralee you called. She'll be glad to hear it."

"Thanks," I said, hanging up, wishing I could do more.

It occurred to me that Em had become EmmaJane again, at least to Tom. It seemed Reggie's direction had been hard to ignore, even after his death.

When I ventured back downstairs, Frankie was nowhere to be found.

I curled up on my purple velvet couch with my skunk and paged through a lovely novel I'd borrowed from the library. These days, Melody only lent me books with happy endings.

My friend didn't call back that night. And I fell asleep without quite figuring out how to handle Ellis and his family.

Still, I knew what I had to do next.

Chapter Nine

The next morning I dressed warm, in a pink fluffy sweater Melody had lent me paired with white jeans and a pair of sturdy brown leather boots. Then I kissed Lucy on the head and slipped out of the house before I ran into Frankie.

The gangster wouldn't be pleased that I'd given him the slip, but at the same time, he would never understand why his presence wasn't needed on this particular visit.

I climbed into my grandmother's old Cadillac and stopped by Sweetbrew for two cups of Lauralee's favorite French roast. The coffee shop was located just down the street from New For You and the rest of the shops on the main drag, so I only had a few blocks to go before I pulled up in front of my friend's charming yellow bungalow.

Lauralee's neighborhood had been built in the 1940s and boasted picturesque homes with postage-stamp front yards and loving winter touches like wooden snowmen on the front porch and pinecone bird feeders hanging from trees that had grown for generations. I smiled at the colorful, hand-painted birdbath in Lauralee's front yard. Her kids had decorated it for her as a present. She'd always wanted a busy house full of love and she'd gotten it.

I just wished I could do something to help her feel
better about her uncle.

Winter boots in a range of sizes and covered with
varying degrees of mud crowded the front porch,
along with a red wagon that contained more gloves
than she had kids. She claimed gloves and socks
tended to escape and multiply, although I wasn't sure
I wanted to know how.

Today was a school day, and if those were the ex-
tras… I supposed I still had plenty to learn about
children.

I knocked on the door and heard a high-pitched
shriek inside. Ambrose, Lauralee's three-year-old son,
smacked his hands against the front window and
wailed his greeting again. In case I hadn't heard him
the first time.

"Hiya, sweetie!" I waved.

The front door swung open to reveal Lauralee, with
hair like she'd been in a wind storm and eyes red
from crying.

"I'm so sorry about Reggie," I told her, opening her
storm door and reaching out to hug her. She clasped
me tight and took several long, deep, shuddering
sighs.

"I just can't understand why anybody would want
to hurt him," she said, drawing away and wiping her
eyes with the sleeve of her shirt.

"How are you holding up?" I asked, following her
inside.

"I've been better," she said, her voice small. I closed
the door behind us as little Ambrose dumped a plastic
bucket of Legos off the coffee table and onto the floor.
Pieces scattered everywhere. "I just cleaned those
up," Lauralee said to herself, her voice rising a notch.
She looked like she was going to start crying all over

again.

"Here." I handed her a steaming cup of French roast. "You sit on the couch. Ambrose and I have got this."

"Oh, so now you're the toddler whisperer?" she tried to joke as she retreated to the tan couch. Both hands clutched her coffee.

I winked at Ambrose and shook the bucket, rattling the three remaining Legos on the bottom. "I'll bet I can pick up more of these than you."

He thrust out his chin. "You can not."

And so, we got to work. We made a game of cleaning up the front room while Lauralee took a moment to herself.

Lauralee had been there for me during some of the darkest periods in my life, from the death of my father to the near loss of my home. I snuck a glance at her. I'd rarely seen my friend so on edge, but it happened to the best of us from time to time. Heaven knew, she'd been through a lot in the last twenty-four hours.

She relaxed into the cushions and took a long sip of hot coffee, sighing to herself. "Lord almighty, that's good."

"Shucks," I said, pretending to be disappointed when Ambrose dumped an armload of Legos into the bucket. He was clearly winning the cleanup game.

Lauralee had dark smudges under her eyes and her skin lacked its usual healthy glow. "You don't look like you slept," I told her.

She rubbed a hand on her forehead. "I can't. I keep trying to make sense of it."

"Me too," I told her, finding two Legos and an army man under the coffee table. I sat back. "Did Reggie discover something out of the ordinary at the bank,

maybe? I don't think Stan has been completely truth-
ful about what happened that morning."

She thought for a moment. "If there was something
like that, Reggie never told me." She leaned forward,
clutching her coffee in both hands. "And he would
have worked it out. Sure, Reggie had his flaws, but he
was a good person. Everybody loved him."

I sat back on my knees. "I sure appreciated him giving me a second chance."

Lauralee managed a small, wavering smile. "He
wanted the best for you." She played with the paper
heat guard on her cup. "Sure, he could get ham-
handed at times," she said, settling back into the
couch. "Did he ever tell you how he romanced my
aunt when they were in high school?" She let out a
small snarf. "Aunt Kelly wanted nothing to do with
him. Mind you, that didn't stop him from declaring
her the love of his life and asking her to prom over
the loudspeaker at the football game. She wasn't one
to hide from the spotlight—she'd been in every high
school musical—but that made her want to die on the
spot. But she did let him take her to prom." Lauralee
sniffed fondly. "Later she said she went out with him
because she was afraid of how he'd ask her next."

"She loved him, though." I'd seen them together
over the years. She'd made a point to come back and
visit Sugarland at least a couple times a year. "She
kept him grounded."

"She packed him a healthy lunch almost every
day, even when he was head of a big firm." Lauralee
swirled her cup. "She'd write him funny notes on
the napkins. He changed after she died. He didn't
laugh as easily. Reggie always did wear his heart on
his sleeve." She sighed. "I think he was trying to find
some part of her here in Sugarland. He wanted that

real connection."

"He deserved it." He was right to come back, even if it had ended tragically.

Lauralee stood. "If we keep talking like this, I'm going to start crying again."

"Then what would you like to do?" I asked her, standing. The Legos were in the bucket once more, and Ambrose had moved on to an attempt to use his head as a doorstop.

"Let's get out of here," Lauralee said. "We can go to the park."

"Sounds good," I said, glad she was shaking out of her funk.

I ran to my car for my winter coat while Lauralee got herself and Ambrose ready. And even though I was grateful to have something warm to wear when a lot of people didn't, I still cringed a bit while drawing my thrift-store find out of the backseat.

Lauralee tried to hide a smile as I shrugged into it. She had the toddler in a red wagon.

"Pretty!" was all he said.

"Well played, Ambrose," I told him.

The red, pink, orange, green, tan, and silver monstrosity had been the only coat left at the thrift shop in my size and price range.

I straightened the collar and ignored how it poofed out to one side. "Joseph had his Technicolor dream coat. I have this," I said primly. Good thing spring would be arriving soon.

Lauralee laughed again, an honest-to-God belly laugh that she tried to wave away as we walked down the driveway. "I don't think I'll ever get used to that thing."

"Don't. As soon as I get a job, I'm donating it back," I said automatically. I'd been telling her that all winter. But now…it looked like I might be stuck with the monstrosity a lot longer than I'd planned.

My friend sensed my change in mood. "It'll be okay."

"I know." I wanted to say the same thing to her, and to have us both believe it.

We walked toward the park, enjoying the sunshine, even though the day was cold. The birds chirped and the occasional car rumbled down the quiet tree-lined street.

"Big Tom said you called last night," she said. "I appreciated it. I just didn't feel up to talking."

I knew the feeling. I told her what I'd seen, everything except for the shocking state of the body. She didn't need to know that. But she deserved the truth about the rest.

We walked side-by-side toward Jackson Park, with Ambrose's wagon thumping over each section of sidewalk behind us.

Lauralee sighed. "Reggie didn't want many people to know this," she said, glancing up at the branches of the bare trees reaching over us. "But he did lose his way in Chicago." We paused our conversation for a mom with a stroller walking the other way, and Lauralee resumed when they were out of earshot. "Reggie was always good at business, and with his personality, he brought in all kinds of clients for his mortgage-lending company."

"I remember he was a big shot before everything crashed a couple of years ago," I told her. Reggie would come to family events and show us pictures of his boats and cars. "Even Em got that fancy car when she turned sixteen."

"A Maserati, and that was after the mortgage industry went bust," Lauralee said. "Some of his clients might have defaulted, but Reggie already had their money."

Ouch. "Maybe he hadn't realized he was getting people in over their heads," I said, trying to be charitable.

"He knew. He talked like he was doing these people a favor—helping them buy their dream homes. But when he was in town for Kelly's funeral, he admitted he'd been lying to himself."

"Wow." I didn't know what else to say.

We stopped at the intersection across from the park and then continued over once the light changed. "Kelly's death did a number on him. The night before we buried her, I found him banging around in my kitchen at three in the morning, making cocoa. He'd stayed at our place last minute because he didn't even want to be alone at the hotel. I think being around the kids made him feel better."

"They always do it for me," I said, turning back to Ambrose, who had found a fascinating bolt on the wagon. Perhaps he'd be an engineer when he grew up.

"Reggie started…telling me things," Lauralee said, shaking her head. "It turns out he'd spent a good part of the housing boom doing all the shady things that a lot of mortgage lenders did"—she cringed—"making bad loans to good people, getting his clients in over their heads."

She glanced at me, as if waiting for me to judge. Only it wasn't my place, not right now. "Did he say why? Other than the money?" He seemed to have plenty without resorting to that.

She shook her head. "He'd told himself he was helping them afford the lifestyle they wanted, but he knew deep down some of the deals he was making were going to hurt people."

We reached the playground and Ambrose just about hurt himself in his haste to exit the wagon and run toward the slides.

"Careful," Lauralee warned him, lending her assistance.

He dashed toward the green and yellow playground equipment. Maybe he'd be an Olympic sprinter someday.

"I've been trying to figure out why someone would target Reggie," I began, needing to be frank. Of course, this was Lauralee. We could be honest. "Didn't Jeb Kemper lose his house in a bad mortgage deal?"

Lauralee shoved her hands into the pockets of her navy puffer coat. "I don't know anything about that," she said, with an edge to her voice, "and I don't think it's kind at all to assume."

I could have been offended, but I wasn't. She was hurting. "I'm just trying to understand what happened," I reminded her. I really wished I could have found a way to talk about Handsome Henry, but that seemed like a bigger stretch than Jeb.

We watched Ambrose run circles around the slide.

"I'm sorry," she said, tilting her head toward mine. "I just...I hate this."

"Me too," I said honestly.

Ambrose abandoned his orbit around the slide and ran straight for a mud puddle just beyond the playground.

"You want me to get him?" I asked, worried.

She smiled. "Don't worry. Toddlers are washable."

And this was a fourth child. We strolled past the slide and the swings and the rest of the expensive playground equipment and stood beside Ambrose and his gooey pile of mud. He seemed to be making pies. "Maybe he'll be a chef."

"You know, Reggie said something strange at Kelly's funeral," Lauralee said after a few minutes of keeping an eye on her son. "He told me he was giving it all up to her, that he'd do what she'd have wanted and he'd start fresh.

"Well, he did start a new life, for better or worse."

Ambrose lifted his hand to smack a mud pie onto the side of his head, and this time, Lauralee intervened. "Do you want a snack?" she asked.

He dropped the mud like it was on fire. Ambrose turned his big, blue eyes on us. "Grapes?"

Lauralee pulled a bag of large purple grapes out of her pocket and you would have thought she did a magic trick. "Get in the wagon and you can have these."

The child flung himself into the wagon like a firefighter jumping into the truck.

Yet another career possibility.

Lauralee wiped his muddy hands before handing over the grapes. Ambrose munched happily and we began our walk home.

"Reggie wasn't the only one who needed to leave his jet-setting lifestyle behind," Lauralee commented. "He kept saying how EmmaJane needed it too."

"To get a dose of reality?" I asked, suspecting where this was headed.

Lauralee shrugged as Ambrose squealed with delight at his grapes. "She'd never held a job. She'd disappear — go to Europe or the islands with her friends — and he wouldn't hear from her for weeks. He'd have to look at her credit card statements to even see where she was."

"I couldn't imagine," I said, glancing back at Ambrose and his grapes. To raise a child and then lose touch.

"Grapes?" Ambrose asked, offering me one in that melodious voice that made my ovaries melt.

I let him feed me one and chewed as he reached into his bag for more.

"Reggie needed this," Lauralee said as we walked the neighborhood. "He needed to come home. He called me the day after he'd returned to Chicago and said he'd made his decision. He said he was going to turn over a new leaf and live a simple, honest life. He said that he and EmmaJane were moving to Sugarland and he'd put an offer in on the Robinson's house down the street from me. The for-sale sign had been up for months, but he gave them their asking price in cash."

I knew he'd moved close to Lauralee, but I hadn't realized they'd been neighbors. "Cash? That does sound like Reggie — direct and to the point."

Lauralee grinned a bit at that. "He told me that he and EmmaJane were going to be a family who cared about each other, no matter what. As if you can just order that up."

"It would make things a lot easier," I joked.

"There's the house, up ahead," she said, pointing to a green bungalow with a generous stone porch on the opposite side of the street.

"Is that Em's car?" I asked, pointing to a sleek Jaguar parked in the driveway. It didn't seem like she'd traded down very far.

"No." Lauralee frowned. "That's Carla's Jaguar." We slowed as we passed. "Strange. Those two normally don't like each other at all."

"Maybe she's making sure Em has everything she needs," I said. No doubt Carla had known Em for most of her life. "She could just be there for support."

"Carla isn't the supportive type," Lauralee mused. "But she's so loyal to Reggie, it would be like her to try."

"Then we should pop by and make sure everything is all right." Heaven knew Em had enough on her plate without having to entertain someone she didn't like.

"Let's," my friend said as I steered Ambrose for the green house across the street. "I've been sticking close this morning just in case she needed anything."

"You know," I said as we crossed, "you might want to call her Em instead of EmmaJane. She likes it better."

Lauralee touched a hand to the bridge of her nose. "Right. I keep forgetting that." She eyed me. "Reggie was so insistent."

"She's no wallflower herself," I began, not sure how to address that elephant in the room.

As usual, Lauralee understood what I was thinking. "I realize Em can be a pill, but oh my word. Did you know Reggie burned her designer wardrobe?"

I bugged my eyes out at her.

"He did it the night he went back to Chicago. It took all five of their fireplaces."

"She must have flipped." Even I would have gotten upset if somebody just burned everything I owned. Not that I owned much anymore.

I steered the red wagon up Em's front drive and onto the sidewalk next to it.

"He sold her car and thrust her into a job and a life she wasn't prepared to lead," Lauralee said. "Now he's gone, and she has to learn to deal with it on her own. She's lost both of her parents in the past year, and she doesn't really know anybody nearby except for me."

I lifted Ambrose out of the wagon and situated him on my hip. "I can't imagine," I told her. I really couldn't. Even after my dad died, I still had my mom and my sister, not to mention my grandmother and friends like Lauralee to pull me through.

Em, on the other hand, had gone from socialite to social outcast.

We made our way up onto the wide stone porch. Lauralee knocked while I held Ambrose.

Em answered the door, her blond hair slicked back into a ponytail, her face pinched with irritation. "Oh, good. More people I didn't invite over."

"Grape?" Ambrose asked, offering her one.

Em rolled her eyes and ushered us into her front room, which she'd done up with modern furniture and accessories in various shades of white, gray, and pink. It was very classy, very clean.

It didn't look like a place where I should put Ambrose down.

Only Carla seemed startled at our small-town drop-in. She sat on the white love seat, with an array of casket sales sheets spread out on the glass coffee table.

"We were out for a walk and wanted to check on you," Lauralee assured her cousin.

"I'm doing great," Em said, scooping up a sales sheet with a shiny brown casket displayed like any other product, with rows of prices underneath. "What kind of coffin do you think Daddy would have wanted, Lauralee? Carla's dying for me to pick one."

"I'm trying to help," Carla said, bringing a hand to her temple. "Your father would want me to help."

To my horror, Ambrose snatched the paper out of Em's hand and began waving it around, crumpling the bottom in his little fist. "I'm so sorry." I tried to get it away from him while he bit the corner of it like a miniature savage. "We just fed him."

Em softened a bit. "Let him have it. There's more where that came from."

"What can we do for you?" Lauralee asked.

Carla stood, her hands clasped in front of her as if she were trying to maintain the decorum of the room. "You can leave us in peace," she instructed. "Emma-Jane and I are working to find some closure."

"She's beyond ready to bury him," Em said, scooping up another sales sheet and handing it to Ambrose the destroyer. "That's our Carla, a paragon of efficiency."

Color rose to Carla's cheeks and she appeared as stricken as if Em had slapped her. "Reggie placed the utmost importance on tradition, family, friends." She hesitated briefly. "You may not care for me, but your father was one of the most important people in my life. He would want us to plan a nice memorial where people can gather and—"

Em turned on her. "Why are you so eager to bury my father?"

"It's a sign of respect," Carla shot back, before she caught herself. She looked to Lauralee for support. "Reggie liked—"

"You don't know what he wanted," Em spat. "Dad left no instructions for his funeral. I'm sick and tired of you trying to force decisions on me, telling me what he wanted." She turned to Lauralee. "And you. If you bring me one more casserole, I'm going to scream."

"You need to eat—" my friend began.

Em glared at her. "Give me space!"

Ambrose screwed up his face and let out a hollow wail.

Em swept the brochures off the table, scattering them over the carpet. "My dad wanted a simpler life," she said, straightening. "Fine. What can be simpler than reducing him to ashes and scattering them to the wind?" Carla gasped and Em relished the older woman's shock. "I'll call the crematorium myself. We'll have it done immediately. He liked ending things in the fireplace."

This was getting out of control fast. "I understand you're upset—" I began.

Lauralee stepped in front of me. "We're not against cremation, but at least think it through."

Em's glossed mouth curved into a calculating grin. "Don't worry, cousin. He wanted to be dirt. I'm letting him be dirt." She strolled past us and threw open the door. "Now get out."

We left, mainly so we could calm poor little Ambrose down and get him back into his wagon with his grapes. It stunned me how quickly the situation with Em had deteriorated.

Carla stopped Lauralee briefly on the front porch. "Don't worry," she said, her eyes reddening, "I won't let her do anything to hurt him."

I hated to break it to her, but I didn't see where we had much control.

Lauralee thanked her for her efforts and we continued our walk. Still, I couldn't keep myself from glancing back at the green house and at Carla's Jaguar as she sped away down the street. "Em's going to leave for Chicago as soon as the police let her." Or Ecuador. I'd seen those brochures.

"We'll lose her for good," my friend said, glum, "and there will be nothing we can do about it."

"Maybe she'll calm down and call you," I said. "You're not overbearing," I added, countering Em's angry claim.

"I don't mean to be," Lauralee whispered.

We turned into Lauralee's drive and Ambrose clapped his hands. "Home!"

"Bath," she told him pragmatically, and he seemed even happier at that.

"I invited her over last night, but she wanted to be alone." Lauralee parked the red wagon near the porch and lifted Ambrose out of it. "I hope she at least has friends in Chicago who will support her. She shouldn't have to do this by herself. She's acting almost flippant about the whole thing, like she doesn't care." I opened the door and she entered first with Ambrose. "When I picked her up at the bank yesterday, she even yelled, 'I quit!' on her way out."

I hadn't spoken with Em much, but I remembered our run-in in the lobby of the bank. "I think she says things sometimes just to shock people." I closed the door as Lauralee began stripping Ambrose out of his muddy clothes.

Lauralee nodded her agreement. "It's like she's afraid to care." She shook her head as Ambrose struggled out of his shirt. "I worry EmmaJane — Em," she corrected herself, "is reacting to Reggie's death the same way she reacted to the move. She's angry and isolated, so she's pushing everyone away."

When she had Ambrose down to his Pull-Ups, she lifted him into her arms. "Big Tom thinks I should take her out for a nice meal. He says we should plan something at a restaurant and not just drop by or invite her to the house."

"He may have a point." The usual Sugarland casserole etiquette hadn't helped.

"It'd feel more social, less like a family intervention, if you came along," my friend said with a cringe. "It might help her connect and feel supported."

Reggie had suggested the same. "As long as you're the one who asks her," I said. I wouldn't be venturing into that particular bear cave. "I'd be glad to help you."

My friend let out a breath. "Good. It's a relief to at least have a plan."

"All the same, I'd give it a few days," I suggested.

"No kidding," Lauralee agreed.

"Bath?" Ambrose asked.

I kissed him on the nose. "Sorry, bub. I'll get out of your way." To his mother, I added, "Call me about that dinner."

"I'll let you know," she said. "And thanks," she added. "For the coffee and the company, and…everything."

"My pleasure," I said. And it was. "I'd do anything for you," I promised her.

Chapter Ten

I steered my big green Cadillac down Lauralee's street, passing Jackson Park and heading up toward Main. Reggie's daughter wasn't the type who would take kindly to being a project—or a suspect—and we'd be careful not to make her feel that way. But if we could help her, and if at the same time I could determine who had killed her father, well, I owed Reggie and Lauralee that much.

How to do it was the question. My usual direct approach wouldn't work.

I'd begun to ponder the problem when flashing blue and red police lights lit up my back window.

A short siren blast barked at me to halt. Mercy. I checked the land yacht's large, round speedometer. I hadn't been over the limit. Then I took a hard look through my rearview mirror and saw Ellis in the squad car behind me.

Irritation stabbed at me. He couldn't just pull me over whenever he felt like talking.

I kept driving.

A loudspeaker crackled behind me. "Pull to the side of the road."

Seems he didn't get the memo.

I ground my car to a stop in front of a tidy blue

house with an American flag on the porch, irritated at myself as much as him. I still didn't know what to say. And after our run-in with Em, I wasn't feeling so confident when it came to interpersonal relations.

I straightened my back against the velvet bench seat and resisted the urge to check my hair in the rearview mirror. I cared, but I couldn't let him know I gave a whit about my appearance. And heavens, I still wore the Technicolor dream coat.

"Quickly…" I murmured, breaking a land-speed record wriggling out of the thing. I tossed it onto the floor near the front passenger seat as Ellis stepped out of his car.

He looked as handsome as ever. He could be annoying that way.

Ellis carried himself like a man who knew how to handle any situation, and he did. He'd saved my hide more than once. His tan and black deputy sheriff's uniform fit over his broad shoulders like a dream, and excuse me if I got a bit of a thrill from the gun belt around his lean hips. In fact, if I wasn't careful, he could melt me into a puddle on the floor.

I lowered the old roller window and leaned out on an elbow. "Ellis," I said, trying for sweet, sounding more clipped and nervous. I tucked a stray lock of hair behind my ear. "I don't need you stopping me like this."

He leaned a hand against my door frame and cocked his head toward the back of my Cadillac. "Your brake light is out."

I sat back. "Really?" That hadn't happened since I owned the car, and I didn't know much about vehicle maintenance. I'd have to figure out how to fix it, not to mention pay for it.

"I can install you a new one," Ellis offered, gentlemanly and just a tad modest.

"It's not going to fix what happened yesterday," I began.

"I heard what she said to you," he said quickly, "the last part at least," he added tightly. "I thought what she did to you was about the wedding money, but what I witnessed at my door, that was personal. I told her it ends now. I'm not going to let her treat you that way."

"What did you say to her?" He might have made it worse.

"I didn't tell her about us," he conceded. "I wanted to, but I wouldn't do that without your okay."

I felt my shoulders relax. Thank goodness for small miracles.

He whooshed out a breath. He still had a slight scar under his eye from when he'd saved me from a killer. If anything, it made him even sexier. "Your brake light is out," he said, as if that justified our entire exchange.

I tried to fight a grin. "Well, then I'm just glad I know a guy who can fight crime and install brake lights."

That was Ellis. He'd learned how to fix a heater so he could maintain Maisie Hatcher's system when she had too little money and too much pride to accept charity. He took extra shifts on holidays for the officers who had wives and children.

If he tamed his mother, he really would be Superman.

He drummed his fingers on my door frame and pretended to consider the question. "When properly motivated," he conceded.

He cocked a grin and I couldn't help but do the same. Dang. If I wasn't careful, I'd fall right back in with this man. Head first.

That could be a big mistake.

I braced my hands on the wheel. "Ellis, what are we doing?"

He let out a huff, his gaze wandering out to the road in front of us. "Hell if I know." His piercing hazel eyes returned to me, hiding nothing.

"It isn't smart," I chastised him, and myself.

"Don't remind me." He leaned a hand against my door frame. "Listen, aside from your run-in with my mother, I wanted to know if you were okay after yesterday. After you left, I called the station and they told me what happened at the bank. How are you doing?"

"Not great," I admitted. "I was there for the whole thing, Ellis. I mean, I was upstairs in Reggie's office when he was killed, but I was down there with Stan, Carla, Jeb, and Em right after Carla found his body."

He shook his head and stepped back. I used the opportunity to get out of the car. "You've got to stop hanging out at crime scenes," he said plainly.

I closed the door a little harder than necessary. "It's not like it's a hobby," I said, crossing my arms over my chest. Dang, it was chilly out here. I winced as a car drove past, kicking up small rocks and debris. "I could have been downstairs with a killer. Although I'm hoping the murderer snuck out upstairs and through the door Jeb wasn't guarding." I really didn't like the idea of it being someone I'd spent time with.

Ellis positioned himself between me and the road, clearly debating how much he could tell me. "The camera in the stairwell shows nobody left that way."

It still didn't mean it was Stan, Jeb, Carla, or Em. "Someone could have been hiding out down there, for days even."

"No," Ellis said. "The night security guard checked the entire floor at the end of his shift."

Yikes. So it had to be one of the four of them.

Or Handsome Henry. I shuddered to think Frankie could be right on this one. The ghost would certainly be able to avoid guards and cameras.

And according to Frankie, a ghost could have shorted out the camera over the vault.

I leaned against the closed car door. "Stan says he was upstairs when Reggie died, but I think he went down there before the killing. I told Duranja. Did that make it into the report?"

"Yes." Ellis braced his hands on his gun belt. "Only your story doesn't bear out." His gaze caught mine. "Stan came down less than a minute before you did, right before Carla opened the door. Jeb also confirms it."

"So he didn't do it," I said automatically, bothered that I hadn't gotten my timeline right and that I'd caused Stan pain in the process.

Ellis drew a hand through his short brown hair, leaving it adorably mussed. "It's easy to make mistakes when your emotions are in play," he conceded.

"Yes," I said, not sure what to do with that. Why couldn't I be one of those people who knew what to do right out of the chute? I always tried to do the right thing.

"Aren't you glad you're also in the clear?" he prodded.

"I already knew that," I said.

"The police didn't," he said as another car blew past. "I did," he added.

The police radio on his belt kicked on, something about illegal parking on Main.

"What about Carla, Em, or Jeb?" I asked.

"We're not sure." Ellis's jaw ground tight. "They were all down there during the killing. Nobody left or entered, save Jeb for a smoke."

"I'm surprised they didn't call you to investigate."
He was the best they had, and I wasn't being biased.

His radio started up again and he turned it off. "After that last murder we solved, let's just say I'm not Detective Marshall's favorite person."

"We did it mostly by the book," I pointed out. Except for the ghostly parts.

He tilted his head down at me. "I read the report and learned you had an urn in your purse when the police searched it. Care to tell me more?"

He knew all about my ghost buddy. Ellis was one of the few people who would understand.

I shrugged. "Frankie wanted a field trip."

"Did Frankie see anything that could impact the case?" Ellis pressed. "Did he talk to anyone important?"

"That's why I stopped by your house yesterday."

"I figured," he said.

I rubbed the back of my neck and tried to think. "This is going to sound crazy if you ever repeat it," I began.

He leaned next to me against the car. "Try me."

"Frankie didn't see the murder, but he believes it looks like the work of a hit man named Henry Hagar."

Ellis froze, visibly shocked.

"What do you know?" I asked quickly.

He blew out a breath and pushed up off the car. "There's been a development," he said, obviously being careful with what he revealed. He glanced back at me. "I suppose I can tell you since it's going to be in the papers tomorrow." His expression hardened. "We found an unusual object in Reggie's jacket — an engraved pocket watch that belonged to 'Handsome'

Henry Hagar, a gangster who died in 1933."

"Oh cripes."

He studied my reaction carefully. "The watch is inscribed to him from his loving sweetheart, Rosie."

"I've never met either one of them," I said, "but Frankie knew Henry when they were both alive. From the way Frankie talks, Henry is beyond ruthless."

He thought for a moment, then asked the million-dollar question. "If Henry is dead, can he kill?"

Heavens. I didn't know for sure. "I believe it's possible. I mean, ghosts have almost killed me before..." I braced my hands on my hips. "Of course, that was when Frankie opened me to the spiritual plane."

He thought for a moment. "I doubt Reggie was in the same boat as you." He quirked a brow. "Unless he started dumping urns onto his rosebushes."

"Even then, Frankie's one in a million," I remarked. "He opened me to the other side after the murder, but I didn't see Henry."

"I'm glad you didn't," Ellis said. "I don't like the idea of you alone with a hit man."

"Neither do I," I admitted, appreciating his concern. "But I'm going to have to talk to him eventually to find out whether he could kill a living person." Saying it out loud sounded bad, even to me, but I pressed forward anyway, trying to reason it out. "Frankie's tried to shoot people, but so far all he has are ghostly bullets. He might be able to shoot himself in the foot, but that's about it."

Ellis thought for a moment. "We'll figure it out."

"We're going to need help. There is a ghost named Matthew Jackson." He was a former Union soldier and one of the most knowledgeable spiritual entities I'd met. "He haunts the old library, and he's a friend. He can talk to me even if Frankie isn't involved."

He looked at his watch. "I'm going off duty soon. I'm coming with you."

I'd like that. "Follow me."

Chapter Eleven

The Sugarland Public Library stood in the middle of the town square, directly across from the bank. Red limestone columns flanked the entrance, and the door resembled something out of a medieval castle. It seemed they didn't get much of a crowd on Tuesday afternoons. I parked in front, and Ellis pulled up right behind me.

I made it out of the car before him and waited near one of the century-old iron lampposts. Across the way, police tape crisscrossed the downstairs entrance to the bank. Two squad cars were parked out front, along with a half dozen other vehicles. It appeared as if at least the lobby had reopened, and the police were still at work below. I wondered what they were finding.

Ellis joined me, his gaze following mine. "Let's focus on our part of the job."

"Right." We had the chance to do some real good here.

"Follow my lead with Matthew, okay?" I wasn't sure if Ellis would be able to see the spirit of the dead Yankee, but it was a distinct possibility. There was no telling with Matthew. He was powerful enough to let me see him without Frankie's help. Matthew was kind by nature, but decades of abuse from other ghosts had taken their toll and he angered easily. We'd have to watch our step.

"Ellis!" a woman's crisp voice called out from somewhere to our left.

A stunning older woman in a fine fur coat had paused on her way out of the church next door. She wore her gray hair in a sleek bob held back by designer sunglasses and set off with glittering red earrings.

She waved, and my handsome companion cursed under his breath. "Mrs. Nellie Holcamp," he ground out.

"Ah, yes," I said, putting on a brave face as I returned her wave. Nellie ran in the same social circles as Ellis's mother. "I've met her." Back when I was welcome in that fold.

I was suddenly very aware of how close I stood to Virginia Wydell's middle son, and what it meant to be seen together like this. Great. I was caught without getting to enjoy any indiscretion beforehand.

There was nothing to be done about it, except to cast Mrs. Holcamp my sweetest smile and wait for the reckoning. With any luck, she'd decide to practice whatever Christian virtues she'd learned in the house of God and leave us in peace.

Unfortunately for us, she didn't seem to be feeling any love for her fellow man.

The society matron advanced on us like a spider stalking fresh prey. My heart beat faster, knowing there was no escape.

I hadn't encountered Nellie since I'd returned her wedding present and her bridal shower gift—in person—this past summer. The hand-embroidered Egyptian cotton bedding and the Waterford crystal candlesticks had both been quite lovely, and very thoughtful, but of course I couldn't keep them.

"Why, Ellis," she called as she neared, tucking her cashmere scarf into her fur collar, taking her time. She had us well and truly stuck. "How interesting to see you here."

He gave her an indulgent nod. "You look lovely today, Nellie." If he were at all disturbed by her presence, he didn't show it.

She stopped in front of us, pursing her red-stained lips in a way that made it clear she'd earned a black belt in society manners. "My, my...you do know how to make a lady feel special," she said to Ellis before her cold gaze flicked over to me. "He was always the sweet one. It's in his nature, dear. Don't let it go to your head."

A chilly wind slammed into me. "Mrs. Holcamp," I said, with more sweetness than self-preservation required, "you have no idea."

Ellis and I were walking uphill with roller skates on. It wasn't just Ellis's mother who would make our lives difficult. We'd have to deal with the opinions of every busybody in town. But right here, right now, I wasn't about to let a bony jerk like her define our relationship.

"My, my...you are confident," she said, as if it were a bad thing. I felt the hardness of her stare and smelled the bite of her French perfume. "It seems you can't leave the Wydell boys alone for a red-hot second, can you?"

I opened my mouth to tell her I was doing just fine by myself when my teeth picked that moment to chatter.

"Mrs. Holcamp," Ellis said, his rich baritone at odds with her shrill pettiness, "you have better manners than this. And more sense."

Her cheeks flushed with color. "I could say the same thing about you, young man," she shot back. "I weep for your mother."

"And I for your husband," he stated, silencing her at last. Suddenly Ellis's warm police jacket settled over me and his hands squeezed my shoulders. "I'm sorry, Verity. I should have noticed you were cold. It's time we went inside."

Nellie's face lit up as if she'd witnessed the rapture. "Will you both excuse me? I have many, many phone calls to make."

"Knock yourself out," Ellis muttered.

I stood, stunned, with his hands still on my shoulders. He might welcome the chaos that came with pushing her buttons, but I didn't. Thanks to my ex-almost-mother-in-law, I had a hard enough time trying to fit into the Sugarland community without this. It was just like Ellis to do what he felt needed to be done, damn the consequences.

Irrational guilt seared my stomach as she crossed the street to the silver Lincoln Town Car parked opposite my land yacht. It wasn't as if she'd caught us at anything, I reminded myself.

We were barely dating, and I was only beginning to rebuild my reputation in town. What could Nellie do to me that Virginia hadn't done already? I shuddered to find out. Ellis had certainly picked the wrong time to be a gentleman.

"Don't let her bother you," he said tightly, helping me with the sleeves so I could feel the full heat of the jacket.

"You can't ask me to stop feeling." Maybe I should have been thicker-skinned or smarter or untouchable. But I wasn't. Her words stung. Virginia's threats scared me, despite Ellis's reassurances. I couldn't help

that. I turned toward the library, lest either of them
see the hurt I wore too plainly. I wasn't some warrior
woman. I was just a regular person and proud of it.

I didn't want to be an outcast in my boyfriend's
family or in the town that I loved. I shoved my hands
into the warm, fleece-lined pockets of Ellis's jacket as I
started up the wide, stone stairs to the library.

He joined me. "It has nothing to do with you."

"You're sweet to say that," I told him, snuggling
deeper into his warm jacket. We both knew it wasn't
true. My reputation's downward spiral began when
Virginia Wydell had gone after me for rejecting her
youngest son. "What was your mother doing at your
place anyway?" She wasn't the type to visit. She usually summoned her sons to the family estate.

He took the next two steps in silence. "Yesterday, I
found out that I applied for Yale Law School. Mom's
doing. You think she could have come clean before
the acceptance letter came. Beau dropped her off to do
damage control. Or maybe he just wanted to see if I'd
let her in the door."

I gave him a wide-eyed stare. "Wow." Leave it to
Virginia Wydell to be that gutsy. I grinned to myself.
I'd known Ellis was smart, but I didn't realize he
had that kind of ability. "You're happy on the force,
though, right?"

His expression hardened. "Of course. I've never
wanted to do anything else." He stared straight
ahead. "She dug up my old LSATs. She forced one of
my dad's law clerks to answer the essay questions."

Imagine if Virginia Wydell chose to use her powers
for good, instead of…this. "She's got to know by now
she can't change you."

He opened the door to the library for me. "That
doesn't mean she'll stop trying. My brothers have fall-

en into line. Beau stopped chasing you." He shrugged stiffly, and I could hear the hurt in his voice. "Now she's going to fix me."

I paused in the doorway. "I'm sorry."

He tried to wave it off like it was nothing. "She needs to feel in control of something." I entered the library and he followed. "At least I managed to dodge the decorator she hired for my place," he added, his voice echoing in the high-ceilinged lobby. "She gave the damned woman my key. I had to change my locks. Now I've got to finish busting out a wall."

Okay, this was one area where I agreed with Virginia that he could improve, but not by force. We headed past the displays of quilting books and British-style mysteries. "Tell her to cut it out."

"The ideal solution for sure. Too bad my mother doesn't respond to reason or logic," he said. "What gets me is that my place does look better without that wall between the kitchen and the dining room," he added, with a measure of irritation.

I cringed. "I could see that," I admitted. It would open up the space. Heavens, though. It bothered me that he'd followed her advice, that he'd take her opinion, even if it was about a wall.

He paused at the entrance to the main reading room. "Look, I don't want to talk about it anymore."

No doubt.

"There's Melody," I said, waving at my sister, who stood behind the long, wooden reference desk at the back.

A group of patrons passed us on the way out. By the time the main doors boomed closed behind them, Melody had made her way over.

Today she wore her blond hair in a side braid that made her look like a Disney princess, with a pink flower pen tucked behind her ear. She glanced from me to Ellis and back to me again in a way I knew meant plenty of questions later.

"How are you holding up?" she asked, folding me into a sisterly embrace while giving a short tug on my hair, same as she did when we were growing up.

"As best as I can," I said, reluctant to let her go.

Ellis stood slightly behind me. She stepped back and eyed him as if she could determine what we'd been doing together. Certainly not that. "Is Ellis helping you with the case?"

"You realize I'm the police officer," he said.

I focused on my sister. "We have a question for one of the library ghosts. Can we visit the stacks?"

She debated in her head and winced when she came to her conclusion. "We have a tour group going through the back. Ellen Haines is leading them. She never misses a beat, but I think I can sneak you down." She motioned us into the main reading room. "Come with me." Melody led us past the rows of reading desks. "After you come back up, we can talk about Henry Hagar. I still need to double-check a few facts, but I think I might have something."

Good. She was working on it. "What have you found so far?"

"Some newspaper clippings and several original photographs." The entrance to the stacks was located in the hall behind the circulation desk. She opened the pass-through on the desk to let us through. "Handsome Henry was a ruthless guy." Melody glanced to the main customer desk. "I have a line," she said. "The door is open. Can you make it from here?"

"Yes." I gave her a quick kiss on the cheek. "Thanks."

"Don't bring any ghosts back up with you," she

added, only half teasing.

There were a lot more ghosts right here than there'd ever be in the basement. The library had been a field hospital during the Civil War, and I'd met a multitude of spooks on my last adventure. They crowded the main floor of the library; she just couldn't see them. Neither could I without Frankie.

Ellis and I slipped past the door marked Employees Only behind the desk and entered the stark corridor in the back. Straight across stood the old oak door that led to the stacks.

It had once been the old coal room, back when the library had needed mounds of it to heat the three-story building. Now when I opened the door wide, cold air streamed from the narrow staircase.

According to Melody, the librarians avoided this place when they could. They were a smart bunch.

"This feels strange," Ellis murmured. He pulled on the string above the dark staircase and lit a single bulb.

The hair on the back of my neck prickled, and I could have sworn something menacing stood directly behind us. I turned, but no one was there.

Courage.

We peered down into the semidarkness. A warning niggled in the back of my brain, the distinct feeling that we were not welcome here.

"To be honest, I'd hoped for a friendlier greeting," I murmured. Matthew could be quite dangerous when he was in a dark mood. "If that's even Matthew down there."

Ellis cleared his throat. "Is there any way to tell?"

"No," I said quietly. "Not without seeking him out."

"All right," Ellis said, taking the first step down.

I had to give him props for bravery.

With each step, the air grew chillier. Goose bumps pricked up my arms.

Ahead of me, Ellis slowly trailed a hand over the rough-cut gray stone wall, taking in every detail. I wondered if he felt the intense loneliness of the place, the utter emptiness and despair.

He reached for the next light-bulb string, his breath puffing out in front of him. It was getting colder than any indoor space should be. "I thought you were on good terms with this ghost."

"I haven't talked to him in several months," I admitted. "He may have moved out to be with his girl." Matthew had found love with a ghost from our last adventure, and I sincerely hoped they were still together.

A low moan echoed from beyond, sending goose bumps skittering up my arms. We pressed forward — foolish or brave, I didn't know which — until Ellis ground to a halt in a pool of weak light at the bottom of the stairs.

Blue emergency lights cast an uneven glow over the first few rows of bookshelves. Beyond that, we saw only darkness.

"Matthew?" I called, hoping it was indeed him down here. My throat felt tight and I couldn't keep from shivering. "It's Verity, and a friend." An icy chill settled over us. I ignored it and kept my voice even. "May we come visit?"

I didn't dare speak again as I stepped into the shadows. I didn't have a choice. Matthew was our best bet to get our questions answered about Handsome Henry and what he was capable of.

"Keep it slow," Ellis murmured as we advanced down the first narrow row. "You don't want to spook him...or it."

I think I was frightened enough for all three of us. My fingers trailed along the shelved and forgotten books on either side of me. Matthew wouldn't hurt me on purpose, but when I'd first met him, he'd been half-wild with madness. I didn't know if he could re-vert back to that state. He should be happy. I'd helped him meet a nice girl and reunited him with his family.

The books under my fingers began to crackle and shudder. I yanked my hands back like they were on fire. The books grew still once more.

"What the hell was that?" Ellis hissed.

"No clue," I said, moving forward once more. The books on the high shelves began to twitch, and I real-ized we were surrounded by potential projectiles. "Maybe we should turn back."

A low, shuddering groan sounded from deep in the stacks.

I stopped and Ellis nearly ran into me. He caught me at the waist and I found a moment of comfort in his strong, steady presence. "I got you," he said against my ear.

We saw a flicker of movement ahead.

Ellis clicked on his flashlight and shone it on that very spot.

We saw nothing. Just an empty concrete floor, then...a dusty hardback book, and another. And an-other. Ellis's light crept up a stack of books that stood taller than either of us, directly in front of us, blocking our way.

"That's it, we should leave," I said, turning around to see that another stack of books blocked our only exit. It stood dark against the weak glow of the secu-rity lights. "Oh, sweet Jesus."

Ellis placed a shaking hand on my shoulder. "Relax. Think."

"I think we're trapped," I whispered, fighting the urge to panic.

"Maybe someone wants to talk to you," Ellis murmured.

Matthew didn't need to corner me to talk.

"Matthew," I said low, but loud enough for the ghost to hear. If he was here, in his right mind, he could help us escape from...whoever had us. "Matthew!" If he'd gone off the deep end or if another ghost had taken over this space, then we could be in real trouble. "Matthew," I gasped when a ghost shot out from the bookshelf to my right.

The face appeared more skeletal than human. It hissed, its teeth bared, its yellow eyes boring into me as it charged straight for us.

CHAPTER TWELVE

"Sweet Jesus!" Ellis tugged me against him, shielding me with his body as the entity advanced on us. We needed help. Now.

"Matthew!" I hollered.

"Verity?" Matthew's voice crackled with energy. It sounded so far away.

A skeletal hand reached for us, its sharp talons closing in for the grip. Ellis wrapped an arm around my torso and I clung to it.

"Matthew!" He was a powerful enough spirit to drive this angry ghost back out. Did he see how much trouble we were in? Why wasn't he swooping in to help?

The ghost halted and bent at the waist as if offering a bow, and a stark realization hit me. I'd seen that move. Only one ghost had ever given me a courtly Southern gentleman's greeting.

"You're Matthew!" I said, praying he realized it, too.

He examined his outstretched skeletal hand as if seeing himself for the first time. "Oh, I beg your pardon," he said, as if he'd been caught answering the door in his pajamas. "This will not do." His voice still sounded farther away than he was. I didn't understand it. "If you'll give me a moment," he said, with a hint of a Southern drawl. "I'll attempt to right myself."

I clung to Ellis, dizzy with the urge to flee, as the spirit turned its back to us.

A blast of cold air set my teeth to rattling as flesh took shape over the ghost's bony arms and hands. As his torso shimmered into focus, I could see his simple white shirt, along with plain dark pants and a set of suspenders.

The spirit turned toward us, and I was relieved to see Matthew's high cheekbones, wary expression, and weak chin. "I apologize if my appearance startled you," he said, producing a Union officer's cap out of thin air. He placed it on his head, somewhat embarrassed. "I've been in a difficult state."

"Apology accepted," Ellis murmured, his body stiff with shock.

I took Ellis's hand—not willing to let go completely—and stepped forward to find out what was going on. "What's the matter?" I asked Matthew. This wasn't like him. He was supposed to be happily engaged to a ghostly friend of mine. "Where's Josephine?"

His features softened at the mention of his fiancée. I'd first met Jilted Josephine while exploring the old Hatcher homestead. The truth of Josephine's existence was very different from the stories I'd grown up with. It seemed town rumor had painted us both in a bad light. Josephine had a tough time at love, and so had Matthew. When they'd met in the haunted woods, it had been pure magic.

The ghost buried his hands in his pockets, the outline of his fists clearly visible under the thin fabric. "My love is staying with her cousin in the country. She says it's bad luck to see the bride right before the wedding."

"So it's coming up soon." It would have been lovely to be invited, but I wasn't one to press. Truth be told, I hadn't expected these old-fashioned ghosts to wait long. And it certainly didn't explain why he was so upset. "When is the big day?"

He began to pace. "Today, tomorrow…never." He clutched his head. "The Confederate chaplain won't marry her to a Yankee, and I can't find our local preacher. I think he went to the light."

"Oh my." I hadn't anticipated the difficulty of finding a proper minister on the ghostly plane.

"She probably thinks I've gotten cold feet, and of course I haven't. But I don't want to go see her until I have a solution, and so far I can't find anyone to marry us." His eyes began to glow and his skin grew thinner and I could see the bones starting to protrude again.

"Stop. I'll help," I said before I could think on it too much.

The poor ghost brightened. "You will? Of course you will. I should have known you would." He sat up a bit straighter and turned to Ellis. "Verity's a good girl."

"Crazy girl," he said, drawing a shaky breath.

I let that one go. We were both under a bit of stress.

Matthew paced the narrow aisle between the bookshelves. "I search the churchyards day and night. I go to wakes. When I'm too sad to wander far, I stack books, I unstack books," he said listlessly as an old green hardback flew off the shelf and into his hand. He held it out to me. "I found this one for you last week. It's on some of the old Sugarland estates. Your family home is listed."

"Thanks," I said, taking it. Considering I'd lost my

best chance at a job, I would most likely have plenty of reading time coming up. I clutched the book to my chest. "I came to see you this afternoon because we had a murder across the street at the bank." He frowned, but I pressed forward anyway. "We have three live people who could have done it, but we're also looking at a dead one."

"Focus on the flesh and blood suspects," he said. "Most ghosts do not actively seek to interfere with your world."

That would be easier to believe if a ghost hadn't tried to kill me a few months ago.

And if I didn't have another ghost who insisted on keeping a rosebush in my house.

Ellis tried a different angle. "The man was shot with a real bullet, which we're assuming was fired from a real gun," he said, "but Frankie thinks it looks like the work of a hit man he knows. Have you ever met Handsome Henry Hagar?"

Matthew snorted. "I try to avoid that lot. I don't even like unhandsome Frankie." He shook his head. "I realize the gangster is your friend, Verity, but Frankie has no idea what he's suggesting."

"Probably not," I admitted. My ghostly house-guest didn't think beyond what was expedient at the moment. But that didn't change what we'd come to learn. "But we both know it's possible for a ghost to manipulate an object in the mortal world." I lifted the book Matthew had just floated over to me, as if there were any doubt.

He stopped to think about it, and I found it eerie the way the weak rays of the security lighting shone clear through his head. "I can think of only one reason why a ghost might try to kill a living person, and that is if his land and his peace were being invaded. But even then I don't know why he'd choose such a difficult way to go about it." He sighed. "It makes no sense. He'd have to be extremely angry and gain energy from that rage."

"That sounds like a poltergeist," I said.

"So we may have a powerful, murderous poltergeist," Ellis said to himself, clearly working out a way to arrest the entity.

"I don't approve of you going after a murderer, whether the person is dead or alive," Matthew said, using his hand to float a book off the shelf next to me. He guided it through thin air and placed it on the stack behind us.

"But you do know Henry," I pressed. Matthew hadn't denied it, and he'd done his best to redirect me. Too bad for him I'd been through the maze of Southern society talk more times than I could count. "You can help me, or I can stir up a lot of ghosts and make a lot of noise looking for him."

"Don't." He turned quickly, knocking over his stack of books, not even reacting as they crashed straight through him. "You must not go near Henry Hagar. He's evil, conniving, ruthless." Matthew advanced on us. "He's sick in the head and completely unpredictable. He's the type to haunt you for the fun of it."

"Oh boy," I muttered.

Ellis cleared his throat. "Is this what it's like for you every time?"

"Pretty much," I said, regretting that I'd ever walked into the bank yesterday morning.

But Lauralee needed me, Em had lost her dad, and I was here to do what I could.

"I absolutely refuse to help you find him," Matthew said, as if that were the end of it.

"All right," I said. Maybe I wouldn't have to find

Handsome Henry. Right now, at this very moment, the police could be breaking the case wide open. Perhaps the only help I'd need to give my friend would be a friendly ear and a shoulder to lean on.

I exchanged a glance with Ellis. We could hope.

***

We left Matthew underground, restacking his books. I had to find a preacher for him and Josephine. Soon. Both ghosts had been prone to depression in the past, and I wouldn't let them get down in the dumps over something that I could fix.

Ellis and I climbed the steps to the main floor of the library.

"Maybe Henry Hagar isn't attached to the crime," he reasoned. "The only evidence we have is Frankie's word that it appears to be a Handsome Henry-style murder."

"That and the pocket watch," I pointed out.

"Which is the kind of thing someone would leave if they wanted to pin it on Henry," he countered.

I followed him out the door. "All right. Which of our three potential killers would have known enough about Henry to pin it on him, and how would one of them get his watch?"

"That's what the police have been trying to discover." Ellis closed the door behind us. "I'm sorry I involved you in this."

"I was in this before you were."

He shook his head. "I don't want you going after that guy."

Ah, so Matthew had succeeded in scaring at least one of us. "Do you have any other evidence yet?"

He snorted.

"Like it or not, you need me," I pointed out.

He rested a hand on his gun belt. "As of this morning we're stuck," he admitted, "and we will be until the murder weapon turns up. That's not common knowledge, so—"

He didn't have to finish. "Of course I won't tell anyone."

I pushed out the door that led to the main part of the library. Melody stood behind the reference desk, going over paperwork.

"How did it go?" she asked, hurrying over.

"We learned a little." We knew the hit man could do it, but whether or not he did? That was the million-dollar question.

"Come with me," she said. "I have some things set up for you in research room two." She led us toward one of the spaces just off the main reading room. The library had four research rooms in total, all with thick wooden doors and old-fashioned windows that looked out over the courtyard below.

She closed the door after we entered, which wasn't a good sign.

On a heavy dining-room-sized table at the center, she'd laid out several newspaper articles dated from the late 1920s and early '30s. The headlines shouted Handsome Henry Hits Again! and South Town Strikes Back.

"The man wasn't exactly trying to hide his crimes," Melody said.

Ellis studied an illustration of a victim with a deep, exaggerated X slashed into his right cheek and a bleeding bullet wound to the heart. "He killed a certain way so everyone would know he did it."

I scooted around a chair and picked up the nearest black-and-white photograph. It showed a couple posing in front of a Model T. The man dressed well, in a suit and tie, but his forehead, nose, and chin all stretched too wide. A jagged scar cut down the left side of his face, from his eyebrow to his chin. He reminded me of Frankenstein's monster. "Is this Handsome Henry?"

"With his girlfriend, Miss Rosie Baker, infamous in her own right as a bootlegger," Melody said, picking up another photograph. "They carried on as lovers for quite some time according to what I've found." This time, they sat at a table in a club. He appeared stern in both while the pretty blonde smiled.

"Sweet mother," I ground out. His fingers clasped the chain of a pocket watch. "Is it the same one?" I asked, passing the photo to Ellis.

He cursed under his breath. "I don't think he'd have two."

"Here's another one of them." She showed us a photo of the couple posing outside a dinner club. Again, he wore the watch. This time, it was perfectly clear.

"You'd think he would have been buried with it," I mused.

Melody shot me a quizzical look. "Are you saying someone has his watch?"

"It's a long story," I said, not wanting to get into it. But if he had it with him all the time, if he wore it constantly, then perhaps someone had taken it after he died.

Melody drew a photo from the file she held. "This is the last thing I could find. It's a 'death' photo, taken after he was gunned down in 1933. A photographer from the Sugarland Gazette took it to run in the paper."

She held out a photo that showed Henry shot to death in bed, covered in blood. It reminded me of the

graphic pictures I'd seen of the St. Valentine's Day
Massacre.

Okay, he obviously hadn't died with his watch.
"Did he have relatives that would have collected his
things?"

"Not a single one," Melody said. "His mother was
ostracized from her family for having him out of wed-
lock. She supported him alone. He grew up hard, and
when she died, he dropped out of school and joined
the gang. It's all in the article." With no one in town to
inherit or hold onto it, I didn't see why the real watch
would suddenly surface now, after all these years.
And on another murder victim.

Perhaps Henry Hagar himself would know that,
among other things. I'd have to persuade Frankie to
show me the other side and hope he knew where to
find the infamous hit man.

Ellis handed the picture back to Melody. "We'd like
you to keep this under wraps for the time being."

"Too late," she said. "Ovis Dupre came in first thing
this morning."

Of all the… "You showed him the picture?"

"He saw everything, same as you. It's part of the
public library record," Melody said, matching my
snit. "I'll research for you, but I'm not going to with-
hold information from anyone else who needs it."
She glanced at Ellis. "Ovis is publishing the pictures
tomorrow as a special guest feature in the Sugarland
Gazette."

"Why can't that man retire?" I wondered aloud.
Lauralee had enough to upset her without the whole
town knowing the lurid details of her uncle's death,
not to mention the gangster connection.

Ellis braced a hand on his gun belt. "I want to know
how Ovis found out about the watch."

I had to admit the old reporter was good at his job. And in publicizing it, he'd stir up just the kind of sensationalist gossip that would have the town buzzing.

"Are you finished with these items?" Melody asked. "I really do need to get back to the desk."

"Yes, but can you keep them handy?" I asked as she gathered them into a large brown folder.

"You have other requests, don't you?" Ellis asked.

She glanced up at him as she gathered the last of the photographs from the table. "I'll bet we will tomorrow."

Dang it.

I left the library more frustrated and confused than when I'd gone in. I understood it was Melody's job to make information available, but she could have been choosier with who she shared it with. I hurried down the steps, bracing against the chill.

"Slow down or you're going to fall down," he said, keeping pace with me.

"What? So we can run into another one of your mom's friends?" I asked.

"So what if we do?" he challenged. "I'm not going to tiptoe around you, and I'm not going to pretend nothing happened between us. Is happening," he corrected as we reached the bottom of the steps.

Wasn't he even a little bit afraid? "You heard your mother's threats."

"And I shut her down," he insisted.

Maybe for now.

It all came down to one simple truth. "I have no idea what you want from me," I confessed, "or what I can even give." I glanced down the street toward the church.

"Dinner," he answered.

I stared at him. "What?"

The corner of his mouth tipped up. "I want dinner.
You know. A meal. Like normal people." He warmed
to the idea as he spoke. "Give me the pleasure of an
evening with you, just you, and no ghosts or felons or
nosy relatives. I'll pick you up, take you to my place.
Let's do it tonight, and if it doesn't feel like the right
thing to do while we're doing it, then we'll know and
it'll be over."

He had me at a loss. Tonight? It felt too soon.

My entire body flooded with warmth and my legs
moved on their own as I began retreating to my car.
He walked with me, refusing to let me slip away this
time. "You want me to just hang out at your place,"
I stated, digging in my purse for my keys, trying to
think of a reason why I shouldn't.

"Actually, no," he said.

I turned to him, surprised to find myself more disappointed than relieved.

He gave a small, uncomfortable laugh. "My place
is a disaster. Before I changed the front door lock, my
mom's decorator added orchids," he said, as if the
plants were out to eat him. "I'm afraid to sit on the
new antique furniture in my family room, and the
dining room is a construction zone." He scratched
his chin. "There's a fainting couch in my bedroom. I
should hand in my guy card right now."

"At least you don't have a yard-waste can in your
kitchen like I do," I said, trying to make him feel better.

He thought for a moment. "Tell you what, I'll pick
you up and take you out to Southern Spirits. You can
see what I've done to the place lately. It's really coming along."

"I'll bet it is," I said, glad to be on more solid
ground. Ellis had bought the old property with his

uncle, and was working to remodel the historic distillery into a one-of-a-kind restaurant. He worked hard
on the old property. That had been one of the first
things I'd noticed about him—his work ethic and how
he cared for old buildings and traditions, rather than
just tearing them down in favor of the new.

It would be fun to see Southern Spirits again. And
I wanted to get on solid footing with Ellis, even if it
meant we decided to end our budding—and falter-
ing—relationship.

He grinned. "Stop thinking so much. I'll serve you
dinner and we'll see if we can make this work."

I shrugged out of his jacket and handed it back to
him. "Let's do this," I said before I could change my
mind.

Chapter Thirteen

I tried to keep my cool as I drove home that afternoon. I'd agreed to one night that would decide everything. It seemed crazy to put that kind of pressure on a single dinner date, but at least I'd know where I stood by the end of it.

I'd come to know Ellis well enough by now to see that he looked at life in terms of black and white. To his thinking, I either liked him or I didn't. Either it would work or it wouldn't. No gray area, no games.

What I didn't understand was his pure boldness, as if he could somehow control Virginia Wydell.

I pulled my car along the side of my house and parked in the back.

Dark clouds hung low in the sky. Two brave birds clung to the bare branches of my apple tree, fluffing their feathers against the cold.

I wrapped myself in my coat and hurried up the back porch stairs and into the semi-warmth of my kitchen.

The interior of the house lay in shadows.

I slipped off my coat and left it on the kitchen island. Hopefully, Frankie was resting in the ether where he wouldn't notice my return. I wasn't eager to run into him after sneaking out this morning.

Of course, I also had a more pressing, very real obligation. I went to the olive-green wall phone and dialed up Lauralee. She needed to be warned about Ovis's story in the paper tomorrow.

My friend answered on the second ring and sounded better than she had earlier. It made it a little easier to break the news about the dead gangster's watch and the sensationalism that would follow.

Lauralee groaned under her breath. "I know all about it. Ovis showed up at EmmaJane's house this afternoon. She was so upset she called me. Glad she did, though. He showed her pictures of some hit man and tried to interview her about what she thought, as if he really believes a dead gangster killed her father."

"I'm sorry." I wished I could have spared her.

"It's insulting," Lauralee stated. "Even worse, you know some people in this town are going to actually believe there could be a homicidal ghost running around."

"Only the crazy ones," I told her. And me.

I heard kids scuffling at my friend's house and then quiet as Lauralee found a place to hole up, most likely in her laundry room. "I tried talking to EmmaJane after Ovis left," she said. "She kept dropping the phone, and when I went down the street, she barely opened the door. It was like we were back to square one."

"Was Carla smothering her with helpfulness?"

"She was alone. From what I could see of her, EmmaJane looked almost panicked. I've never seen her like that. Now she's refusing all calls and contact. She won't even talk to the funeral home." She sighed. "At least I got her to agree to let us take her to dinner tomorrow, after she made me promise not to drop by unannounced or bring her any more casseroles or homemade cookies. But, Verity, she needs to vent or she's going to explode."

"Let's just take it one day at a time."

"I told her we'd stop by near seven, once Big Tom gets home to watch the kids."

"I'll meet you at your place." This was such a mess. I admired Lauralee to no end for the way she was able to be there for both her cousin and her own family, but I worried she'd worn herself a bit too thin. "It'll get better," I promised. It had to. "In fact, I saw Ellis this afternoon. The police are working real hard on this."

She paused for a beat. "Why are you seeing Ellis again?"

Because I couldn't help myself. "It's not important," I said. We could dissect my love life another time.

"I'll give you a pass this time," she said, "but only because I'm sitting on top of my washing machine with a light-saber battle going on outside the door and my cousin in tears down the street."

I wished there was something I could do for my friend. Perhaps I should try to at least talk to Handsome Henry. Matthew had said it was dangerous, but so was having a killer on the loose. "I'm going to try to find a way to help," I promised.

"You did this morning," she said. "Seriously, it felt good just to talk. Thank you."

It only made me want to do more.

I braced a hand against the wall and stared real hard at the gnarled, twisted loops of the kitchen phone cord. Maybe I should tell her my secret and exactly how I could help. "This is going to sound crazy," I began. Lauralee of all people would love me anyway. I wound a hand in the hopelessly tangled cord. "You remember that ugly urn that I found in my attic, the one nobody wanted…" I hesitated. Now wasn't the time. She didn't need her world rocked any more. "Never mind. Just know I love you."

The smile in her voice came through over the phone lines. "I'm counting on it."

I hung up more determined than ever to make a difference. I just had to figure out how.

I turned and nearly jumped out of my skin to see Frankie standing mere inches away from me, so near I could make out a faint stubble on his neck that I'd never noticed before.

He lowered his chin and gave me a pointed glare. "Way to sneak out on me," he said, as if I had some obligation to cart him around town.

I blew out a breath. "Excuse me for going to the library. Now kindly remove yourself from my personal space," I said, inching around him. He made me feel like a bug pinned to the wall.

He followed me so close I could feel the chill. "The library's where I like to play poker."

Sheesh. The gangster needed to learn a lesson in boundaries. I slipped past him and headed to the cabinet to grab a granola bar for a late, late lunch. "You realize I can't take you everywhere with me."

"Why not?" he asked, too close for comfort.

I turned and closed the cabinet door. "Because not every girl wants a long-dead gangster trailing her around town." I took a bite of my Chewy Oats & Honey bar. "And you're not exactly good at keeping your opinions to yourself."

"Excuse me if I call it like I see it." He crossed his arms over his chest. "What bug bit you?"

"I have no idea what you mean. I'm having a perfectly lovely afternoon," I said, like every steel-spined Southern girl before me.

Frankie rolled his eyes. "Fine. You want to play

some chess?"

"I have a date in an hour," I said, finishing off my granola bar and hoping he didn't see the color that rushed hot to my cheeks.

He smirked. "You can thank me later."

"Depending on how it goes, I may make you sleep on the porch," I said, tossing my wrapper and going to rinse my sticky fingers in the sink.

The gangster leaned up against my kitchen island, with the back half of him sinking straight in. "So where is he taking us?"

"There is no us," I warned him. "I am going to the Southern Spirits property with Ellis."

He lit up at that. "Hotsy-totsy!" he said, standing. "The South Town Gang haunts that place." He raised his hands and his eyes to the ceiling. "This is my reward."

"For what?"

"For how I make your life easier," he said.

"That's debatable," I told him.

"You owe me a night out with the fellas," he said, as if it were fact. "Now that the poltergeist isn't holding them down, they might even be able to point me to my lucky gun."

I still didn't see how a firearm was going to free him. "I can't take you on my date." It had gone badly enough when I'd brought him along on my job interview. "Ellis and I want time alone."

The gangster glided away from me, towards the trapped rosebush. "Believe me, I won't be paying attention to you."

"That's good to hear. But be practical. Why would a bunch of ghosts have your gun?"

He ran his fingers among and through the thorny branches. "That's easy. Self-defense." He dropped his hand. "Too bad it didn't help. They were all shot down in the speakeasy underneath Southern Spirits."

I stared at him. "What?"

He fidgeted with his sleeve. "It happened the night I died."

I'd wondered what Frankie had been up to while I had my hands full ridding the property of the angry ghost. "Are you investigating your death?"

He gave me a steely glare. "I don't want to talk about it."

"All right," I said, holding my hands up in surrender. I wouldn't push him. "But tell me this. When we did the job at Southern Spirits and you disappeared, you were at that speakeasy, weren't you?"

"I do have an afterlife," he groused. With a shrug of the shoulder, he added, "Our old watering hole is underneath what's now the kitchen at Southern Spirits."

Oh my word. "Does Ellis know about this?"

Frankie's lip curled with distaste. "He'd better not. South Town guys only."

"Darn it, Frankie. You're putting me in a terrible spot." Ellis and I needed to work things out. Alone.

Yet he had a multiple murder scene underneath the place where he was treating me to dinner tonight. Surely, this was reason enough to alter the agenda. Ellis deserved to know what lay beneath his property, and this could be a great opportunity to track down the hit-man ghost. I wasn't sure how my life had gotten so strange, but it had definitely started with the gangster in front of me.

I eyed Frankie. "If I take you on my night out…" and truly, this was the only instance where I'd consider it, "you have to show me and Ellis the speakeasy."

Then Ellis could decide I was too crazy and that he never wanted to see me again.

Frankie scoffed. "I ain't showing Ellis the other side. I don't have that kind of power."

"I wasn't asking that." I knew his resources were limited. "I need to see. Ellis can look at whatever is still there."

He ran a hand over his chin, thinking. "I don't want to lose my feet in front of the guys."

"You can hang out while I have my date; then we'll go down after. We'll get your gun if it's there, and I'll ask a few questions. We'll be gone before anyone knows parts of you are missing."

"That might actually work." The gangster fiddled with his collar, edgy. "I gotta tell you, you may not like some of the wiseguys you meet."

I had no illusions otherwise. "But Handsome Henry knew some of them, right?" I asked.

The gangster stiffened. "Yeah. What about it?"

"Did Henry die down there?"

Frankie's eyes narrowed. "I don't know. I was too busy getting plugged." His hand shifted to the gun in his coat as if it were second nature. "But, yeah, Henry might be hanging out. He used to tip a few with the gang from time to time."

All right. "Then it's a date."

***

Ellis picked me up promptly at six o'clock. And he arrived at the front door, instead of sneaking in the back as he had on numerous occasions before. The man had taken a stand. I just hoped I was ready for it.

He looked gorgeous in a button-down shirt that showed off his broad shoulders and made me realize just what I might be passing up. He stood with the setting sun to his back. It had already begun to sink under the horizon, throwing off shots of red and gold over the place. "You look beautiful, Verity."

"Thanks," I said. I'd tried to dress nice.

After agreeing to my ghost friend's demands, I'd gone upstairs and changed into jeans and a soft white sweater. White wouldn't be the best for going underground, but I only had three nice sweaters. One had skunk water on it and the other I'd already worn to the library today. That was the thing about a limited wardrobe—it made dressing for a date much easier.

"I hope it's okay, but I told Frankie he could tag along." I reached for my bag that I'd left hanging off the end of the bannister and resisted the urge to show him the urn inside. Ellis had seen Frankie plenty of times, and I'd rather not dwell on why the gangster had insisted on joining us. We should at least get out of the driveway before Ellis decided this wasn't going to work.

"I'd rather it be just us," Ellis said, disappointed—in me or in the situation, I couldn't tell which. Lucy tried to climb his leg and he bent to greet her. The skunk didn't like to come out when Frankie was around, but she appeared to have made an exception for my date. She nudged her nose against his leg and grunted happily.

He scratched Lucy on the sweet spot behind her left ear. She responded by flopping against him and twitching her left back leg. Okay, that made me melt a little.

"I realize it's a bit odd." Not the petting-the-skunk part, but the fact that we had a third-wheel ghost.

"But you already told him he could come," Ellis said, guessing the truth as he glanced up at me.

"Something like that," I winced.

Frankie chuckled behind me. "He'll be okay once you take him ghost hunting. You two ain't happy unless you're fixing something."

I smoothed my sweater and tried to relax. I didn't need Frankie playing Dr. Phil. I had this handled.

Ellis stood. "Ready?"

"Sure." I tucked a lock of hair behind my ear. I'd tried to style my hair into an effortless, Melody-style messy updo, but only managed to appear as if I'd just finished cleaning the attic. So I brushed my hair down into its usual, simple style and decided to let things happen naturally.

It would be my theme for the night.

We made our way outside and I saw Ellis had brought his personal vehicle, a black Jeep Wrangler. He opened the door for me, and I placed Frankie's urn in the back so that the gangster could have his own space. Perhaps he'd take the hint and not infringe upon ours.

No such luck. Ellis hadn't even started the engine when Frankie shimmered into view in the space between us, with an arm around the back of each of our seats. "Ask him if he's got any Benny Goodman CDs."

"I don't think Ellis listens to your kind of music," I said, with quite a bit of certainty.

Ellis slipped his key into the ignition. "I assume that was aimed at Frankie and not me. You can tell him I've got satellite radio," he said as the engine rolled over. "Has Frankie ever listened to the Big Band station?"

"There's an entire station for that?" I asked, a little disturbed as Frankie whooped and did a fist pump.

Ellis grinned, gravel crunching under his tires as we pulled out. "They're doing a whole hour on Paul Whiteman tonight." Ellis hit the button for the station and soulful, jazzy swing music filtered through the car.

Frankie flopped onto the backseat like he'd just been

let out of jail.

"I'm making an executive decision," Frankie said, eyes closed, tapping his fingers to the music. "I'm hanging out with him even if you don't."

We talked about little things on the way there, both of us fully aware of our smart-mouthed chaperone. Although Frankie hardly seemed to notice us while bebopping and playing air-trumpet.

Ellis took Highway L over to the old logging road on the west side of town. As the sun set fully, we drove past barns full of antiques and a series of orchards in hibernation, waiting for spring.

Whitewashed fencing gave way to a battered limestone wall and I knew we were close. Ellis had partnered with his uncle to buy the fifteen-acre Wilson's Creek spread, with the idea that they'd renovate the old Southern Spirits distillery building and turn it into a modern restaurant and bar. Only his uncle had died before they could complete it. Ellis had been in the middle of renovations when I'd helped him rid the property of a frightening poltergeist.

We turned onto a wide, black-topped road. A large brick building stood at the end, with broad wooden carriage doors at the front. New outdoor lights lit up the building, making it feel welcome and open. Tall windows lined the first and second floors. The wood turret off the back had been completely refurbished. Old-style painted lettering, done in white on the brick, read "Southern Spirits since 1908."

The Jeep drove over a smooth, newly paved parking area.

"The place looks great," I said, truly happy for him. Ellis was one of those people who could envision something new and then find a way to make it real. It made me proud to know him.

He seemed pleased at my response. "I hope you like the rest," he said, leading me to a set of newly refinished arched wood doors. He opened one for me. Frankie floated inside ahead of me, and I could see his glowing form zip straight into the kitchen area at the back.

The space inside appeared dark at first, until I noticed dozens upon dozens of battery-powered tea lights lining the bar inside the door, and the window-sills, and illuminating a path laid out on the gleaming hardwood floor. Strands of white lights twinkled from the rafters above.

The large space, with its high rafters and red brick walls, seemed like it belonged in another world entirely.

"What is this?" I asked, hesitating, feeling my face go warm.

The building had been a carriage house before the gangsters had used it to run whiskey. Along the left wall, Ellis had set up a table for two under one of the arched doorways. He took my hand and led me inside. "I dressed the place up for our date."

I'd known he was resourceful, but wow. It appeared so…magical. And real. And a little frightening. He seemed to be expecting a lot from this date and from me.

"What's the matter?" he asked. "I thought you'd like it, but you look spooked."

My heart rattled in my chest. "No one's ever done anything like this for me before," I admitted.

"Then relax and enjoy it," he said, leading me to the table.

He pulled a remote out of his pocket and the music system switched on. Frank Sinatra began singing "Angel Eyes."

Ellis pulled out a chair for me.

I cleared my throat. "Thank you," I said, determined to let myself be taken care of. Aside from my sister and my friends, I was used to relying on just me.

Beau had never gone out of his way like this.

A bottle of Malbec rested on the table. Ellis took the seat opposite mine. He began to open the wine.

Everything looked so wonderful. He was a great guy, but none of this solved our real issue. In fact, it almost felt like a tease. Like I'd learn to enjoy this and then have it taken away. "I appreciate all of this. I really do." He'd gone through a lot of trouble. "But it doesn't solve our real issue."

He placed the bottle back on the table. "Okay, what does?"

Just like a man. "This isn't a three-step process." Or a twelve-step one. Or heaven knew what it would take to placate his mother. "I don't have the answers. That's the problem."

He scooted his chair forward and planted his elbows on the table. "I told my mom that if she ever threatened you again, if she hurts you, if she tries to take anything from you, she'll lose me."

"Wow. I never expected that," I said, tossing my hands out and accidentally knocking a tea light off the table. I let it go and we both watched the light skitter across the floor and into the darkness. "She may be... difficult, but she's your mother." She'd forced him to choose and he had, but at the same time, "You still have to live with her."

"We do," he corrected.

"Oh, no. She'll never accept me."

"Not right away," he conceded.

"Not ever." Trying to join Ellis at family events would be torture, pure and simple, for both of us. He had to accept that. "Then there is the small matter of her sway over the town. And her friends." They'd be after me even if she and I called a truce. "You saw what happened when you gave me your jacket outside the library."

Ellis bit back a curse. "You were cold!"

I stood. He had an answer for everything, but I called bull on that one. "You gave mean old Nellie Holcamp gossip for a month. Don't even pretend you didn't realize that."

He abandoned his chair and it toppled over behind him. "I don't care about her. I'm not afraid of this. I saw it when my mom threatened you. Making this a secret gives it power. I say you admit you like me, you date me, and damn the consequences."

I huffed out a breath. "You make it sound so easy."

"It is."

I recognized the incident with Virginia Wydell for the threat that it was. He thought of it as a way to set us free. "You stood up for me against your mom and I appreciate that, but you're missing the point. I'm the one she's after." I held up a hand when he started to protest. "Maybe she'll stop going after me directly since you told her to, but her minions won't. The town is still against me. I'm taking all the heat for this."

He watched me carefully. "And you care more about heat than you do about me?"

Of all the... "That's not fair."

"You're afraid," he said, skirting the table. "I get that. I'm with you on it. But hiding isn't the answer. If we don't face this, we're always going to be on the defensive, and that's not right. We haven't done anything wrong."

I'd been on the offensive before. I'd shown up at my

almost-wedding reception to give Beau and his mom a piece of my mind. It wasn't all it was cracked up to be. "You don't know what it's like."

He stood over me, too close. "You take risks in other areas of your life, but not for me."

"That's not fair." With the ghosts, I didn't always have a choice.

The lights cast shadows over his handsome features as he ground his jaw tight. "You adopted a skunk because you found her hurt in your yard."

"Well, of course." He couldn't go by that one decision. "Lucy needed me."

But Ellis wasn't finished. "You let a dead gangster live in your house."

I held my arms out. "He can't exactly go anywhere else."

He took a step forward. "You tore up your garden trying to free him."

"We were running out of options."

He refused to let it go. "You stormed into what would have been your wedding reception and smashed my brother's face into the cake."

"That was kind of liberating." I also threw the ring that accidentally hit Ellis in the forehead. "Your brother cheated on me."

"He deserved to lose you," Ellis thundered. "I don't."

His words hung in the silence between us, and I could see a thin sheen of sweat on his skin. "I've made it clear I'm serious about you. But I can't do this alone."

I stood frozen, hating that he was right.

He swallowed, as if he'd said too much, but he stood his ground. "Either you end it tonight and leave me be, or you make room for me and let me in."

Heavens. It terrified me to leave, and to stay.

"How do I know you're really serious about this?" I asked. He'd let me go before. He hadn't fought for me at the beginning, either.

He took my hands in his. "I've been saying yes for a while. I'm saying yes right now," he said, more determined than I'd ever seen him. "Are you?" He frowned when I hesitated, and his grip loosened. "I'm not going to beg you. You have to want to be with me."

I felt his hands slipping from mine.

I wasn't ready. But at this point, it didn't matter. This was my one chance and I had to grab it or let it go for good.

"I want to try this," I said quickly, tightening my grip so he didn't slip away. I wanted to be with him. Despite his family and the town and all of it. "I'm just not used to deciding." Beau always chased. I always let him. Things sort of happened.

Of course, that hadn't ended well.

Beau had done everything for show. Ellis wanted the real deal. He wasn't playing at all, and while I appreciated his sincerity, that terrified me as well.

"I can work with a good try," he said, squeezing my hands, "so long as it's an honest one." He drew me closer and bent down for a sweet kiss that was all promise, and maybe a bit more.

I let myself enjoy the moment, and him.

Because in a second, he was going to notice the cold spot forming next to us.

Chapter Fourteen

I drew back from Ellis's warm embrace, feeling… wonderful.

Then I saw Frankie chain-smoking behind him.

A trail of smoke curled over Ellis's right shoulder. "Good," Frankie said, flicking ash off the end of his smoke. "You're done."

Hardly.

Go away, I mouthed to the gangster. Frankie of all people had to give me this moment. He knew how much it meant.

Ellis drew me close and bent down for another sweet kiss when I felt the back of his neck go cold. He flinched, then glanced behind him. Even though he couldn't see the ghost, the cop in him knew who did it. His eyes narrowed. "What do you want, Frank?"

The gangster stepped back, more offended than accommodating. "You believe this guy?" he asked, gesturing with his smoke. He held a mixed drink in the other hand. "Your man should be thanking me. I talked you back into him."

He did nothing of the sort. "Shoo." I rested my head against Ellis's broad shoulder. "We're busy."

Frankie stirred his drink with his finger. "Tell him

the candy shop's closed." He shook off his finger and sipped the cocktail. "Ahh... Sticky Pete pours 'em the best."

"I thought you were going down to the speakeasy," I said. "Why are you back so soon? Did you find your gun?"

"Yeah," Frankie said, "and it's going to be another eighty years before I get it if I wait for you two."

Ellis jolted my head off his shoulder. "What are you saying about a speakeasy?" he asked me, his tone gentler than I would have expected. "I thought Frankie couldn't leave the property."

I sincerely wished there were a better way to tell him this, but Frankie had beaten me to the punch. "There's one in your basement," I told Ellis. "Surprise." At least he'd agreed to date me before this all happened.

It took him a second to process it. "How long have you known about this?"

"Frankie told me tonight," I assured him, hoping that would make it better. It wasn't like I was holding out on him.

"You're missing the point," Frankie said, as if we were a trial to him. "While you two were canoodling, I learned Crazy Louie has my revolver."

"Is the gun located in this realm?" I asked.

Frankie rolled his eyes. "I wouldn't need you otherwise." He took a long drag from his cigarette. "Louie's body is down there. Slumped over a bar table with my gun stashed in the front pocket of his suitcoat." He pointed his smoke at me like I was about to go back on my promise. "You gotta get me that piece." He took another drag. "We bury it with my ashes and I bet I'll be free by midnight."

Stranger things had happened.

Then again, we were in the middle of my date.
Things had been going so well, after our argument at
least. Ellis had been really sweet, but this was a big
boyfriend favor.

No, I don't need you to kill a spider or move a
couch. I just need to stop kissing you so we can go
to a haunted speakeasy and reclaim my gangster
friend's gun before he chain-smokes himself to death.
Wait. Scratch that.

To his credit, Ellis did seem to be taking the news of
the hidden mob hideout fairly well. He rubbed a hand
over his chin. "I thought I'd been over every inch of
this property."

The South Town Gang hid their bar well. "These
are criminals," I said, trying to make him feel better.
"They're sneaky."

Frankie took another drag from his cigarette. "Stop
trying to butter me up."

I took Ellis's hand. "Handsome Henry could be
down there. His friends certainly will be. This is our
best shot to track him down."

Ellis shook his head the same half-astonished, half-
enticed way he did when I told him I had a ghost in
the first place. "Show me where to find my speakeasy," he said plainly.

"Yours?" Frankie chuffed and put out his cigarette
on the floor. "I think lover boy is in for a surprise." He
glided away from us and into the darkness beyond.

"This way," I said, following.

"Just a sec." Ellis flipped on the lights just in time
for me to see Frankie go straight out the back wall.

"We need to go outside," I said, heading for the back
door about ten feet from where Frankie had disappeared.

"Frankie doesn't waste time," he said, digging for

his keys.

"Not when guns and booze are involved."

"Well, aren't we lucky, then?" he asked, honest-to-goodness amused.

We shared a knowing glance, and it lit me up inside. Dang. Where else was I going to find a guy who talked me through my issues, forgave me my mistakes, found amusement in my resident ghost, and would help me track down a hit man, no questions asked?

I had to make this thing between us work, because if we ever broke up for good, I'd be doomed to singlehood for the rest of eternity.

"Hold it," Ellis said as we headed for the door. "This isn't all fun and games. I want you to be careful." He gave me a long look. "I've dealt with the mob in New York. These are violent criminals. Pay attention to every move you make around them."

"I understand," I said, glad that he wanted to protect me. When Frankie tuned me in to the other side, the ghosts could hurt me, even kill me. Still, if one of them went poltergeist and got violent, Ellis could be in just as much danger as I was. He'd drawn a poltergeist off me the last time we solved a case, and it had nearly killed him.

We found Frankie outside in the clear, black night, lighting up another cigarette. "I bet on a racehorse as fast as you once," he mused as the end of his smoke went hot. "I shot him."

"I don't see what we're even doing out in the open," I said, stepping cautiously into the night. "This is a bad place for a speakeasy."

"You'll see," Frankie muttered, turning his back and gliding farther away from the building.

Ellis stuck close to me as we made our way out into the yard. The ground still felt wet from all the rain we'd had this past week.

"They'd want the entrance near a main road, but not visible to traffic," Ellis said, catching me when I slipped on a patch of mud. "Back here, there's plenty of parking and you can get people in and out pretty easy."

"All those smarts but he didn't find this," Frankie said, stopping in front of a circular wooden lid with a modern padlock in place over a circle of rough-cut stones.

"Here?" I asked.

"This is the old well." Ellis bent down and began entering the combination into the lock. "Why didn't I look at this closer?"

"Because you're not me," Frankie scoffed, throwing his leg over the stones and using a ladder I couldn't see to lower himself down. "I helped pick this spot."

"Ready?" Ellis asked. He lifted the lid away from the dark, round opening. "This reminds me of the last time you and I went underground," he mused.

True. "You kissed me in the tunnel," I reminded him.

He grinned. "Why else do you think I want to go down there?"

"Pipe down!" Frankie's voice echoed from below. "You're gonna have the police on us if you keep up that racket."

"Truly, Frankie?" I asked. "You're worried about the police?"

Ellis glanced down into the hole. "Should I remind him?"

"No," I said. It would just make him mad.

"I'm heading in," I said, throwing my leg over the edge. Maybe I'd say something nice to Frankie when I got down there. I caught the ball of my foot on the top rung of an iron ladder bolted to the side.

"Wait," Ellis said, catching me at the waist. "Let's test this thing first."

"Good point," I said, easing my foot back. "I should have thought of that."

He tugged at the ladder, making sure its bolts remained securely fastened to the stone. "Patience," he reminded me.

I shrugged. "I'm an action girl." At least with everything but my personal life. Which only went to show how deeply mucking up a relationship scared me. I was scared now, but not enough to stifle my curiosity about what was happening in that haunted club. When Ellis was satisfied I wouldn't plunge to my death, I kicked a leg over the edge again. "Let's do this."

"I'm right behind you," he said.

I descended into the old pit and tried not to let claustrophobia get to me as the dusty rock walls closed in on all sides. The rusty grit of the ladder felt slippery under my boots, and I made a point of clinging to the roughened sides.

Frankie's groans echoed up from the darkness.

He sounded like a tortured spirit haunting the moors, instead of an impatient mobster who wanted his gun back.

Blackness surrounded me. "This is deeper than I imagined," I said, feeling the air cool.

"Keep going," Ellis said from above, the ladder jerking with his heavy movements. A wave of anxiety hit me when I realized he blocked my escape from underground. The stench of the place kept me from taking a deep breath. I can do this.

This wasn't even the worst part. If we were lucky, we'd run into a killer.

I continued down until I reached the sandy, rocky

bottom. I could feel the rounded stones through the soles of my boots.

Frankie leaned against the wall at the bottom. "So nice of you to join me, your highness." In the silver glow he gave off, I could see the rough rock at his back and the outline of a dark tunnel just to the left of him.

"Is that it?" I reached into my bag for my key light and shone it down a seemingly endless passageway. Rotting planks of wood crowded the entrance.

Ellis crunched down onto the rock behind me. He shone a light over rusted hinges. "Somebody broke in the door."

"Recently?" I looked to Frankie, who merely shrugged.

"Hard to tell." Ellis stepped into the passageway, the powerful beam from his Maglite bounding off the walls. "A friend of my uncle's told him there was something funny about the covered well out here." He ran a hand along the stone ceiling and bent over to keep from hitting his head. "You'll never guess who it was." Where there had been an echo in the well, the stones here seemed to absorb his voice.

"I'm not sure," I said, trailing along behind him in the passageway.

Frankie appeared a ways down the tunnel.

Ellis glanced back at me. "Jeb Kemper."

"Oh my."

"He looked in on the place for us sometimes. I think my uncle even gave him a set of keys." Ellis shook his head and advanced along the corridor. "Hale and I never looked into it. We were more concerned with security in the actual distillery building. If Jeb did venture down here, he didn't say anything to us."

I placed a hand on Ellis's back, for his comfort — or so I told myself.

"Watch your step," he murmured as we encountered a fallen stone. I hoped this part of the passage was stable.

I could see Jeb coming down here, although if he did it alone, that would be brave. I wondered if he might have come across Handsome Henry's possessions when he was poking around.

I slipped on a patch of loose rock and steadied myself against the rough brick wall. A lot of wiseguys died down here. No doubt they left plenty of valuables, other than the gun in Louie's pocket.

"Frankie's right in front of you," I said as we neared the gangster. He stood outside a rusted steel door complete with an envelope-sized slider that I assumed was a peephole.

"I need to see," I said to the ghost. "If I'm going to find your gun and figure out if Henry is around."

"Gun first," he warned.

"I promise."

I felt the air around me prickle with ghostly energy. My senses sharpened, my muscles throbbed, and the space filled with a familiar silver, otherworldly glow.

Jazz music filtered from the other side of the door, along with voices and clinking glasses. "Sounds like quite a party," I said.

Frankie smirked. "We have some good times," he said. "I should take you to Mick's gin joint." He frowned. "Although that's under a parking lot now. I don't know if anybody still goes there or not."

"It would be private," I reasoned.

"Yeah," he said, lighting up.

The peephole slid open. A beady-eyed ghost scrutinized us and I heard the unmistakable sound of a pistol cock on the other side.

"I thought these were your friends," I hissed.

"Shh..." Frankie waved me away. "I got this."

The man on the other side cleared his throat. "A toast to those who wish me well."

Frankie chuckled. "All the rest can go to hell."

The door swung open. "Frankie!" said a skinny young ghost in a suit. "Where you been, you old skirt chaser? It's been so long I almost didn't recognize you."

Frankie shook his hand and rubbed the top of his head. "Shut it, you egg." He gestured me forward. "Brewer, this is Verity. She's with me."

The guy looked me up and down like he had a chance. "Nice stems."

"Thank you," I said, taking Ellis's hand for support. "He's also with us."

The guy shrugged. "As long as you ain't the law."

"Ha," I said, distinctly uncomfortable. That earned a glare from Frankie.

"Watch yourself," he said under his breath, with a level of concern that surprised me. "Your boyfriend was right to warn you about us."

We stepped into a dark alcove separated from the party by a flowing velvet curtain. I caught a strong waft of cigars and sweat.

"Smile," Frankie said, muttering close to my ear. "Act natural. And follow me if we have to run."

Run? What had I gotten myself into?

I didn't have much time to worry about it before Frankie opened the curtain.

CHAPTER FIFTEEN

It was an entire night club. Scratch that—a jazz club, filled with smoke and music, men in suits and ladies showing off glitzy flapper dresses with feathers in their hair.

"Frankie!" Two skinny guys in suits greeted him, patting him on the back as more wiseguys took notice and stood up to say hello to my gangster buddy. Soon, he had a small crowd around him. Frankie ate it up, shaking hands and kissing the cheeks of the girls that hovered on the edges of the mob reunion.

"Well, look at that," I muttered to myself. "Everybody knows his name."

An ornate wood bar with a mirrored back took up the entire right side of the place. It was crowded with patrons turning to see what the commotion was about and wiseguys grabbing drinks from two young bartenders that should have been carded themselves. A five-piece band played on a stage in the back. Every member wore gray suits and matching ties. They jazzed out a lively rendition of "Sweet Georgia Brown" over the animated conversation of the crowd and the clinking of glasses.

"You're popular," I called to Frankie over the din of

the partygoers when I could get a word in edgewise.

"I'm home," he hollered back, still greeting his friends.

Ellis eased forward, exploring the party without the benefit of rose-colored glasses. He paused close by, at a circular table crowded with wiseguys, and I winced as one used the decorative candle at the center to light a stinky cigar.

Ellis's breathing grew shallow. "This is unreal."

I squinted and tried to see beyond the ghostly party. I'd never been in a room like this one before, with every stick of furniture, every art deco light fixture the same on the ghostly plane as in real life.

It felt so real, so vivid, that I had to work to see past it, to the wide underground room cluttered with dusty tables and the skeletal remains of guests. They wore tattered party clothes and lay as they did when they died. Many slumped in their chairs or sprawled over the once-festive tables. One guy had made a barricade out of a bullet-riddled table. Bullet holes peppered the bar at the back, and the long mirror behind it barely held itself together, a shattered, gaping shell of its former glory. Dusty bottles, many of them broken, lined the bar, as cold and dead as the patrons.

Frankie joined us, drink in hand, as Ellis took in the crime scene. "This was a mass murder."

"Yeah," Frankie agreed. "But it was a hell of a lot of fun before that."

"What happened to everyone?" It looked brutal.

"Shot mostly," Frankie said, ever the practical one. "The Irish got the jump on us. That and drunk guys don't shoot so straight." He took a swig of his drink. "Happened the night I died, so I would have been a goner anyway. Didn't miss much. In that way, it's kind of nice."

No, it wasn't. "They just…gunned everyone down?"

Frankie shrugged. "We shot 'em back. They had orders from the higher-ups," he said, as if that made it right. "It was nothing personal." He grinned at a rather large gangster who patted him on the shoulder as he walked past.

"So you all just drink and party?" It seemed both a waste of time and a fabulous way for Frankie to spend his afterlife.

"Until you came along," he said, his humor fading.

I was beginning to see how he might have gotten frustrated when I'd taken him on multiple trips to the library, not to mention the dollar store.

Ellis made his way toward the bar as he mapped out the scene. The ghosts shifted out of his way, muttering under their breath.

Meanwhile Frankie greeted two fellows who came up on us from the left, weaving through tables, the bulges in their jackets making it abundantly clear they carried multiple firearms. "Hey, ya losers!" Frankie shouted by way of greeting. They clapped him on the back and seemed happy to see him. "Verity," Frankie said, turning everyone's attention to me, "you gotta meet Dime Store Bobby." He drew an arm around a blond gangster with a lock of hair that fell stylishly over his forehead. He'd be handsome, if you were into the bad-boy type. "Bobby takes care of the bribes."

"An important job," I said, opting for a wave instead of a handshake. Bobby grinned at me like he was up to something. He probably was.

"And here's…hey, wait." Frankie looked around. "Where's Icepick Charlie? She needs to meet him, too."

"Aw," Bobby said, "he's got a thing going with one of the Irish. Mikey accidentally shot Icepick in the skull yesterday, so now Icepick is gonna get back at him today." He made a motion that suggested Icepick would stab the poor man through the ear.

I stifled a gasp. "We have to stop him."

I searched for Ellis. He'd help. He was bent down one table away from us, examining bullet casings, much to the dismay of the ghosts, who crowded together opposite him, avoiding his touch. Now if I could only locate an ice-pick-wielding gangster with a mind to murder...

Frankie pointed a finger at me. "Don't you dare," he warned. He leaned so close to my ear my entire lobe went numb. "Nobody's got a problem with this but you. Everybody's already dead. Think of it like a sport."

"Murder?" I prodded. "You want me to equate murder with Monday Night Football?"

Frankie shrugged. "More like paintball. It stings a little, but then you're fine in no time. The real pain is keeping score."

Frankie had a point. It wasn't like any of the ghosts could die again. I was the only one who could get truly hurt or killed if ghostly bullets started flying or if I drew the wrong sort of attention.

Dime Store Bobby watched me, his expression gone hard.

"I'm fine. Everything's fine," I said, drawing away from Frankie before I lost feeling in the entire left side of my face.

Bobby took a menacing step toward me and I felt my blood pressure rise. "You got a problem with the way we do things around here?"

"I just want everybody to get along," I said, trying to keep my hackles down and my voice sweet.

Bobby wasn't convinced. "The Irish deserve to catch hell every now and then," he bit out. "They're the ones who shot up the place. They even smoked the band. I mean, did they have to kill the band?"

I turned to Frankie, but he'd abandoned me to greet a table full of guys and gals who seemed to think he was incredibly funny. I glanced to Ellis. He stood examining a bullet hole in a man's rotting jacket, as if I wasn't in a pinch here.

Bobby cocked his head toward the gangsters crowded onto low couches. "We make the Irish sit in the back and drink their own liquor. We ain't gonna waste our booze on the guys who murdered us."

It appeared as if the Irish tried to ignore the South Town Gang as well, for the most part. Despite the skeletons and the ice-pick-wielding ghost, this seemed to be a happening death spot.

I stepped away from Bobby—hoping he'd get the hint—and scanned the crowd for Handsome Henry. He should be easy to spot, with his tank of a body and scarred face.

Meanwhile Bobby looked me up and down, a wiseass grin tickling his lips. "Whatcha looking for?" he prodded. "Because if it's a good time, I'm it."

Of all the nerve. "You were threatening me less than thirty seconds ago."

"That's part of my charm," he said, drawing too close for comfort. The man was going to get a real shock if he kept it up. He'd obviously never hit on the living before.

I stepped away. "You're not my type," I said, my gaze finding Ellis, who was examining a long butcher knife jutting from the ribs of one of the victims. I liked the ones who solved problems instead of creating them.

"What? You like that clown?" Bobby prodded. The stabbed man's ghost stood just behind Ellis, sipping a cocktail. The knife was still sticking out of his chest. "He brought a knife to a gunfight," Bobby chided, "then he got stabbed with it."

"Not him," I said. And I wasn't going to point out Ellis, either. This was my chance to get what I'd come for. "I'm looking for Handsome Henry. Have you seen him around?"

Bobby frowned and I caught a vulnerability in his expression that almost made me feel sorry for him. Almost. Until he slammed his fist on the table next to us. "Why do dames always go for the assassins?"

A gangster wearing all black came up behind him and handed him a mixed drink.

"Ice Pick!" Bobby said, accepting the drink and taking a long swig.

Ice Pick stirred his own drink with his finger. "Henry doesn't come around much, not after his death anyway. He mostly stays hitched up with his girl," the droop-eyed gangster said in a high-pitched voice that would have probably made him a target if he weren't so talented with deadly kitchen tools. "Bobby's just mad 'cause he danced the tango with her, too."

Bobby crossed his arms over his chest. "If he ever brought her in here, she'd be looking at me."

Ice Pick smacked his friend on the back of the head. "That's 'cause you're a clown."

"How can I find Henry?" I asked them, trying to keep the conversation on track.

Ice Pick took a long sip of his drink. "Ah, that's the stuff." He tipped his glass at me. "You want to see Henry and Rosie both, head to the Holy Oak Cemetery. They're homebodies now — always at each other's graves. You want Henry on his own, wait a week or so." He shrugged. "He'll show up in some dark corner."

"If you go see him at the rock garden, bring flowers," Bobby said. "He likes ladies who like flowers. Reminds him of his mamma."

"I think that's nice," I said of the gangster who liked

his mamma. At least I understood it better than I did Bobby. One minute, he was having a violent outburst, the next, he stood there talking about flowers.

Ice Pick chuckled. It was a hollow, empty sound. "Bobby just wants you to nab Henry so Rosie'll give him another chance."

Bobby held up his drink, his pinkie in the air. "She don't know what she's missing. All dames like a sharp suit."

The left side of my body went cold as Frankie sidled up to me. "I'm gonna borrow her for a second, fellas." He led me away, weaving through tables like he was in a hurry.

"What's going on?" His tone had changed and I didn't like it.

Frankie turned and drew so close I feared he'd touch me. "Nobody's looking at us anymore. We can sneak my gun."

"Wait. Why do we need to sneak it?" I sidestepped to avoid a drunk flapper swinging her beads. "It is your gun, right?"

"Crazy Louie has it," Frankie hissed, glancing over his shoulder. "He don't like to be touched."

"Darn it all, Frankie," I started.

"Quiet down. He's right over there." Frankie pointed to a table near the bar. A girl in a shiny dress, with pixie-cut hair, sat on it while a guy in a plaid coat stood and lit her cigarette. "His body's slumped over the table, with the gun in his left front coat pocket."

I strained to see past the ghosts to the two partially rotted corpses lying on the table. One of them wore the plaid coat.

"Be casual," Frankie said as I started forward.

Did he hear himself talking? "If I don't touch his body" — his skeletal, dead body — "I can't get the gun."

"Not so loud," Frankie said, grinning at the gang-sters at the next table. They stared at us. "She knows not to lay a mortal hand on anything," he assured them.

Wait a second. I wasn't born last Tuesday. I drew closer to him. "You're going to pretend you don't know anything about this, and then you're going to blame me when Crazy Louie's gun goes missing."

"Only if they see you," he said, relaxing a bit as the other gangsters returned their attention to the party. "I want to be able to come back here."

"Consider this." I stared up at my hook-nosed, beady-eyed jerk of a friend. "You want me to steal from a dead gangster's body, thereby angering the man while he stands about two feet away from me with a loaded weapon." Louie died with the gun and that meant he'd have the ghostly version on him for eternity.

"Exactly," Frankie said, completely missing my sarcasm. "Everyone will see I didn't take it. And," he seemed quite proud to point out, "nobody's hunting me down later at your house."

Except for one detail. "What if they hunt me down later at my house?"

He straightened his suit coat collar. "It's not like you're going to get caught," he said, as if it were a logistical impossibility. "And worst-case scenario, if you do jack it up, you won't be wanting to borrow my power ever again. You can spend your time drawing goofy signs for mortals and we'll all be happy."

He didn't even believe I had a legitimate business.

I edged too close to a fat man and the chippie sitting on his lap and shuddered at the bone-searingly cold wetness that seeped through me as my knee passed through his elbow. He cursed and dropped her.

"Sorry," I began.

"Move," Frankie said, urging me forward while the guy was busy picking his date up off the floor.

Darn it all. Frankie had me pegged. Right about now, I was fine with never seeing the other side again. There was only one catch. "I still have to talk to Handsome Henry. Your friend Ice Pick says he's probably at the cemetery."

"Fine. I'll plug you in at the cemetery. I won't even complain. We'll do it quick and none of these guys will even notice."

"Frankie…"

"They don't even hang out there," he added. "Besides, you're not gonna get caught."

I wasn't sure I wanted to take the chance. "Unhook me." We were only a table away. If I wasn't on the ghostly plane, I'd be safe like Ellis.

Frankie practically snarled. "You throw off sparks when I do that. You don't want that kind of attention." Frankie leaned closer. "Do it fast. Do it now and nobody's gonna shoot you."

I stood directly in front of the dead mobster's body. Frankie moved to block me from his view.

"All right." I could handle this. "Now?" I murmured to my houseguest.

Frankie shrugged. "I don't know what you're talking about. I'm just an innocent bystander."

Cute.

Stomach tight, I drew closer to the dead body. This wouldn't be pleasant even without the prospect of getting shot. I braced one hand on the grimy table. Crazy Louie's bare skull lolled on the table, a gaping hole in the back revealing a dusty mess that I didn't even want to think about. Bloodstains marred his once-white shirt and the jacket hung in tatters from his bony shoulders.

Think of it like a mannequin.

One with bones and dried-up organs and…

I slipped my hand inside the jacket, hoping I didn't grab anything gross as I felt gently and found a large lump in his pocket. I reached inside and felt the fragile fabric rip as I closed my hand around the handle of a very real, very deadly gun.

"Don't touch any of this. It's a crime scene," Ellis said, standing over me. Cripes. It wasn't like I could tell him about the gun, not at the moment, anyway.

Louie turned to look at us, as did his girlfriend, the man next to her, and a dozen more gangsters.

I felt the heat of their stares as I drew my hand slowly out of Louie's pocket. Surely these guys wouldn't fault a girl for stealing what wasn't Louie's anyway. "It's not like we can call the police." I tried to chuckle, and failed.

Without missing a beat, Ellis cocked his head. "I am the police."

A chorus of metallic clicking echoed through the bar as every gangster in the place drew his gun and pointed it at Ellis's head.

But they weren't looking at me.

I grabbed Louie's gun.

"Get 'em!" Louie hollered.

Dozens of gangsters opened fire on Ellis, their bullets passing straight through him. The wiseguys dropped like flies in their own crossfire.

A chair crashed to the floor and the ghost of Crazy Louie staggered for me.

I jerked to the side and the jacket tore. The body lurched and Louie's head fell off.

"Gaaah!" Louie scrambled for his head, which he couldn't hope to catch because he couldn't touch it.

I ducked under the table. Of course I'd never start a mob fight or knock off Louie's head on purpose, but that didn't stop the insane gangster from pulling a revolver and pointing it straight at me.

Frankie tackled him with a head to the stomach, and he went down, his shot going wild just as I realized he'd shot at me. Shot at me!

My bag went flying, sending Frankie's urn skittering across the floor, and someone yelled, "Bar fight!"

The Irish started firing in the back. The band struck up "Ain't Misbehavin'." And the fat gangster next to me smiled and plugged Frankie in the head just as he was standing up to yell at me about his urn.

The bullet hit Frankie square between the eyes and he went down.

Then a bullet whizzed straight past my left ear. I had to move. Now.

A girl with a feather in her hair kneed the fat gangster in the groin and he collapsed to the floor near me, still smoking his cigar as he fired his gun up at somebody.

I crawled to Frankie. "Turn your power off!" He lay on the floor, not moving with his eyes wide open. Two round bullet holes now marred his forehead. "Frankie!" I grabbed him by the shoulders. "Wake up!"

A bullet hit the floor next to me, throwing up biting shards of concrete, and I stared in horror down the yawning barrel of Crazy Louie's ghost gun.

"Verity!" Ellis passed straight through the gangster, startling him.

"Wave your arms," I pleaded. Bless the man—he did it without question and nailed Crazy Louie. The gangster cursed and dropped his ghostly revolver.

I scrambled for it and got it before he did, feeling the rush of power and the cold steel against my skin. Now I had a gun in each hand. A ghostly one in my right and a real one in my left. I made a break for the urn, passing through two cowering flappers under the next table.

"Why you little—" Crazy Louie drew another gun, so I shot him in the leg with his ghostly gun. I felt the kickback reverberate up my arms as he cussed and went down.

I felt awful that I'd shot a man on purpose, even if he was already dead. I was also a bit surprised I'd actually hit him. I barely knew how to shoot, and here I stood double-fisted in a mob fight.

I found Frankie's urn under the next table and shoved it into my bag, along with the real gun.

Ellis ran straight through Frankie's motionless body and pulled me to my feet. "Let's go!" he said, half-dragging me in a full-out haul for the front door.

He cut a path through the ghosts like Moses through the Red Sea while I ran next to him, out of breath and scared to death I could go down at any second.

We plowed through the velvet curtain and made a mad dash down the passageway.

"We clear?" Ellis barked.

"No!" I stumbled over debris in the tunnel. Gleeful shouts rang behind us.

I took the ladder first, climbing for my life with Ellis right behind me.

Classic cars parked five deep in the yard. I dodged past Packards and Model Ts, not willing to risk the consequences of running into them, while Ellis on the mortal plane plowed through them all.

We dashed alongside the old distillery building, and I hollered for him to run faster when I heard the engines starting up behind us.

I jumped into his Jeep, tossing my bag with Frankie's urn onto the floor, along with the real re- volver, which hit the floor and went off.

"Be careful!" Ellis snapped.

"I didn't know it was loaded!" I bit back. Cripes. Of

course it was loaded, it was in Crazy Louie's pocket. Why would Crazy Louie carry around an unloaded gun? I aimed my ghostly gun out the side window as Ellis started the car.

These guys had been insane when they were alive, and now killing was some sort of a game to them. Except as long as I held Frankie's power, their shoot-'em-up antics could actually kill me.

"Unload it!" Ellis ordered.

"I am! I am!" I shouted. "Just drive!"

We sped away.

I placed the ghostly gun on the dashboard and dug the real one out of my bag. I struggled to unload it with shaking fingers. At least three pairs of headlights bounced up the grassy area we'd just abandoned.

Ellis peeled out of the distillery, and my ghostly revolver slid down the dashboard.

The gangsters started firing.

A shot flew straight through his back window and whizzed past my ear, out the front of the car. "Sweet Jesus!" I dropped the mortal revolver and the bullets onto the floor of the car and grabbed the only weapon I could use off the dash.

A Packard rode our back bumper, two guys leaning out the side with handguns, whooping and grinning like they were riding the Rockin' Roller Coaster at Disney World.

I fired at the front left tire and missed. I saw the flash of their guns as they returned fire, and felt the bullets whiz past.

I ducked, too late and uselessly anyway. The bullets could pass straight through the mortal car and end me.

"Hold on." Ellis stomped on the gas, flying down the narrow two-lane country road.

The car behind us swung into the oncoming lane,

and for a second, I thought the driver had lost control. But no, he quickly passed and pulled in front of us.

Then a second car pulled up the side. Dime Store Bobby leaned out the front passenger window, waving at me with a wild grin as somebody handed him a Tommy gun.

Oh my Lord. "Don't shoot!" I called.

I fought down a wave of panic and fired at him, taking a straight shot, right through Ellis.

"What the — ?" He stiffened and swerved like I'd dropped an ice cube down his back.

I fired again. Missed. I pulled the trigger again and my gun clicked. I was out of bullets.

Bobby laughed and aimed his Tommy gun directly at me.

Chapter Sixteen

Dime Store Bobby actually smiled as he took aim at my head.

"Ellis!" I pointed and ducked.

Ellis slammed on the brakes and the car carrying Bobby shot out in front of us. The Jeep whipped to the left and I banged my head on the dash as we went careening off road, straight into a fallow cotton field still tangled with the remains of last year's harvest.

I scrambled to see out the Jeep's cloudy soft-top back window, where three pairs of headlights turned around and left the road to follow us.

They weren't giving up until I was dead.

"Frankie!" I called.

No response.

I had his urn. He had to be...somewhere nearby.

"My Jeep was made for this," Ellis gritted out.

That was well and good, but it couldn't stop a ghost bullet.

"Tree!" I gasped. Ellis's high beams caught a large trunk straight ahead.

"I see it." He remained completely focused, whizzing past it and dropping us down straight into a creek. Water flew up on either side of us and I couldn't see. I didn't know where the gangsters were.

We bounced up the bank and I squinted through the glistening water clinging to the back window. The glare of headlights bore down on us. I could almost hear the guns cocking.

Shots erupted and I ducked again, but I didn't feel bullets whiz past. And when I craned to see out the back, the headlights had faded. "I think they're losing power." Or maybe I was. It was the only explanation.

Ellis refused to take his eyes off the road. "Hang on."

He steered us through a fallow wheat field and past a barn before we came out on the Old Mill Road near where he grew up.

Unbelievable. "I can't believe I'm not dead. Do you realize how many times they shot at us?"

"I'm hard to kill," Ellis said, making a sharp turn down another side road. I didn't think the ghosts were following, but I suppose it paid to be extra careful.

"That was some amazing driving."

"Told you I was a good date," Ellis said, steering us toward the highway and home.

"Sinatra, candles, and now this." I shouldn't have been surprised.

"You didn't even get to taste the dinner."

At least I knew now that we'd be trying it again.

I propped my elbow on the windowsill and stared at the scenery flashing by. My brain was a mess. I kept seeing ghostly buffalo out the window — entire herds of them moving alongside the road. And just when I'd accepted the buffalo, they faded and we zipped past a group of men on horseback. They wore fancy chest armor and helmets that looked exactly like the kind Spanish explorers wore.

I hoped Crazy Louie wasn't contagious.

We drove past the diner and I saw a Native American encampment in the parking lot, complete with a bonfire and old men smoking long-stemmed clay pipes. I didn't understand any of this.

Frankie's power usually left me when I removed myself from a property, but now it flowed freely, if erratically. I wondered what that meant, if Frankie lay dying for real, bleeding his power into me.

Ellis remained focused on the road and didn't slow until we neared my home.

"I lost my gun," I said, searching the seat next to me, unable to find the ghostly revolver. Ghostly objects never stuck around long after I touched them. It seemed this one had disappeared as well.

"The real gun is right next to the hole you made in my floorboard," Ellis remarked.

Sure enough, Crazy Louie's gun lay black and deadly beside a gaping bullet hole in the rubber floor runner. "Sorry about that."

He hazarded a glance at me. "Are you all right? What happened back there?"

No doubt I looked a mess.

"They didn't let us go easily," I said, eyes trained on his dash. I was afraid to look out the window anymore. I didn't want to think about my mishandling of a deadly firearm.

I pulled Frankie's urn from my bag, just to make sure that it was okay, and found a fresh dent near the top. When I looked closer, I saw a circular indentation where it had taken a shot. Probably from my bad handling of Crazy Louie's real gun.

It seemed my gangster friend couldn't dodge a bullet to save his afterlife.

"We need to get him home," I told Ellis. The lid was gone. I rooted around in my bag. Then I took everything out. "No," I gasped. I'd lost it. It was probably under a table at the speakeasy. This was really bad. I drew a hand to my mouth as the horror of it sank in. "We might have spilled Frankie out in the speakeasy." Maybe that was why his power faded when we got too far away. "We could have left him behind with a bunch of murderous thugs."

Of course, those were also his friends, but still...

"Breathe." Ellis turned into the long driveway that led to my house. "We'll take it one step at a time."

That was easy for him to say. He hadn't dumped his friend's ashes out. Again.

Would Frankie be trapped in both places?

Was that even possible?

Ellis parked out front, and once he shut the car down, he gently took Frankie's urn from me. "Let me see." He hazarded a glance at me, the light casting shadows over his features. Then he clicked on his light and shone it inside. I held my breath as he examined it closely. "Looks like there's a big chunk of dirt on the upper left curve of the urn."

I felt the fist in my chest ease just a bit. "That's good."

"Plus some more dust at the bottom." He clicked off the light and took my hand. "You did everything you could back there. You stood up to the mob for him."

"I hope it's enough."

Now that we were home, I simply wanted to go to bed. Or cry. Maybe both. I'd shot a man tonight. My bullet wouldn't kill Louie, but I'd still pulled the trigger and felt a thrill when I took him down. Frankie had been trying to drag me into a life of crime for as long as I'd known him, and it turned out he didn't need to ride me about it. He just needed to put his afterlife on the line and I'd start shooting. What kind of person did that make me?

"Let's get you both inside," Ellis said. He eased out of the car, cradling the urn, and walked around the back to open the door for me.

"You're lucky you didn't see that chase," I said, my legs a bit weak. Good thing he'd been with me for it. "Where did you learn to drive like that?"

"Advanced Vehicle Operations course," he said, letting me get out. He picked up Frankie's favorite gun from the floor, examined it to make sure it wasn't loaded, and tucked it into the back of his jeans.

We made our way up the back steps and I let us inside, holding the door open for Ellis and what was left of Frankie.

I lit a fat, orange, three-wicked candle with shaking fingers.

"Come here." Ellis opened his arms to me and I went gladly, letting him pull me close while I rested my head against his chest.

"I hope Frankie's okay." He had to be okay. We couldn't have come this far for nothing.

He placed the gun on the counter, next to the urn. "Me too," he said, drawing me close and simply holding me.

I didn't know what I would have done without him tonight. "You were amazing."

He huffed and I felt the vibration against my cheek. "You were pretty brave yourself." We stood in my kitchen and enjoyed a moment of peace. He wasn't mad about his car. He didn't go on about the speakeasy under his property. He simply drew circles on my back with the lightest touch of his fingers and I let him.

We listened to the crackling of the candle and the howl of the wind outside. I felt safe, ensconced in the quiet darkness with him. I enjoyed the warmth and the peace, and vowed to hold onto it for as long as he'd let me.

His stomach growled and I couldn't help but smile.

"Sorry about dinner. I'm sure it was delicious."

"It was. Lauralee made it at the diner."

My heart lurched. "So she knows." I'd wanted to be the one to tell her about us.

He drew away slightly in order to look down at me. "Give her some credit. She and Tom had odds going on when we'd make it official." He nestled me back into his arms and rested his chin on my head. "Thanks to us, Tom's doing dishes for the next week."

"In his house, that could be a full-time job," I joked, still nervous but also giddy and flush with the possibilities that lay in store for us.

He grinned and brushed his lips against mine for a sweet lingering kiss that would have turned to more if an impatient gangster hadn't cleared his throat.

I stepped back. Frankie stood way too close and appeared as if he'd swallowed a bug. "Is this my life now?" he asked, impatient. "I gotta wait until you two get done canoodling?"

"Frankie!" I nearly hugged him without thinking. "You're all right!"

He stepped away and held up his hands like he was afraid I'd hug him, too. "Easy there, sweetheart."

A round indentation marred the skin next to the bloody bullet hole on his forehead. "Oh, you poor thing."

"I bled out all over the floor," he said proudly. "It was a mess."

"I'm happy for you. I think." I turned to Ellis. "Frankie is fine." At least as fine as he ever was.

"Sure, I passed out," he said, clearly enjoying the telling. "And when I woke up, I was standing on your porch. Woulda been nice to see what happened to the rest of the guys, but all in all, it was a good shooting." He looked past me to the counter. "Hot dog. You got away with my gun." We stepped aside so Frankie could run his fingers through the cool metal as if he could actually touch it. "I love this gun," Frankie said fondly. "It was my second-favorite gun."

Wait. "I thought that was your favorite."

"Nah," he said, shrugging it off. "My favorite didn't turn up down there."

"So you had me risking my life over your second-favorite gun?" I'd been willing to go after his favorite gun, the one he'd had on him when he died, the one that might help to set him free. But this one? Of all the reckless, stupid, insensitive moves. "I could have been killed!"

"But you weren't," Frankie said, as if that made it right. "Now what do you say we bury this sucker?" he asked, rubbing his hands together. "Most of the guys should have woken up by now. I want to go back to the party."

I wasn't about to let him off that easy. "After I risked my life for you, the only thing you're worried about is your party? I was afraid we'd left part of you back there, that you were trapped."

"I wish," he mused.

"Fine." I grabbed his precious gun and his urn, and I carried them over to the trash can.

"Let me," Ellis said, sounding as frustrated as I felt. Of course, he'd overheard my part of the conversation. He helped me dig a nice, deep hole while Frankie watched. Then I placed the revolver in it and covered it over with dirt.

"There," I said. "I hope that works." Even though I had serious doubts it would.

Frankie stood anxiously, like a kid ready to try out a toy for the first time. "This is gonna sound nuts, but I feel it. It's like…I'm lighter. On my way to free," he added with relish. He pointed a finger at me. "Now don't go all soft on me. See you around." With that, he disappeared.

So much for a fond goodbye.

"Is he gone?" Ellis asked.

I waited for a moment. "I'm not sure."

The kitchen remained silent. The candle flickered and a rosebud, half bloomed, tickled my elbow. I even saw Lucy emerge from the parlor. Perhaps Frankie had gone.

But Lucy fled with the swish of a tail when Frankie reappeared next to the trash can.

"I'm still here!" he said, throwing up his arms, as if he'd been the one risking life and limb. "I got up to the property line a little easier, but when I tried to walk through—no dice!"

Matthew had said he could be free if he buried the thing he loved above all else. I was pretty sure his second-favorite gun wouldn't count, but I didn't want to discourage him. "Maybe it takes a little time."

"Because I haven't spent the last five months waiting," he bit out.

"Well, in the meantime," I said, trying to take his mind off his problem, "there's another issue that we can solve tonight. I still seem to be hooked up to your power."

"For the love of…" He eyed me and I could tell he was looking at me carefully for the first time tonight. "Stand still."

He yanked it back so fast even Ellis felt the spark. He jumped back as if I'd given him a huge dose of static electricity.

"What was that?" Ellis demanded.

I bent over, getting my bearings. "That was Frankie being a jerk."

The gangster smirked. "Be careful. It backfires sometimes."

"No kidding. I thought I was supposed to lose your

power the minute I leave a property," I told him. "What changed?"

"That's my little rule," Frankie said, "not a natural law. Otherwise, I know you. You'll take advantage."

"You mean like when I shot Crazy Louie in the leg to get your gun?" I challenged.

Frankie grinned wide. "You should have shot him in the balls."

"They chased us," I said. "I had to dodge bullets. Ellis took us off road."

"You're just trying to make me jealous, aren't you? Now I'm going to have to hear all about it when I go back and see the guys. If I ever get back," he added, frowning at his memorial trash can.

"We'll figure it out," I promised. We would.

"Yeah?" Frankie challenged, planting his back against the wall, staring at the rosebush in the dirt, "Well, I'm not leaving this spot until we do."

Chapter Seventeen

Ellis stayed until well past midnight, and when I woke the next morning, I found Frankie sitting in the same spot as before. He still squatted with his back against the wall, staring at the trash can.

"Anything yet?" I asked, wiping the sleep from my eyes and squinting against the bright clear day. I really had to find some curtains. Maybe Goodwill had gotten some cute ones in.

"No," the gangster muttered. Just the one word to acknowledge my presence.

"All right." I gave him his space to brood and headed to the kitchen to peel a banana for my skunk and me to share. That was when I missed the chilly, wet kiss of Lucy's nose on my ankle.

Looking up, I saw the swish of her tail as she disappeared into the laundry room.

I divided the banana onto two plates and began slicing it into bite-sized chunks. "Have you been staring at that trash can all night?" I prodded.

"Yes," he said, not moving.

"Ah, so you're not in the mood to talk about it," I said, reaching into the cabinet for the Vita-Skunk mix. Lucy required a special nutritional supplement, seeing as not one pet-food supplier made actual skunk food. She didn't think it tasted so good, so I mixed it in with her favorite treat to make it better.

Too bad there wasn't a Frankie version of mashed banana.

"Maybe you can take a break and, I don't know, make a few cold spots," I suggested to the ghost. "I'll watch your trash can." He needed to find something more constructive to do.

"I'm fine," he gritted out.

"Offer's open if you change your mind," I tossed over my shoulder as I headed to the laundry room to deliver Lucy's breakfast. She obviously had no intention of sharing her space with the ghost, and considering his mood, I didn't blame her.

She and I sat on the floor and broke our fast together next to a washing machine and dryer that were probably older than me.

"This just isn't like him," I confided to my girl. The gangster still hadn't moved. "He usually bounces back faster than this."

Lucy grunted and ate with gusto. She liked my cooking.

Afterward, Frankie stared at the trash can while I cleaned up; then he stewed some more while I did some work calling local businesses to see if they might be interested in meeting with me about their marketing and branding needs.

None were. At least not today.

I also noticed that some of the rejections had gone from polite but firm to downright terse. Yes, Reggie had died in the middle of a meeting with me, but I hardly thought it had anything to do with our plans to work together.

I lost my pep after the twelfth rejection, even though I reminded myself that I was a dozen nos closer to a yes. I'd made progress. All the same, I decided to call it a day and try again tomorrow.

Frankie didn't even offer to commit armed robbery or suggest I open up my own money-laundering business.

He moped through lunch. Afterward, he ignored me while I swept up a few tiny bits of dirt we'd spilled while digging last night. I returned them to the trash can and then went ahead and hand-scrubbed the floors on my hands and knees, cleaning around him when he didn't feel up to moving.

By late afternoon, I couldn't take much more of his gloomy mood.

"Frankie," I said, approaching him. With a sigh, I slid down the wall and sat next to him. "I'm worried about you."

He narrowed his eyes and refused to turn his head to acknowledge me.

He'd seemed okay at the speakeasy last night. He'd even had fun seeing his friends and getting his gun. But that joy had dissipated with every hour that passed since we planted his gun next to my rosebush. I'd never seen him this down. "I'm sorry you got your hopes up."

He glared at me. "You're sorry, sweetheart?" he snapped. "My entire future is in your dented old trash can. It doesn't get any sorrier than that."

"I'm trying," I said. "Do you still feel different? Last night, you said you felt a little lighter."

He stood up off the wall. "Maybe. It's hard to tell. Whatever it is, it don't matter. I still can't go anywhere. I can't live." He took two steps away from me and turned back as I climbed to my feet. "Do you know what it was like to be in the middle of that bar fight last night?"

"Yes. It was awful." I'd been terrified.

He opened his arms wide. "It was amazing! Best

time I could've had in fifty years, and that includes when I was laid up with a bullet to the skull."

"I'm so glad you're okay." I could hardly see the dent anymore.

His nostrils flared. "Now those guys can do it all again tonight. Or they can smash booze bottles. They can run numbers, lay cash on the ponies. They can do whatever they want, and I gotta sit here watching you play house with a skunk!"

With that attitude, it was no wonder Lucy didn't like him. I ignored his harsh words and tried to focus on what had truly upset him. I understood what it was like to want something badly and not be able to have it. "We got your gun. We're making progress. Focus on how good it feels to be on the right track."

"On the…" He spun in a circle, clenching his fists. "I got my gun. I should be free. Not in bits and pieces, but now!"

Well, the world didn't work on a Frankie time schedule. We'd done everything we could. I'd even got shot at last night. For him. "I'm trying!"

He ripped off his hat and threw it straight through my back wall. "This is a demented scavenger hunt! And it's only the beginning! How much stuff do I gotta find to end this?"

I scrubbed my hands over my face. "Matthew said whatever is going to free you has to mean something to you, Frankie. It can't be your second-favorite afterthought because ooh, look, it's shiny." There were no quick cures, no instant fixes. "What did you really care about in life?" I demanded.

The gangster clammed up and refused to even look at me. He dropped back down to his place on the floor and wrapped his arms around his knees, staring at the trash can.

I cleared my throat and fought the urge to apologize. I had nothing to be sorry for. "I'm going out in about an hour," I told him. "Lauralee and I are taking Em out to the diner. Would you like to come?"

He didn't bother looking up. "No."

I considered tempting him by describing the Native American encampment I'd seen in the diner parking lot last night, but opted to leave the gangster in peace. Even I knew sharing a bonfire with a native tribe wasn't the same as knocking over an armored car.

"I'll be back later tonight to take you to the cemetery," I told him.

He leaned against the wall, one leg up, one leg stretched out in front of him. "Maybe Henry will be there," he said absently.

I hoped for both our sakes that he was.

***

Frankie wasn't any better when I left to pick up Lauralee for our dinner date with her cousin.

Focus on what you can control.

When I got to her house, Lauralee stood waiting on the porch. "Did you see the Sugarland Gazette?" she asked, holding up a copy.

"No." I couldn't afford the paper. I probably didn't want to see it anyway. "Ovis's article came out today, didn't it?"

She handed it to me. "You can read it on the way. I'll drive." She walked around to the driver's side of her blue minivan. I opened the passenger-side door and two bottles of Elmer's glue spilled out onto the driveway from a seat packed with white and brown felt, a packet of huge googly eyes, acrylic paints, a broom, a flat section of acrylic PVC pipe, and an assortment of plastic fruit.

"Do I want to know?" I asked.

"Gosh." Lauralee cringed. "I forgot that was in here." She went to move it to the backseat, but both back rows appeared to be in worse shape than the fairgrounds after the carnival had been through town.

"I'll drive," I said, quickly, sparing her any explanations. Her children were happy and well-adjusted. She didn't need to have a clean car, too.

"Tommy Junior landed the role of the Sugary Molar in the Happy Tooth Opera," she gushed, cheering up, "only he needs me to make him a costume. I just figured out how to make him a life-sized toothbrush. Thank God for Pinterest."

"Let me know when it is and I'll put the show on my calendar," I said as we walked to my car.

"I will." She slid inside. "Now, about the paper. Since you can't read for yourself, I'll tell you. Ovis is claiming some awful things. He said Reggie had a stolen watch in his pocket, from a dead gangster's grave, no less."

"I heard," I said, starting up the engine.

"And this Handsome Henry is Reggie's great, great uncle. Which makes him my relative, too. We always knew we had a mobster or two in the family, but I never thought Reggie knew much about it. And I have no idea why he'd have the man's watch."

"Wait." I paused, my hand on the gearshift. "So Handsome Henry Hagar…"

"His mother was a Thompson," Lauralee said. "They'd had a falling out with the family, and we don't have any stories or pictures, but he's buried next to her in our family vault. I've seen his name there in the crypt, I just didn't realize who he was."

"Wow," I said, throwing the car into reverse and pulling out. "I don't know what to make of that."

"Henry sounds like a really ruthless guy from what Ovis found, and my uncle died the way Henry used to kill people," she said, tearing up. "When I read it, I rushed right over to see Em, but she refused to answer the door. She's not answering her calls," Lauralee said, her breath catching. "It's awful." She strained to see out the passenger-side window, as if catching a glimpse of Em's house would make everything better. "I don't know if she's going to be any better tonight. She barely talked to me through the door last night, but I got her promise to come out with us."

"This will be good for both of you," I said, driving the short block to Em's place. "Just take a deep breath and try to relax. I'm nervous sitting next to you."

"This whole week has me twisted in knots," she said, running a hand through her wild auburn hair.

That was because she felt so deeply. I felt lucky to be counted among those she cared for. "We'll work this out," I promised, firmly believing we would.

I found a parking spot on the street one house away and took that instead of pulling in the driveway. I didn't want to be presumptuous and assume Em would want to ride in my beat-up old car. Although my old Cadillac should go a long way toward making her thankful for whatever modest car Reggie had purchased for her.

The porch light shone, a bright spot in the rapidly darkening neighborhood.

"Ovis thinks that gangster could go on a murder spree," my friend scoffed as she got out of my car. "I worry it'll give some nutcase an excuse."

I walked with her to the front porch. "Let's just worry about what we can control."

The small green house stood dark inside, which didn't sit well with me. Lauralee and I exchanged a glance as she rapped on the black front door. "Em? We're here," she said. "Yay!" she added, with forced merriment that was more depressing than helpful.

"Maybe we should go somewhere that has wine," I suggested. A tart, strong bottle of Pinot could go a long way to soothing all of our nerves.

"Ha," my friend said, trying not to fidget.

Em still hadn't answered the door. I rang the bell again. "Maybe she needs extra time to get ready." It wouldn't be at all surprising if Reggie's daughter were the high-maintenance type.

Lauralee pulled out her phone and checked the messages. "She didn't call." She dialed a number and waited. "It's going to voice mail." Lauralee peered in the window closest to us. "What if she's hurt?"

"Let's not jump to conclusions," I said. "Maybe she's listening to music through her earbuds and she can't hear the bell. Let's try the door. Maybe we can just peek inside."

It was locked.

"You're right. We need to go in," my friend said, hopping off the porch.

"Not if she didn't leave her door open." Most everyone in Sugarland did, but Em definitely clung to her big-city ways.

But Lauralee wasn't listening. She'd landed in the yard and had begun rooting under a prickly grouping of holly bushes. "Voila," she said, producing a plastic rock. "Reggie showed me this." She opened a compartment on the underside and slid a key out.

"I suppose if we're desperate." I glanced at the door, afraid we'd scare a city girl like Em if we just waltzed inside. She might still be in the shower. I rang the bell again. The bing-bong echoed throughout the house.

But still no answer.

Lauralee's fingers shook as she inserted the key into the lock and pushed the door open.

The front room stood dark.

Lauralee walked in while I found the lights. "Em-maJane?" she called.

"She wants to be called Em," I reminded her, closing the door.

She chewed her lip. "I've got a bad feeling about this."

So did I.

I didn't want to find Em hiding or hurt...or worse.

The house had an open floor plan, with a kitchen straight past the front room. "Em?" Lauralee asked, walking past the empty dining area to the darkened hallway on the left.

She flipped on the lights. "It's us, Em. We're here for dinner."

The house remained eerily silent.

I stuck close to my friend. "How about we stop giving away our location," I murmured.

"What?" she asked, not understanding.

She hadn't been hunting any killers lately.

"This is her bedroom," Lauralee said, approaching a darkened room on the left. I touched her hand to keep her from turning on the lights as I stepped into the doorway. A thin stream of moonlight poured in from the window. I caught a glimpse of my reflection and gasped.

"What is it?" Lauralee turned on the lights and we saw a long mirrored dresser.

"Heavens to Betsy." I clutched my chest, feigning a heart attack even though it may not have been that far from the truth.

Lauralee giggled. "You said I was a nervous wreck."

I'd venture to guess no one shot at her last night.

"Let's just take this one step at a time," I said, entering the room.

The decorations reflected old Hollywood, with an elegant white faux fur throw over a sleek gray silk bedspread. Vases of pink roses graced the dresser and nightstand. I crossed the room and found Em's tiny bathroom dark. "Maybe she's using the master," I suggested, with the sick realization that if Em were here and able to speak, she'd have found us by now. "Be cautious," I said, crossing the hall to the only other bedroom in the house.

Looking away, I flipped on the lights.

"It's empty," Lauralee said over my shoulder.

At this point, I truly hoped it was.

It soon became clear Em had taken over the larger room after her father's death. Green and brown bedding lay in a heap in the corner next to the dresser while fresh pink sheets and another faux fur throw rumpled the unmade bed. I smelled expensive perfume and something earthy underneath.

"I don't know if you want to go in here," I said, bracing myself as I advanced toward the master bath. I didn't want to proceed, but I'd seen tragedy before, and I barely knew Em. This was Lauralee's cousin, her blood kin. If the killer had murdered Reggie's daughter in that bathroom, I should be the one to walk in and see it first. If I could do anything for my friend, it would be to protect her from that.

Now or never. I hit the lights, turned the corner, and saw chaos—but no body. I braced a hand on the door jamb and blew out a breath. "She's not in here." Thank God.

Cream blush bled out all over the counter and a mass of towels exploded all over the floor. I drew closer to the tub, where a black silk shirt soaked in muddy water.

Muddy black jeans lay crumpled outside the tub. I could smell the tang of minerals and dirt. "Correct me if I'm wrong, but Em doesn't strike me as an outdoor girl."

"She won't even touch Ambrose when he has Oreo hands," Lauralee said, staring at the mess on the floor. "I don't know what she could have been doing."

Whatever it was, I doubted she wanted anyone to see her.

"Let's get out of here," I said softly.

Lauralee let out a frustrated sigh. "We're only trying to help. She knew we were coming."

Not for this. "Come on," I said, ushering my friend out of the room.

"What could she have gotten into?" Lauralee continued as I hurried her down the hall.

I didn't even care. "When we see her," I started, "if we see her, don't mention this." She wouldn't tell us the truth anyway.

My friend's eyes widened. "She might have run back to Chicago."

"Without burying her dad?" That seemed cold even for her. "No." I had a feeling she was up to something else.

"I was afraid she might get overwhelmed and bolt," Lauralee said, her nose going red as tears threatened to form.

A knock sounded at the door.

We exchanged a glance.

I motioned Lauralee forward and we walked silently to the door.

The knock sounded again, impatient this time. Lauralee stood next to me as I opened the door.

Carla stood on the porch, and she seemed equally shocked to see us.

"What are you doing here?" I asked, forgetting my manners.

She held her shoulders back and gripped the strap of her purse with both hands. "I could ask the same thing of you."

Not really. Lauralee was family.

"Come in," my friend said, with all the sweetness she could muster.

That made Carla appear even more uncomfortable. She kept her eyes forward as she walked into the house like a prisoner returning to her cell. "I would like to speak with EmmaJane privately," she said, making it sound more like an order than a request.

"Then you'll have to get in line because we don't know where she is," I said.

Carla's eyes widened slightly, with surprise or fear, I couldn't tell. "When did you see her last?"

Lauralee crossed her arms over her chest. "When did you?"

Carla glanced toward the darkened front window as if she wished to make an escape. Her lips quivered and turned up into what I was sure Reggie's protégé meant to be an appeasing smile. "When we made our appointment."

Lauralee eyed her. "That doesn't answer our question."

The front doorknob rattled and Em walked in. She dropped her purse by the front door and stared at us like we were out of our minds. "What are you doing in my house?" she demanded.

"You're okay!" Lauralee gushed, rushing to hug her cousin, who ducked away from the embrace and tried to keep walking as if Lauralee were an overly enthusiastic Labrador.

"We had plans tonight," I reminded her.

She checked her watch. "I was only ten minutes late," she snapped. "And you barged into my house?"

Guilt washed over me.

Lauralee cringed. "Welcome to Sugarland."

Em stared at her. "You people are unbelievable."

"Okay," Lauralee said, trying to rally. "Why don't

we head out to dinner?" She gestured to an equally surprised Carla. "You're welcome to join us if you'd like."

"She's leaving," Em stated, holding the door open for Reggie's assistant. She turned to us. "You are, too."

"But what about dinner?" my friend asked as Carla brushed out the door.

"Oh, you think now is the time for Sugarland hospitality?" Em demanded. "Not on your life. People say Chicago is so dangerous and Sugarland is so safe, but when I was in Chicago, nobody killed my father or broke into my home," she shouted.

She had a point.

Lauralee sighed. "Oh, Em. I never meant to make you feel—"

"You don't know how I feel. You and my dad have been shoving this town down my throat since the second I got off the plane. Newsflash: I'm glad I can go back to living a normal life, that I won't have everyone watching my every move. You can psycho stalk me all you want, but it doesn't make me your friend."

"I'm your only family," Lauralee pressed, more understanding than I would have been.

Em huffed, almost amused. "And you think that's what I need." Her expression hardened, and she pointed at the door. "Get out. Leave. Now."

Lauralee stared at her, rooted to the spot.

"Sorry to blow your little minds," Em said briskly, "but if I did this the Sugarland way, we'd be here all night."

We filed out the front door and stood dumbly on the porch as Em closed the door and locked it behind us.

"Oh my gosh," Lauralee fretted, tears springing to her eyes. "I really messed up this time."

I wrapped an arm around her. "It'll be okay," I said,

hoping I was right.

We watched Carla stride down the walkway ahead of us and slip into the Jaguar parked in the driveway.

There was something bigger going on, and I was going to uncover it if it was the last thing I did.

Chapter Eighteen

When I got home to pick up Frankie and take him to the cemetery, I found him sitting in the same spot, still staring at the trash can.

I turned the lights on. "How are you holding up?"

He shrugged. "Suds came to visit."

"That's great," I said, making my way to my un-friendly ghost. "How is your friend?"

Frankie shrugged a shoulder. "He's right next to me," he said, indignant, as if I should be able to see the deceased mobster. "Now that he knows he's a ghost, he's too depressed to rob the bank."

"I hardly think he should give up his goals," I said, worried. "Unless he'd like to help us look for Hand-some Henry." We could use all the help we could get.

Frankie stood and addressed the empty spot next to him. "You should run by the speakeasy, have a few laughs." He listened for a moment. "Yeah, ask about Henry, too."

"Thank you," I said to both of them as I slipped Frankie's urn into my bag. "Suds can let himself out," I said, whether it be through the door or a wall.

Frankie was strangely quiet as I started up my car and headed out. He remained a small, flickering light in my passenger seat as we drove through downtown

Sugarland, toward the town's original graveyard.

I substituted a granola bar for dinner and tried not to worry.

It just wasn't right. I'd seen him that way before, usually when he was overtired or recovering from an evening of ghost hunting. But this time I hadn't overtaxed his powers. His current situation had to be wearing him down.

He wouldn't want me pushing or sticking my nose in, but it didn't feel right to ignore him either. I sighed.

"It's a pretty night," I said, making conversation as we turned left past Pearlman's Gas Station and Auto Repair. "Although the temperature's dropped, so we might get some fog."

I found myself slightly amused by the idea of visiting a dark, foggy cemetery with my ghost friend. Even stranger, I was looking forward to it.

Life could change on a dime—for worse, but also for better. I held onto the better part. Frankie and I were due for something good to happen.

"Ellis is meeting us right after he gets off shift," I said to the ghost. "It'll be nice to have him along because I think it's illegal to be in a cemetery after dark."

Perhaps breaking the law would cheer Frankie up.

The flicker snapped and disappeared.

Maybe not.

We passed Fitzer's Memorial Monuments and Engraving, and I made a mental note to see if they were in the market for new signage. They'd kept the same black and white look since Gerald Fitzer passed away in the late '90s. He'd probably had it done in the '60s. It would be a nice project because Fitzer's had the only gravestone-carving place in town. Everybody would have to go there eventually, and they'd see my work when they did.

I pulled up to Holy Oak Cemetery, glad to see Ellis had arrived before us. His squad car stood on the street near the main gates. I parked behind him and retrieved my bag with Frankie's urn from the floor of the passenger side. I'd placed a white paper-wrapped bouquet of yellow roses on the passenger seat and retrieved those as well. They'd cost more than I could afford, but roses seemed like a classic choice, and yellow signified new beginnings. I hoped that wouldn't be lost on Handsome Henry.

A sharp wind hit me the minute I opened my car door and I sincerely wished I'd gone ahead and worn my ugly monstrosity of a coat. It would be toasty and readily visible. Instead, I wore two sweaters, the freshly washed pink one over the white one Ellis had seen last night.

"Hey," he said, greeting me with a warm hug. "How's Frankie?"

"Upset," I told him truthfully.

"You?" he prodded, opening the back of his trunk and retrieving a Maglite. He handed it to me.

I smiled. "I'm glad to have a hot date tonight."

He grinned and slammed the trunk. "Those better not be for me," he said, eyeing the flowers.

"No, they're for Henry," I said, smelling them. They really were beautiful. "I have to tell you, I just had a strange encounter with Em and Carla." I related the story as we walked to the tall iron entry gates. I also filled him in on the article that connected Reggie's family to Handsome Henry. "I don't know what to make of it." There was obviously more going on than I could learn from real, live people.

Ellis buried his hands in his pockets. "That's not the only new development. I probably shouldn't mention this, but one of my buddies at work said Jeb opened up a big bank account out of town last week."

Yikes. "That doesn't look good."

"It doesn't," Ellis agreed. "Maybe Henry will have some answers for us."

We needed to visit the Thompson family vault. "I can show you where to go." It stood in an older section on the left side of the sprawling memorial park.

"Lead the way," he said.

A tall stone wall surrounded the entire cemetery. Neatly trimmed bushes clung to the base. Holy Oak Cemetery closed at dusk, the sign said. The gates stood shut and locked.

Ellis would have to boost me over the wall. Or perhaps we could scale one of the old oaks that had given the land its name.

Instead, he pulled a key out of his pocket.

"Where did you get that?" I asked, impressed as he inserted the key into the gate's padlock.

"I talked to Steve, the manager." He swung the heavy gate open. "What did you expect us to do? Break in?"

"Well…"

He laughed at my expression. "You did."

"It would be more like trespassing," I said, heading back toward his car so he couldn't see the pink on my cheeks. It wasn't as if he hadn't bent the rules for me before.

"I refuse to be corrupted," Ellis joked, settling in next to me, "at least not tonight."

"I'll hold you to that," I said as we drove through the gates. "I don't have time right now anyway," I added, unable to resist flirting with the man.

Fog blanketed the ground. We passed the caretaker's cottage and the landscaping shed at the entrance. I could have sworn I saw the fog take shape among the tombstones just beyond.

Don't look for trouble.

We glided down Resurrection Avenue and through the oldest section of the cemetery, dating back to the early 1800s. Worn grave markers thrust from the ground at odd angles.

A low moan sounded from behind me, sending my heart skittering. "Frankie?"

I sincerely hoped it was him.

He didn't answer.

"Left," I said to Ellis as we reached a fork in the road.

"Yeah, I know," he said gently, uneasy. Century-old crypts clustered in the foggy night.

"Did you hear it, too?"

"I think so," he murmured, eyes on the road. Our headlights cut through the fog and shone upon the older vaults in this section of the cemetery. "At least we're moving away from it."

I stopped just short of telling him the truth: it didn't matter which way we went within the cemetery; we were on their turf now.

"Just a little farther down," I said as we passed under a pair of old oak trees on either side of the road. Their branches leaned toward each other and had grown into a canopy that spanned the pathway.

"Here." I motioned for Ellis to pull over next to a white marble obelisk with a weeping angel at its base. Dark shadows cloaked what lay beyond. "We've got the Ward vault and then the Thompsons," I murmured. Maybe if I kept talking, I could distract myself from the unease that prickled up my spine.

Our Maglites cut through the black of the night, sending a small animal skittering away through the dead grass. We stepped beyond the obelisk to a lichen-encrusted stone vault with the name Ward carved across the top.

The muddy ground felt slick under my tennis shoes.
Old stone tombs rose up all around us, and I felt very
much like an unwanted tourist in the city of the dead.

"This one," Ellis said, his beam coming to rest on a
bleeding green bronze plaque that read Thompson.
I knew it well. Lauralee and I had been here many
times over the years to visit and leave flowers for
her grandparents. We'd also stood graveside for the
funeral of Em's mother.

"Hi, Henry," I said, placing the roses in a built-in
bronze flower holder, making sure he understood
these were for him. Four generations of the Thompson family rested inside.

An iron door with crisscrossed bars covered the
sealed entrance to the tomb.

This was where Reggie would be buried as well,
assuming Em didn't go through with her threat to
cremate him.

"Frankie?" I asked, not wanting to pressure the
ghost, but needing to see all the same.

He sighed and shimmered into view next to the
entrance to the vault. "Nobody ever leaves flowers for
me."

My heart squeezed a bit. "I'm sorry. But you're not
buried in a cemetery," I reminded him. His remains
rested in my purse…and in my kitchen. "You do have
an entire rosebush," I added.

"It's not the same," he grumbled.

It wasn't, and I vowed to do something about it as
his power settled over me.

It felt pricklier than before. I winced as it hit my skin
like a thousand tiny needles. "You mind easing up?"
I asked. The sharp, bristly feeling reached down into
my bones.

Frankie wasn't playing. He really was upset.

Ellis drew close to me.

"I don't know if it worked," I murmured to him, taking a step back. The aged vault appeared as it had before. A sharp wind whipped around the corner and I shivered. "Henry?"

The doorway remained dark and abandoned.

"Don't blame me," Frankie said. "He's got no reason to answer the door. He don't know you."

True. "You're his friend, though," I reasoned.

Frankie shrugged. "Nah. He don't like me after I hit on his mother."

"Frankie," I said, shocked.

"What?" He pulled out his cigarette case. "I was single at the time and she was a total Sheba." He selected a smoke and perched it on his bottom lip. "You oughta thank me. The way to get to Henry is to piss him off. Bringing me with you was your best chance to get his attention."

Oh sure. Anger the man who murdered for a living, and quite possibly for fun. "Well, he's not answering. What do you suggest I do?"

Frankie lit up. "Disrespect his grave," he said around his smoke.

"That's a truly awful idea," and one I'd never consider.

I turned back to the looming, dark vault.

Frankie took a long drag and exhaled through his nose. "You have got to learn to be more ruthless." He held the cigarette in his mouth and studied the vault. "The door looks too solid to bash in, but you could probably remove these screws here… hell, do you have some dynamite?"

"No." But I had a plan of my own. Dime Store Bobby had said Henry liked flowers. What would the hit man think if I took the roses back? I'd neglected to take the paper off anyway.

Frankie measured the gap between the iron gate and

the stone base with his fingers. "You could fit at least two sticks of explosives in here…"

I reached down and tucked the bouquet of roses into my bag.

A howling wind descended over the grave, scattering dead leaves and brush. "Leave 'em alone!" ordered a booming voice.

"Henry?" I asked.

He shimmered into view. I recognized him from the photo in the library, with his wide face and the uneven red scar that marred the left side of his face, from eyebrow to chin. "Handsome Henry," I whispered. He stood in front of me in his underwear.

Sakes alive. I tried to keep my eyes off his threadbare gray boxer shorts and focused on his scarred chest with one, two, three…four bullet holes and a tattoo of a pinup girl wearing a short dress and thigh-high stockings.

He glared at me with murder in his eyes, and I had no problem believing this man killed people for fun.

I quickly replaced the flowers. "My apologies." I'd always heard that it helped to picture an intimidating person in their underwear, but in this case it might have made things worse. Henry was the scariest man I'd ever seen, even in his skivvies. "I did get them for you," I added, glad that my voice didn't shake too badly. "I didn't want them to go to waste if you weren't…er…home."

"You looking at my underwear?" he asked, narrowing his eyes.

There was no good answer for that. "Erm," I turned to Frankie for help, and the hit man eyed him as well.

"Not everybody gets shot while wearing their best suit," he said of my friend.

Frankie lifted his smoke in a respectful salute. "How's it going, killer?"

He looked ready to tear Frankie apart. "I ought to pop you," he said, a pistol materializing in his hand.

Frankie smiled and drew his own gun.

No. There was too much riding on this conversation to let a firefight break out. "That's it. Nobody's shooting anybody," I ordered, fully aware I was speaking to two men who could gun me down, one of whom would probably enjoy it. "We came here to talk."

The corner of Henry's mouth lifted. "I ain't shootin' at you, dollface. You're a cute one." He frowned toward Frankie. "You with this rat?"

"No," I said quickly as Frankie said, "Yes."

"The thing is," I interjected, determined to skate over the unpleasantness, "I'm a friend of your distant cousin." At least, that was how I thought it went. "She's concerned about some property of yours."

I cringed inwardly. I hadn't meant to bring up the watch, but I was making this up on the fly. I just hadn't expected him to be angry or mostly naked or an old rival of Frankie's. "An engraved pocket watch of yours was found on the body of a bank president who was killed a few days ago. We were hoping you might be able to tell us something about it."

"My watch?" he demanded, getting scary again. "Who stole my watch? Wasn't I buried with it?"

"I don't know," I told him. He slammed back into his grave and I directed a frightened glance at Ellis, who stood at the ready. "I don't think he knew his watch was missing."

"Well, nobody broke into the crypt," Ellis said, "at least not recently. I got a look at the vault door through the iron gate. The seal on the door appears to be intact, although it looks like somebody tried."

Henry's head thrust through the stone. "It's not in there!" He stormed outside. "First I can't die with the damned thing, and now I can't take it to my grave!"

Poor ghost. He hadn't known. Even if it had been in his coffin, he couldn't have used it. Every ghost spent eternity with the things they had on them when they died.

"The watch is gone," I told Ellis. "When was the last time this vault could have been opened?"

Ellis eyed me. "When they buried Reggie's wife."

"Did he open it?" Henry demanded, pointing his pistol at Ellis's head.

"Stop!" This was getting out of hand.

Henry turned and pointed the gun at me.

"What's the matter?" Ellis demanded.

"Boys, boys!" An elegant ghost shimmered into view wearing a pearl bracelet and a short silk teddy. Her perfectly curled and coiffed blond flapper hair was styled with a silver art deco comb encrusted with emerald-cut gems. She played with the long string of pearls draped between her breasts, knowing that was where both Henry's and Frankie's eyes immediately went. She really could have used a bra, but I wasn't going to tell her that when she might have just saved my life. "What seems to be the trouble here?"

She twisted her hips like the sex kitten she was while she looked me up and down, clearly judging. "I know you're not fighting over her," she added, apparently taking issue with either my double sweater look or my simple ponytail. "No offense, doll."

"None taken." She'd given the mobsters something to focus on besides their guns. And she bore a striking resemblance to the woman in the photos from the library — Rosie.

Henry rubbed at the back of his thick, gray neck. "Somebody nabbed my pocket watch," he grumbled, "then planted it on some dead banker."

"I thought he should know," I said to them both.

"Even if it is bad news."

She nodded to me, as if my efforts meant I deserved a bit more respect, or at least consideration. "Come on over to my place," she said. "We'll discuss this in a more civilized manner."

I didn't miss Frankie's wolfish smile. Neither did she.

She turned and began gliding deeper into the cemetery. A trio of raw bullet holes raced across her spine, in stark contrast to her white teddy.

"We're not going," I said to Frankie. Our business was with Henry.

She stopped near a broken Celtic cross and glanced over her shoulder. "Do what you like, but you're coming with me if you want answers."

She must have done well with the gangsters. She could certainly read a situation. "Excuse me, are you Miss Rosalind Baker?" I asked, needing to be sure.

Her cupid's bow mouth curved. "Call me Rosie."

"This way," I said to Ellis.

He joined me without a word as we wound deeper into the cemetery, on the trail of Rosie's ghost. Henry glided beside her, an arm absently wrapped around her neck, while Frankie trailed back with us.

"She's the only one who can calm him down lately," Frankie said as the pair disappeared into a decrepit vault under a weeping willow tree.

"Lately?" I asked.

"Since '29," Frankie clarified.

"All righty then." I stumbled over roots that had broken the path and glanced at Ellis in surprise when I saw the iron door gaping open.

"Families are responsible for maintaining the individual crypts," he murmured as his flashlight traced over the worn, dirty stone and a broken angel. "Looks like her line died out."

I didn't know of any Bakers in town, which said it all.

"Come on in," she said, passing through the half-opened crypt door.

Oh, boy. I didn't like the idea of visiting anybody's grave from the inside.

"We've been invited in," I said to Ellis, as if this were a normal social call.

"Very kind," he murmured as I slipped in ahead of him. Ladies first.

The heavy door squeaked as I pushed past it. I shone a light inside, over the stone casket that rested in the middle. Opposite it, high up, grime caked a stained-glass window set over the far wall. The stone walls on either side contained no other burials. Dirt and refuse littered the floor. A spiderweb caught my hair and I tore it out, rubbing the sticky goo on my pants.

"My apologies, doll." Rosie shimmered into view behind a ghostly bar cart in the back. "The maid's dead." She mixed a cocktail like we stood at a party.

I stepped inside. "Where's Henry?" I didn't see him or Frankie.

This better not be a trap.

"He's outside, making sure the coast is clear. Someone followed us," she said, wary.

No good. "A ghost or a mortal?"

She reached for a glass on the bottom. "Mortal."

"Ellis?" He stood by the door, looking out. "We might have been followed. Somebody living. Can you check it out?" He seemed reluctant to leave me in the crypt. "I'll be fine."

He nodded. "I'll be right back. You yell if there's trouble."

I had no problem doing that.

Rosie eyed me as she poured the bourbon. "He's a

cute one."

"Hands off," I teased.

She fought a grin. "When Henry gets back, best way to settle him down will be with an old-fashioned, heavy on the bitters. Luckily I died while holding onto the bar cart."

"You've been together for a while?" I asked, trying to think back to the article.

"A while." She plunked two ice cubes from a silver bucket. "So how did they find Henry's watch?"

"The president of the First Sugarland Bank was murdered in the bank vault. He had Henry's watch in his pocket."

"So he was a thief," she concluded, pouring a scotch and taking a sip from it straight.

"We don't know that."

She lowered her glass. "I've been around a long time, babe, and I'll tell you one thing. Greedy thieves always get caught because they're too greedy. Sooner or later, somebody always evens the score."

"Reggie didn't steal it. Some people have suggested Henry left it behind after a hit—" I began.

"He didn't." She placed her glass down.

Just then, I felt a pricking on the back of my neck. I turned my head to see that Handsome Henry loomed behind me.

I stepped aside, and Rosie crossed the room quickly, handing him his drink. "Remember, hon? Your watch broke on the McKinley job."

Henry perked up. "That's right. Old man McKinley busted the chain while begging for his life," he said, relieved.

"I got it fixed for you, but it was still on my dresser when I died. My sister put everything in my safety-deposit box. Whoever stole it must have taken it from there." She sipped her drink. "What do you want to bet it was the banker?"

"It couldn't have been," I protested, standing up to Henry's cold stare. I knew Reggie. "He wouldn't do that."

"Somebody followed us," Frankie said, in the uncomfortable silence that followed.

"I sent Ellis," I said.

"Not Ellis," Frankie muttered, replacing his pistol in his coat. "This one got away."

"So you found my watch and now you think I'm back in business," Henry concluded, like the stone-cold killer he was.

Oh boy. I really wished he wasn't standing between me and the door. "The person who killed Reggie used your signature style—a shot to the heart and an X slashed across the cheek. I saw it myself. I was there when they found the body."

"What?" Henry demanded, growing so large he took up the entire doorway. "Somebody's posing like me? There's only one Handsome Henry. Me!"

"So, it's safe to say you didn't—" I began.

"I'll kill 'em. Slow and painful," he snarled. He began glowing red at the edges. Oh, shoot. He'd better not be going poltergeist.

The air crackled around us.

When a ghost got angry enough and emotional enough, it could manifest startling amounts of violent power.

Henry turned and crashed out of the doorway, shooting across the cemetery in a blaze of silver light.

Ellis stood just outside the crypt, shocked as if he'd witnessed the ghost pass. "You feel that?" he asked, patting himself down.

"Where'd he go?" I asked Frankie, who shrugged.

Rosie strolled to the doorway to join me, drink in hand. "I'd say he went to check it out for himself."

Chapter Nineteen

We dashed to Ellis's squad car. I wanted to be at the bank when Henry uncovered the truth behind the haunting there.

"How long do you think it'll take him to make it across town?" I asked, buckling my seat belt.

"He's a ghost," Frankie barked from the backseat. "He's already there."

I figured.

Ellis pulled out and sped as fast as he could through the cemetery. We passed a wisp of a woman, her lower half missing, weeping over a lichen-encrusted headstone. Near the canopy of oaks, I saw a ghostly family enjoying a picnic in the grass.

A light mist had begun to fall and the windshield wipers swept it away.

"Please keep me plugged in," I said to Frankie. It would avoid the power whiplash and I'd need to see once we reached the bank.

He folded his arms — what was left of them — over his chest and sulked in the backseat. "This is what happens when I get lax on the rules," he groused.

"Your arms…" They misted out below the elbows. "I hoped finding your gun would make you stronger." Or at least more able to resist the power drain.

Frankie stared out the window, glum. "I don't need more energy. I just need to be able to leave." To zip away, like Henry. Poor ghost.

"Hey," I said, trying to cheer him up, "you might see Suds at the bank."

"Great. In the meantime, I get to hang out in the back of a squad car. At least it feels familiar."

"That's the spirit," I told him.

When we'd exited the cemetery, Ellis started up the blue and red lights on top of the cruiser and I got a bit of a thrill speeding through town.

We arrived at the bank only minutes later. Ellis parked in front and I quickly gathered Frankie's urn and stuffed the Maglite in my bag.

The lobby lights glowed inside the bank and all appeared well from where we stood. Of course, we all knew looks could be deceiving.

"Let's go down to the lower entrance," Ellis said, keeping an eye out. The misty rain and late hour left the sidewalk out front deserted.

We had only the buzz of a nearby streetlight for company.

"Stick with us, Frankie," I said as we navigated the concrete steps in the dark. Security lights shone yellow over the lower entrance, but did nothing for the shadows at the top.

"Look," Ellis said, pointing out movement just inside the door. He edged out in front of me, one of his hands hovering over the curve of his back. In typical Ellis fashion, it appeared he had a gun holstered there.

Breathing heavy, and keeping his weapon in reach, he knocked on the glass door of the bank.

Jeb's face appeared on the other side. "Ellis," he said, relieved. He pulled out a key and unlocked the door. "I heard sirens and almost wished they were

for me," he said, opening the door a crack. A thin
sheen of sweat coated his upper lip and his hands
shook. "We're getting even more paranormal activity
since Reggie died, and it's not my imagination." He
winced, his lower lip trembling. "Did you hear that?"

"No." I hadn't, but I was sure he had Handsome
Henry in there.

Jeb directed his attention to me. "What are you doing here?"

"We're on a date," Ellis assured him.

Jeb gave a quick nod. "It's happening right now,"
he said to Ellis, as if pleading for the officer to believe
him.

Ellis took a look inside, past the guard. "Did you
call anyone?"

"And tell the police I think I hear a ghost?" Jeb
scoffed. "The interim president would sack me good.
He's a real hard-ass."

A metallic crash echoed from behind him and Jeb
dropped his keys.

"Right there," he demanded. "I didn't make that up.
I'm not crazy."

"I'll check it out," Ellis told him. "And Verity, she'll
stick with me."

I was glad Ellis carried himself like the law officer
he was. Jeb didn't even question him as we entered
the bank.

"Be careful," the guard warned. "Try to get a picture
or nobody's gonna believe you, either. I think I saw
mist once." A low unearthly creaking echoed throughout the marble lobby, stopping us just inside the door.
I froze in place and Jeb grabbed my arm. "You hear
that, too?"

I cleared my throat. "Yes."

The trick would be to calm him down.

"You stay here," Ellis assured him. "Keep watch."

"All right," he said, frozen with fear. I gently extricated myself from the guard's grip. "I'm not allowed to leave my post," he said, as if talking himself into staying. "It's not like this is any kind of an intruder I can stop."

True. This was most likely an angry hit man in his underwear. I didn't think they covered that in security class.

Jeb retrieved his keys from the floor and practically clung to the locked exit. Ellis and I ventured closer to the sealed vault.

"Hold it," Ellis said, pausing near the thick round door. "You hear that?"

I did—a faint scratching sound. "It's coming from inside the vault."

Jeb swore and made a sign of the cross.

"I need you to let us in," Ellis told him.

He hesitated, then gave a sharp nod. "The scratching, it's the same as I heard the morning Reggie died." Sweat stains pooled under the arms of Jeb's uniform. "I let him in just like this."

Lucky us.

Jeb inserted two sets of keys in two separate locks and twisted them both. Then he turned the heavy vault wheel until it clicked open. Ellis helped him drag the door away from the entrance.

I paused at the threshold. Flickering streaks of white and yellow light shone from the spot where Reggie had met his end. I'd experienced soul traces once before. It marked the place of a recent death.

"Looks empty to me," Jeb said, coldly surveying the space.

A low chuckle echoed through the vault. We stood frozen at the entrance. It ended almost as soon as it began.

"I gotta watch the door," Jeb said, backing away.

Silence descended over the vault and I sincerely hoped that creepy laugh wasn't the last thing Reggie heard before he died.

Ellis stood at the entrance, making sure I had my privacy, while I took one step inside, then another.

"Hey, Henry," I said lightly. Show no fear. I kept my voice even and opted for his first name as if I belonged there talking to him. "I know revenge is great, but whoever did this is long gone."

The hit man appeared, walking straight through the wall of safety-deposit boxes. He stood, murderous, in the middle of Reggie's death spot, glaring down into the shards of energy as if he could see the body. "My box is empty!" he raged. "Rosie's jewelry is gone. My mamma's wedding ring is gone." He had the red glow around him that warned of a possible descent into poltergeist. "Some poser thinks he can act like me."

I cleared my throat. "Think of it this way. It's good that people want to imitate you. You set the standard."

He snarled. "I promised my mamma I wouldn't kill no more so she could go to the light. She ain't gonna like this."

"You didn't do anything," I reassured him, hoping I was right.

He swallowed hard. "She don't know that." He hurled his ghostly gun straight through the floor. "What if she comes back? She worked hard her whole life, and she couldn't even rest after she died until I promised I wouldn't kill no more," he shouted. The gangster scrubbed a hand over his ugly mug. "What if she thinks I screwed up? She might never be happy again."

"Calm down," I told him. "Please, just…work with me. I feel like we're close to an answer here." The more I talked with him, the more sure I was that Henry hadn't killed Reggie. A man like Handsome Henry was proud of his work. If Reggie's murder was his doing, he'd want everybody to know. And he seemed really serious about upsetting his mother. "Can you tell me more about your safety-deposit box?" I pressed. It made sense that someone had cleaned it out in the years since Henry died. "Do you have any idea who could have taken everything?"

"I don't know, lady. I ain't no security guard. Good thing, too. They sure scare easy." He chuckled low in his throat. "I coulda given that guard a heart attack, but that ain't my style." He pointed at me. "You're gonna find the creep who's trashing my reputation, and you're gonna stop him."

"Absolutely," I vowed. "Bringing Reggie's murderer to justice is our top priority. We're going to solve this."

"We will," Ellis promised, stepping into the vault. "We want this murderer as much as you do."

The ghost grew three feet as he stared past Ellis. "Hey! What do you got there?" Henry demanded.

Henry zoomed through the wall, cursing, as the door slammed closed.

We listened in horror as someone on the outside spun the wheel, and something inside me died a little when the massive lock clanged into place.

Chapter Twenty

Ellis shoved against the door. He cursed under his breath. It didn't budge.

"That did not just happen." I desperately searched for a handle or an inside latch, the gravity of our situation slamming down on me. The vault was airtight. And we were trapped.

"Henry?" I hollered. I couldn't hear him anymore.

I dug in my bag for my cell phone, knowing it probably wouldn't catch a signal, but I had to try. It scrolled, searching...and finding nothing.

"Frankie!" I called.

"You don't need to take that tone," the ghost said, rising from the floor, obviously not recognizing that we were in a desperate situation. "Suds and I weren't up to anything."

Yeah, right. "Go outside," I told him. "Find Jeb, and get him to let us out. And for the love of God, don't scare him away."

The gangster nodded and slipped through the front of the vault without so much as a complaint. Now I knew for sure this was bad.

Ellis examined the vault door. "I'm pretty sure Jeb's the one who locked us in."

It made sense. Jeb was the only one who knew we

were in here.

And now he wanted to get rid of us.

"He was also familiar with the security here. It's an older system. He could have shorted out the camera over the vault door," Ellis said grimly.

"Any chance it's working now?" I asked, letting myself hope.

He shook his head. "Marshall took it with the rest of the evidence. They were supposed to install a new one right away, but I didn't see it up there."

I nodded, preserving my oxygen. I didn't get it. What could we have discovered at this point that would make someone want to kill us? We didn't have all the pieces yet...or did we?

"Jeb lost everything in the housing crisis," I said, trying to put it together. "Reggie might have written him those bad loans. The two were old friends."

Ellis glanced at me. "It would explain a lot." He kept working on the door. "Especially with Reggie getting on with his own life, and Jeb still paying the price."

We had to get out of here.

"Henry?" I called. I didn't see him anymore, but maybe he was still within earshot. He was a criminal. Maybe he knew how to bust out.

Frankie reappeared. "Henry split. I don't see the guard, neither."

Sweet Jesus. Was it me or was it getting warmer in here? "How much air do we have?"

Ellis strained against the vault door. "Don't go there yet," he warned, out of breath as he tried another tactic. He moved to a half dozen bronze administrative storage boxes to the right of the opening. They stood out from the wall and were all different shapes and sizes. None of them were locked, which was a very good thing. "People who designed banks—even years ago—were well aware of the danger of getting locked in a vault. They always have a telephone or hidden key to get out."

"Good," I said, joining him, searching the wall for a phone box or an emergency key. "Here," I said, popping open a square enclosure marked Bank Personnel Only.

An age-scarred key holder thrust out, empty. Behind it, in black paint, I found the outline of a key, as if to taunt us. My heart sank. "It's gone."

"Okay," Ellis said, as if this were somehow routine. He opened a larger square box above it.

Empty.

I checked the signal on my phone again. Still nothing.

Frankie paced next to me. "This is a disaster." He hovered over my bag near the door. "What happens to my urn after you die? Did you even think of that?"

"I'm not dying," I snapped. At least I'd better not. I shoved my phone in my pocket and opened a tall, rectangular box. Empty. "Did they ever have a key and a backup phone?" I asked Ellis.

He pried the fourth box open, another tall, rectangular one. "Let's hope so."

He found an umbrella.

Seriously?

I checked my phone again. No signal.

"Do you have a will?" Frankie pressed. "Who gets your house when you die?" I went for box number five, a wide one above the other two. "Your sister?" he prodded. "God, I hope not. I can't break in another perky blonde."

"She'd be just as thrilled with you," I said, my fingers snagging on the edge as I pried the box open. Empty.

I looked to Ellis. We were running out of options. He

forced open the final box, a wide rectangular one that could have easily held a phone. Old wires tangled at the back, but the receiver was missing.

"No," I whispered.

"That's right," Frankie said. "Keep your voice down or you'll just use up your air faster. Besides," he instructed, "nobody can hear you anyway."

Was it me, or had the air grown warmer and less breathable? I tried for a slow, easy inhale and exhale, but I felt like I wasn't getting enough oxygen. I hoped it was in my head.

Ellis studied the room as if he could find some way out of a locked vault just by looking around.

Think.

We had wire, an umbrella… Oh cripes. I wasn't MacGyver. "Suds was tunneling in through the floor," I said. "Maybe we can break out that way. Frankie, where's the tunnel?"

He sank down into the pink marble, and a moment later, his head reappeared out of the floor. "Here," he said. "All set to go. Suds did a good job. It's even set with a charge."

I scrubbed a hand over my face. "How are we supposed to set off dynamite?" Ellis and I couldn't reach it, and Frankie and Suds would pass straight through it.

We stood surrounded by locked safety-deposit boxes, at least a foot of steel in all directions, and a marble floor with four feet of concrete underneath. I had to admit, it didn't look good.

I stomped on the floor. "Suds told me they'd cleared through the concrete and only needed to break through the marble floor. How hard is marble?" I could feel the air thinning, or perhaps I truly was panicking now. "Break, break, break!" I hollered, jumping up and down on top of it. But the pink marble floor remained solid. I grabbed the umbrella and drove it down into the floor, breaking the handle and the tip and sending pieces of it flying.

"Damn it!" I yelled, sweaty and spent.

"Hey." Ellis wrapped his arms around me, stopping my rant, shoving my cheek up against his chest to calm me. He felt uncomfortably warm and his heart beat like crazy. "It's going to be okay," he murmured into my hair.

I lifted my head and looked straight into those gorgeous hazel eyes. "You don't believe it, though, do you?"

The crinkles at the corners of his eyes deepened, but he didn't answer. Great. I finally found one who couldn't lie, and we were about to suffocate together.

"Ellis?" I began as I tilted his chin down and kissed him. It was sweet and desperate at the same time. A pledge of loyalty and trust and — my blood heated — a fair bit of lust. Dang. Even now, he could drive me to distraction.

He stroked my cheek as I pulled back. "You always kiss me at the end."

"I'm glad we worked it out before we died," I said, a little sad.

Ellis tried to smile and failed. "Don't say that."

He had to know. "I'm proud to be dating you. We could have made it work."

He kissed me hard, then drew back just as quickly, resting his forehead against mine. "When we get out of here, I'm taking you to dinner at my mother's."

I laughed despite myself. "Are you trying to make me feel better about being trapped in here?"

He huffed out a chuckle. "Okay, how about a nice dinner out and a movie at the drive-in?"

I nipped him on the bottom lip. "That's more like it."

He held my head in his hands. "Verity, I…" He lowered his gaze.

"What?" I asked, leaning into his touch. "You can tell me."

"I—"

Suds popped straight up out of the floor next to us. "Aww, come on!" He turned away. "You weren't kidding, Frank." He forced himself to turn back to us. "Enough with the smooching. Frankie and I have a plan, and it starts with you ending the lip-lock."

I didn't get it. "What can two ghosts possibly do?"

"I'm going to forget you just asked that," Suds said. "You're gonna change your tune anyway when Frankie and I set off my charge."

Heavens to Betsy. "You're going to blow the vault? How?"

Ellis appeared as surprised as I felt. "I thought you said they can't touch anything."

"They can't."

That didn't stop Suds from grinning like a maniac. "I could touch all kinds of things before I knew I was dead. I just need to think like I'm alive!"

"You can't just decide that," I protested.

"I do believe that's a dare," Suds drawled, sinking back into the floor.

Frankie watched him go. "He just needs to push down on the lever. It's a solid inch, but if anybody can do it, Suds can." Frankie grinned as if pleased to see his friend in such high spirits. "He always did like to blow things up."

"Go cheer him on," I said, hoping they could do it.

Ellis placed a hand on my arm. "Let's get back. We don't know how much dynamite is down there."

"Plenty, I assure you," Frankie's voice echoed from under the floor.

"Do you think they can pull this off?" Ellis asked.

"Maybe." They certainly seemed to think they could. What choice did we have but to believe in them?

Of course, Suds had believed he could break in eighty years ago.

"This way." Ellis led me to the far end of the vault, as distant as we could get from the gangster's explosives. "It could get ugly," he said low under his breath. "I still have my duty vest on. I'm going to cover you and protect you as well as I can."

"A duty vest is for bullets, not explosions."

He huffed out a breath. "It's a lot better than nothing." He caught my eye. "We're going to make it through this."

I wanted to believe that. "You actually sound kind of convinced this time."

"I am," he said, hugging me close, trapping me safe between his solid chest and the steel of the vault. "We're doing this. You and me."

The air grew chilly. I pressed my forehead against Ellis's upper chest and we braced ourselves.

"You can do it!" Frankie shouted like he was an Olympic coach. "Come on! You've been waiting for this your whole afterlife!"

"Urrrrrrgh!" Suds groaned. "I'm alive, I'm alive, I'm alive…!"

I slammed my eyes shut and gripped Ellis's shirt in both hands, holding on tight.

Then, silence.

"Huh," Frankie said, his voice echoing through the floor.

"Let me try it another way," Suds said, sounding a little desperate. "I'm alive…and there's money!"

I kept my head down and my eyes shut even though I didn't see how they were ever going to be able to—boom!

The floor shook and I held on to Ellis as the explosion rang out against the metal walls of the vault. I pressed harder against his shoulder, choking on the dust.

"Did it work?" I stammered, daring to look.

As the air cleared, I saw Frankie's head pop out of the middle of a hole in the floor. Just his head. Everything below the shoulders had gone missing, but he didn't care. He grinned like a gangster who just broke into the vault at the First Sugarland Bank. "That was fantastic!"

Suds shot up out of the hole past him. He looked like a kid on Christmas morning. Tears filled his eyes as he threw his hands up in the air. "At last!"

Frankie grinned. "Aww… Look at that. He needs some joy before he realizes they took out the gold in 1946."

"You okay?" Ellis asked, his hair coated in white dust.

I smiled. "Yeah."

We pulled out our flashlights and I shone mine down into the hole. Jagged, blackened concrete lay at the bottom, mixed with shards of the floor and Lord knew what else. I hoped we could make it all the way out. Parts of the tunnel might be sealed up or caved in by now, but it was a start.

Ellis squeezed my arm. "I'm going to check it out," he said, dropping down into the tunnel.

Suds cursed at the empty vault. "What are we gonna say to the Chicago guys?"

"It don't matter! The good news is they're dead," Frankie explained happily.

Ellis shone a light down the passageway. "Verity!" he called from below. "Quick as you can. We've got to get out of here before this tunnel caves in."

"Oh boy." I dropped down onto the largest piece of

concrete I could find. Ellis grabbed me when I stumbled and helped me down. It smelled like sulfur and gunpowder down here. That and dust. At least this section of the tunnel walls had been bolstered with wood planks.

"How far is it?"

"I don't know," he said, pressing forward in front of me.

I could barely stand. The remains of shovels and axes littered the ground. I shone my light forward and it hit Ellis several yards down.

"Keep quiet and keep moving," he said, pointing to his left, where part of the wall had caved in. Dirt and rocks rained down from above.

"We're officially crazy," I said, hurrying after him through the rickety old tunnel.

"He's got it reinforced pretty good, but these boards have been down here for generations. And that explosion didn't help."

Ellis's light hit another partial cave-in about ten feet ahead. At least it looked old. The air grew more stale with each step, and I wondered if we were trading one grisly death for another. My brain swam and I forced my legs to keep moving. We'd find out soon enough if this place would hold, if we had enough air, and exactly what lay beyond.

Frankie's urn clanked inside my bag. He'd be following us as well. The gangster didn't have a choice.

The tunnel went on for way too long. It made me nervous, the feeling of being closed off from the world, ever since Ellis and I had almost been buried alive at the distillery.

We saw nothing but inky blackness, both ahead and behind.

Keep moving. It wouldn't do any good to panic now, even if the earth was closing in above us.

I about wept when Ellis's light caught an old wood door at the end of the tunnel.

"Beautiful," he said, hopeful. Ellis tried the handle and it broke off in his hand. "Damn it." He tried to reattach it, but the neglected metal had actually snapped with age. He flung it to the ground. "We gotta catch a break that doesn't involve ghosts with dynamite."

"Let me try," I said, winding my fingers into the door mechanism, trying to get a grip on a latch. We couldn't make it this far only to be cornered at the end.

Nothing.

"Help!" I beat on the door. "Anyone! We're trapped back here."

"Be careful!" Ellis hissed. "Noise could set off a cave-in. Besides, we don't know who's on the other side of that door."

We should have asked Suds when we had the chance. Of course, he only knew what was there ninety years ago. "If we don't make noise, we might never get out." It wasn't like the door was going to open on its own.

"Give me a second," he said.

We had to get out. Jeb would not get away with murder so long as I had breath in my body.

I dug out my cell phone again. Still no signal. I fought the urge to smash it on the floor along with the broken knob. It was about as useful.

Ellis shoved his shoulder against the door and we heard a loud crack. I didn't know if it came from the door or if he broke something. He rushed the door again.

Crack.

"Shoot it," I told him.

He hit the door again. "That only works in the movies."

He was going to kill himself. "Ellis!"

He rushed the door a fourth time. Crack! This time, it flew open.

On the other side, a ghostly couple kissed like the ship was going down. With a start, I realized that I recognized one of them. That meant I knew the other, too.

"Matthew," I said, a little harsher than I intended. He had to forgive me. I was surprised. He spun around, and sure enough there was Josephine with him.

She startled and quickly drew up a hand to cover the hickey forming on her pale, translucent neck. "This isn't what it looks like," she stammered.

For their sakes, I hoped it was exactly what it looked like. But I didn't have the time or the inclination to explore the details. "I'm so relieved to see you two. We need help."

Chapter Twenty-One

"Verity!" Matthew stepped aside, and we rushed into what appeared to be an old coal room in the basement of the library. Tall brick walls stretched up to an iron chute.

Josephine fidgeted, her hands fluttering at her neck. "I was just visiting," she stammered, "to see if there was any news on the preacher."

They'd get no judgment from me.

I located the door to the stacks. "This way," I said, opening it and beckoning Ellis to follow. "We're working on getting you kids a preacher, I promise," I called to the ghosts as we hurried through the stacks.

The library above stood silent as a grave. "It must be late," Ellis said, taking the stairs two at a time. I rushed to keep up. We'd lost all sense of time down in that vault. I was anxious to see what had happened above ground while we'd been trapped.

My flashlight beam cut through the darkened hallway above. "It's well past closing time."

"Keep your guard up," Ellis warned, pushing out through the door that opened up to the main reading room. "Jeb might have heard us escape."

"He'd have to know where the tunnel led to find us here," I said, keeping my focus on the main doors and away from the moans of the ghosts who occupied the field hospital in the main reading room.

Ellis pressed ahead as we made our way for the doors at the front. "Jeb's already tried to kill us once. I don't want to take any more chances."

"Wait," I said to Ellis as he threw the bolt on the main doors. The library had installed new security since the tragedy we endured a few months ago. I went to the key panel next to the door and typed in the code 1-2-1-2.

"That's a terrible password."

"Even worse is that I know it," I said, hitting Enter. I'd learned from watching Melody one morning.

The system gave a beep of recognition and the alarm switched off.

"First thing tomorrow, I'm holding a security meeting with the library staff," Ellis vowed as we slipped out the front.

Alarms blared at the bank. "Flashlights off," he cautioned as we hurried down the stairs. "Jeb may be long gone, but I want to get the jump on him if he's not."

He drew his gun and held it low as we ran across the square to the bank. Lights blazed inside. Ellis's squad car sat out front. His was the only car in the square.

"Stay here," Ellis ordered. "I'm going down for a look."

He had to be crazy. I wasn't standing all by myself in the dark in front of a haunted bank that might or might not be stalked by a live killer.

"I'm not separating," I said, following him down the stairs. Not with Jeb on the loose. Lucky for me, there was zero time to argue.

Ellis made it to the bottom of the stairs first and stopped dead in his tracks.

"What?" I asked, joining him.

Jeb Kemper lay on the floor of the bank in a pool of blood, eyes open and glassy. He'd been shot through the heart. Blood oozed from an X slashed into his right cheek.

Ellis attempted to open the glass door separating us from the guard, but it was locked. The bank was as secure as it had been when Jeb locked us all in with Henry.

"Holy hell." Ellis shoved off the door. "It might actually be a ghost."

"Henry might have locked us in and then killed Jeb." He'd certainly been angry enough. "But Henry said he had changed. He promised his mother he'd go straight."

"And gangsters always tell the truth," Ellis said, letting the words linger between us. Ellis stared down at the body. "You said he was mad enough to kill." He turned to me. "Now how do we stop him from doing it again?"

"Rosie can help us find him." I still wasn't convinced he'd done it, but he'd seen something right before that vault door closed. "With any luck, she's still at her grave."

We made a break for the car and sped back to the cemetery. "The police are going to need us for questioning at the bank," Ellis said, lights blazing as we raced away from the scene.

"There's no way the police could know we were there," I said, breathless. Jeb was dead. The back stairs camera couldn't see us and the main camera had been blown. "Besides, what are we going to say? That a ghost gangster locked us in the vault, but two more ghost gangsters were kind enough to blow up the vault and lend us their secret passageway to the library?"

"This is my life," he mused, hitting the gas hard around a turn.

"Believe me, I feel that way a lot," I told him.

The hour was late and there was hardly any traffic. We made it across town in record time.

I braced a hand on the door as he made a sharp corner at Pearlman's gas station. "Are we breaking the rules by doing this first?"

"You'd like that, wouldn't you?" he asked, his eyes on the road. "As it so happens, this is part of the investigation," he reasoned as we passed Fitzer's Memorial Monuments. "It's just not one I can ever talk about."

"You can always tell me," I said, earning a smirk as we pulled into the graveyard.

"We left the gates open." Ellis winced.

"We were chasing a homicidal ghost." We needed to cut ourselves some slack.

The fog had thickened in this part of town, and I could barely see the road as we made our way past the timeworn graves at the front and into the section that held the family vaults.

We were the only ones who could confront the hit man. We couldn't leave this part to the police.

Ellis pulled over next to the white marble obelisk. Thick fog obscured the weeping angel at its base. The fog felt unnatural. Wrong. As if something had created it in order to hide.

The Baker mausoleum hunkered near the back, past the broken Celtic cross.

"Lights off," Ellis said as we exited the car. It was the wisest course of action, but it didn't feel so good in the middle of a dark cemetery.

I didn't even have the gray light of Frankie to lead the way.

No doubt the ghost had used up his energy down

in the tunnel with Suds. I'd seen him go from half a body to only a head. Then a whole new worry hit me—what would happen if my share of Frankie's power suddenly ran out? I hoped my ghost friend had enough energy left to let me deal with Handsome Henry.

Old stone tombs loomed on both sides, surrounding us. The temperature plummeted as we neared the Thompson mausoleum. "You feel that?" I asked Ellis.

"No," he murmured, "but somebody's back there."

He paused behind a vault with matching Greek-style urns at the top. I drew up next to him and heard a rough strike, like a shovel hitting dirt.

We waited. I held my breath.

Scraaape.

Crunch.

A figure in a heavy black coat bent in the doorway of the Thompson family vault. A metal clip light shone down into the corner. Henry hovered close, glowing red, his pistol aimed inches from the figure's skull. "What do you say I try something new and blow your brains out?"

Oblivious, the figure kept digging.

Henry cocked his ghostly revolver. Oh my God. The hit man appeared perfectly willing to kill.

And he certainly wasn't thinking of his mamma.

I dug my elbow into Ellis's side. "Do you see the figure in black?" I prodded.

"Yes," he murmured.

That meant the person was in the land of the living. Henry shouldn't be able to touch the intruder. Unless the ghost got angry enough to go poltergeist.

"Stay back," Ellis urged, heading to the left as if to flank them.

I zigzagged forward and slipped behind a large headstone.

The iron door with its crisscrossed bars lay open, and I knew what had set Henry off. The gangster didn't even like me taking flowers back and this person was trying to open his grave. He glared at the hooded figure with a hate that reached down to his soul.

Henry aimed his revolver at the figure's head and squeezed the trigger.

His gun clicked, out of bullets.

Handsome Henry, ace hit man of the South Town Gang, had died with an empty revolver.

Henry threw the gun down to the ground and bellowed his outrage.

The grave robber kept digging.

"Stop," Ellis said, stepping from the left and taking the intruder by surprise. I drew my Maglite and shone it on the person's face.

"Carla," I gasped, my beam catching her as she pointed a black revolver at Ellis's chest and fired.

He staggered back a step.

"Ellis!" I cried. Thank God he wore his duty vest. Please let it work. My heart stopped as I saw him clutch his chest where the bullet hit.

"Stay where you are," Carla ordered, aiming her gun at Ellis's head as he cursed and struggled to remain upright.

"That was a bad move, Carla," he grunted out.

She smirked.

I couldn't believe how callously she'd shot him. We were looking at our murderer. I had no doubt of it.

"I have a better idea," she said. "Toss your weapon."

Ellis hesitated briefly, then did as she asked.

"You," she called out to me. "Place your light on the ground and step out here now."

I had no choice but to follow her crisp, efficient orders. I placed my light so I could see her and the tomb.

"Against the vault," she said. I shared a glance with Ellis as I planted my back to the cold stone grave. She huffed out a breath, as if she couldn't quite believe we'd interrupted her. "You Sugarland people are nuts."

"You don't have to do this," I told her.

"That's where you're wrong." She aimed the gun squarely at my chest. "I'm having trouble digging through the seal," she said. "Break open the door for me," she ordered Ellis. "You try anything and I shoot her."

A pickaxe leaned blade-down near the corner of the door. She'd bashed in a solid foot of the seal near the bottom.

He glared at her, breathing heavy, a bullet hole torn in his shirt.

With grim determination, Ellis hefted the pickaxe. He swung hard and hit the seal, opening up the entire left side of the door.

Sweet heaven. Ellis was too strong for his own good — and mine. It would take him no time at all to break through. And then Carla would have no reason to keep us alive.

We needed help. Now.

I turned to a fuming Henry. "She wants to destroy your grave," I murmured.

Ellis struck the seal once more. Henry roared as the portion over the door fell away.

Ellis and I couldn't fight back, but if there was ever a time for the ghost to get angry and go poltergeist on Carla, this would be it.

He'd been mad enough to shoot. We needed him furious now. The gangster's chest heaved, the bullet wounds stark against his pale, gray skin. "She thinks you're weak, standing there in your underwear."

"Have you lost your mind?" Carla barked. "Shut up," she ordered me, her attention on Ellis.

The red aura around the gangster intensified.

"Let's not even talk about how she tried to peg you for murder," I hissed. "She doesn't care about your mamma. She could even go after mamma's grave next."

"Not my mamma!" His image expanded, his face hollowed into a skull. A cold wind whipped through the cemetery and I felt the harsh thrumming of negative energy. Almost there.

"Wait a second. Babe!" Rosie shimmered into view next to Henry. She placed an arm on his shoulder, and I watched in horror as he exhaled some of his anger.

The wind calmed. The thrumming lessened.

She rubbed his arm and he shrank back down to normal size. "Whatever it is, let's talk about it. It's gonna be all right."

No. "It's not!" I whispered hotly. "He's got a grave robber! Right there!" Maybe Rosie could at least get mad for him.

"Enough!" Carla shoved the barrel of the gun against my chest, and I knew she wanted to shoot. Badly. I could tell by the way her finger tightened on the trigger. Ellis had stopped working and was watching us, probably wondering if he had time to take out Carla with the pickaxe before she blew me away.

"Dig," she said to him.

Ellis shot her a look as he swung the axe again. His blade hit true, breaking off a large chunk of the seal.

"Hey!" Rosie barked. "That dame's wearing my earrings." She zoomed straight for Carla and reached to snatch her jewelry back, but her hand passed straight through. "You little thief!"

Carla flinched and tugged at her hood, briefly exposing a flash of silver art deco earrings with glittering green gems.

Rosie looked ready to girl fight. Maybe we didn't need Henry's anger after all.

"She took what's yours," I said to the ghost under my breath, risking Carla's wrath, trying to stoke Rosie's rage. Carla couldn't shoot me until she got that door open. I might have enough time to push Rosie over the edge. "Are you going to let her get away with it?"

Rosie's eyes hardened.

"Faster," Carla warned Ellis. One more good hit and he'd break through.

Rosie grew in size. Her image strengthened and I could see her rage building. This was it. This was what we needed.

Until the ghost halted. "Balls. I need a drink."

"No!" I shouted as she smoothed her hair and turned to Henry.

"Let's get out of here," she said, wrapping both her arms around one of Henry's and kissing him on his scarred cheek. For the first time, I saw the gangster smile. And I watched in horror as he led her away.

We were alone when Ellis broke through the last of the seal.

CHAPTER TWENTY-TWO

"Open it," Carla ordered.

Ellis shoved against the thick stone barrier and it fell inside the grave with a mighty thud. This was it—the end. I braced myself for the gunshot when suddenly, a flash photograph snapped off to our left.

Carla pinned me to the vault with her gun and turned. "Show yourself! Now! Or she's dead!"

"Do it, please," Ellis urged, hands raised.

For a breathlessly long moment, no one emerged.

Then Em stepped out from behind the large tombstone. She wore dark jeans and a black shirt, and had her blond hair pulled back into a tight ponytail.

"You're the one going down, Carla," Em said, a little too confident for her own good. She held up her iPhone. "I have a great shot of you breaking into mom's grave. And holding a weapon on a townie." Carla sneered and Em froze, as if she suddenly realized the bank VP could turn the gun on her next. The younger woman blinked hard. "I have the picture addressed and ready to text to a girlfriend in Chicago," she warned. "One move and it goes to her, and she goes to the police." Em's expression darkened. "I know you killed my dad."

Carla stared her down. "Prove it."

Em flinched. "I've been trying."

"By following me here the other night?" Carla demanded. "I was ready to slit your throat until I found Verity and Lauralee in your house instead of you."

Em appeared shaken at the threat. Nevertheless, she took one step forward, then another. "What do you want with Mom's grave?"

"Your dad's money," she said, relishing Em's added surprise. "He promised me my share. And if you work with me, I don't see any problem giving you yours."

Em halted. "How much is in there?"

"Everything he took from you," she said, "plus more." Carla pressed the gun hard against my chest. "I don't need it all. But if you want me to turn over your part, you will need to prove your loyalty."

"Hit send on the picture," Ellis urged.

"She won't," Carla said, with too much confidence for my taste. "We all know what's important to EmmaJane, and it certainly isn't any of you."

And she was right. Em didn't push that button.

Instead, she seemed to be considering Carla's offer. "You killed my father and you want me to work with you." Her words were halted, her tone stiff, but she didn't say no.

Carla saw it too, and the corners of her mouth turned up. "You can build a new life," she reasoned, as if this were what should have happened in the first place.

"Don't do it," I warned.

"Oh, why not?" Em glared at me. "So I can stay here and survive on Lauralee's chicken dinners? Play a little bingo at the VFW Hall?" She glanced over Carla's shoulder. "He's getting away."

Ellis had begun moving toward his gun. "Stop!" She shoved the gun barrel against my chest once more, pinning me to the grave. Ellis, breathing heavy, stayed where he was. "Back here," Carla ordered, motioning until he stood in her sights once more. "Good girl," she said to Em.

Em slicked an errant lock of hair behind her ear. "Seems like you need me." Her face went cold, calculating. "If I'm going to work with you at all on this, I need you to admit what you did to my dad." Her voice iced over. "I want to hear you say it."

Carla gave a slight nod. "I killed your father."

Tears formed in Em's eyes. "Say his name."

"I killed Reggie Thompson," Carla stated, her voice betraying hurt. "But admit it. You wanted him dead, too. He promised everything and then took it away. But you're free now. And you can be a very rich woman."

"If I kill these two," Em said, guessing Carla's angle.

"Just one," Carla couched. "We're a team, right?"

"You can't even be considering—" I began.

"Shut up," Em ordered.

"It'll be easy and quick. The cop's gun is over in the grass," Carla said. I watched in horror as Em went to retrieve it.

She came back, holding Ellis's service revolver out in front of her.

Carla observed Em's every move, calculating. "Choose one. He's wearing body armor, so you'd have to plug him in the head. Pick her and you can shoot her wherever you want, as long as she's dead. We store them in the grave…after we take the money."

"They'll blame us," Em said tightly.

Carla pulled off the clip-on earrings she wore. "These came out of the same safety-deposit box as the hit man's watch." She deposited them in her pocket. "We'll plant them on the bodies and blame it on the ghost again."

"The ghosts will get angry," I warned. "The hit man knows what you did to him."

"Yeah, I'm sure he's rolling in his grave," Carla said flippantly.

"I'm serious," I said, desperate, as Em pointed her gun at me. Always me. "I talk to ghosts. That's how Ellis and I have solved murders before." Carla smiled, backing away to give Em a clean shot.

"It's true," Ellis said. "Every word of it." He took one slow step forward, then another. "Your father would never have wanted this for you," Ellis warned.

"My father and I never could agree on anything," Em said, firing.

Her shot went wide.

I ducked and fell to the ground.

"Shoot her again!" Carla ordered.

But Em turned the gun on Carla. "Psych," she said as flashing police lights lit up the night. I saw them speeding through the cemetery toward us. "I called 9-1-1. They've heard and recorded our entire conversation." Em grinned. "It means you're caught, bitch."

And so was I.

CHAPTER TWENTY-THREE

Carla made a full confession the next day. She didn't have a choice. She'd already admitted to murder in front of me, Ellis, Em, and the entire Sugarland police department.

It seemed Carla had gotten into banking for the money, and Reggie had offered her the promised land if she did what he wanted, but he'd yanked the prize at the end. Instead of making her a rich mortgage lender in Chicago, he'd brought her down to Sugarland to change them both.

She'd gone for the payoff instead.

Reggie had lost his life, along with Jeb, who had caught her following us.

The next afternoon, on a cold and blustery day, I gave in and wore my monstrosity of a coat as Ellis and I stood outside the Thomson family vault with Lauralee. The three of us stood vigil as workers re-sealed the tomb.

"I can't believe he hid all this money in my aunt's grave," my friend said, her voice small. "Reggie did tend to act quickly, but still..." she trailed off.

"His mistake was telling Carla," Ellis said. "She admits she came down to Sugarland to get the money. Only Reggie would know if she took it, so she decided he had to die as well."

"And his death would get the grave open," Lauralee said woodenly.

I hugged her. "I'm sorry, honey."

Lauralee wiped her eyes. "Em was too smart for Carla. I wish she would have let us help her."

"So do I." Em had suspected Carla all along, but she'd had no proof. "But Em didn't trust us."

Dead leaves crunched under Em's polished boots as she walked up to join us. "I still think you all are a bunch of crazies," she said somewhat fondly. "I didn't know who to trust. But I knew Carla was way too anxious to put my dad in the ground. I thought that meant she was hiding evidence, not uncovering cash."

"But you followed her to the cemetery anyway," I said.

"I had to know what she was doing," Em agreed. "She'd come over again, insisting I bury him. I lied and told her I'd already turned him over to be cremated. Then I followed her."

"She was hell-bent on getting the cash one way or another," Lauralee said, heartbroken. "She'd already destroyed him. And for what?"

"About twenty million dollars," Em said, wiping a tear. "We had our problems, but I miss him so much." She didn't even flinch when Lauralee embraced her. And a few seconds later, Em even hugged her back.

"You were brave," I said. Em investigated despite her grief and when she had no one to back her. At least I had my friends. And Frankie.

"I wasn't going to shoot you," Em said, wiping her eyes. "I'm a good shot. If I meant to hit you, I would have."

"I believe you." It was all in the report. "Although it would have been nice to know at the time."

"You were perfect," Ellis agreed. "You had me fooled."

"So what are you going to do now?" Lauralee asked her cousin. "I hope you realize that despite...everything, you always have a home here."

Em sniffed, and judging from the shadow of a smile, it appeared as if she almost considered it. "Thanks, but I don't belong in Sugarland. I don't know where I fit in. But I'm going to find out."

"I can help—" my friend began.

"No." Em held up her hand. "I mean, please don't," she said, lowering it. "I'm going to travel, study, take courses and see what I like, what I can do for people."

"For people. I like that," I told her.

"It's a good start," Lauralee agreed.

Em gave a weak smile.

My friend wrapped an arm around her cousin and started talking about how Em used to love to teach other kids to dance when she was small.

Ellis and I attempted to slip away.

"Nice to see you two," Lauralee called after us. "I'm glad you're giving it a go. You both deserve to be happy," she said, with the wisdom of a woman who knew what that was like. "Although if you hurt her, I'll remove your intestines with a fork."

Spoken like a true friend.

We strolled through the graveyard, along no particular path, but one that led to Rosie's place all the same. I'd already told Ellis what had happened on the ghostly side during our ordeal in the cemetery, and how I'd hoped for Rosie's or Henry's help.

When we reached her vault, it hurt me to see the lichen-encrusted tomb appeared even more run down in the light of day. Rust caked the metal entry grate, and sparse grass struggled against ugly bare dirt that made up the path to the once-lovely space.

"Let's fix it up," Ellis said. "It's the least we can do."

"Even after she left us?" I did appreciate rational ghosts, but it would have been nice to have some poltergeist support when we needed it.

"I respect the way she handled herself," Ellis admitted. "She had some nice things that survived the years, and when she found out Carla stole them, she didn't let her anger consume her."

He had a point. "Who knows what else she took from those abandoned safety-deposit boxes."

We knew she'd found Henry's gun and his watch, along with the earrings. She'd also stashed her murder weapon in one of the old boxes. That made it easy to kill Reggie, then walk out without the murder weapon.

"I still don't get how Carla blew out the security camera," I said.

Ellis shook his head. "Jeb was out smoking. She used a simple surge booster." He shoved his hands into his pockets. "Reggie had been in the middle of getting bids to upgrade the security system, and she'd been reviewing them. She knew exactly how to blow the existing system. Her boss had done studies."

"She didn't need to kill him. She could have just quit and earned more money."

"She felt like she had earned it," he said quietly. Ellis wrapped an arm around me. "I'm glad you're okay."

I kissed him on the shoulder. "You're the one who got shot."

He pulled me closer. "Good thing I'm the police."

I couldn't help but smile up at him. "Yeah, good thing."

***

Carla had made her confession to the world, and so

had I. The newspaper printed the transcript of Em's 911 call in its entirety. And it seemed every radio station in the county had broadcast excerpts. I was out of the closet.

The next morning, I uncovered the rosebush in my parlor and prepared for my interview with Ovis Dupre. He wanted to know all about my ghost-seeing abilities and my thoughts on Handsome Henry, as well as the gangster tunnel under the bank, for a Sugarland Gazette exclusive article already titled The Haunted Heist.

It would be a whopper of a story, even if most people didn't believe it.

I borrowed Lauralee's green silk shirt for the occasion. Ovis never went anywhere without his camera, so I might as well look nice.

Frankie shimmered into view behind me. He'd regained most of his body, save for his arms and a portion of his left shoulder.

"Tell him to find some old pictures of me, preferably with my favorite gun. There should be lots of them."

"I'll ask him to give it a try," I promised the ghost as Lucy struggled out from under a blanket on the couch and made a beeline for the kitchen. "You're sure you want to go forward, with…everything?" I asked.

The gangster shrugged. "If it's the only way I can get you to take me out for a little fun, then yes."

I tried not to dwell too much on what Frankie meant by fun. "Then we're ready for our announcement to the paper."

We'd even spiffed up Frankie's final resting place for the occasion. Ellis had gone back down into the speakeasy and recovered the small brass lid to Frankie's urn. He also replaced Frankie's trash can with one of the original whiskey barrels from the Southern Spirits distillery. It may have even been one of the barrels that the gangsters had emptied themselves.

He'd repacked the dirt and now the rosebush stood tall.

"That's nice," Suds said, materializing next to his friend, nodding in approval. "It even matches the rose carved in your urn."

"Where?" Frankie asked, and I couldn't help but smile. He couldn't make out the god-awful drawing Suds had made on his urn, either.

"It's right there on her dress," Suds pointed out.

"Ah," Frankie said in admiration.

Ellis strolled into the room, all sweaty from his labors and definitely comfortable in my space. "While I was outside, I fixed your brake light."

"I'd forgotten all about it." But he hadn't. Ellis was always watching out for me. I went to him and planted a sweet kiss on his cheek. "Thank you."

He gave a slight grin. He wasn't used to me fussing over him.

"Say," I asked him, "do you happen to know of any preachers who have passed recently? Maybe one that has unfinished business?"

He pondered the question. "No. Why do you ask?"

"Hey." Suds waved a hand. "I'm a preacher."

"You?" I asked, too surprised to be polite.

He made an iffy sign with his hand. "I got it out of the back of a magazine, but I'm licensed."

"Good enough. I'm going to host a wedding," I told Ellis.

"Right here?" he asked, looking around.

Yes. "If Matthew and Josephine approve. Suds as well."

"I'd better dust off my tux," Ellis said.

The snub-nosed gangster whistled under his breath.

"I'd better get myself a Bible. Anyone we know die with a Bible?" he asked himself, disappearing.

I'd leave that to him. I took Ellis's hand and together we walked over to Frankie, who stood admiring his new resting place. "It looks nice," I told him.

He crossed his arms over his chest. "For now. You know I'm getting out of here soon."

"Right." We'd figure this out.

"We just need to keep trying," he told me.

Because our plans always worked out so well.

"Frankie's strategizing his escape," I said to Ellis.

He wrapped an arm around my waist. "Oh good. Just let me know what I need to do."

"That's a promise you may live to regret," I said, handing him the design I'd started for my new business: Verity Long, Ghost Hunter.

Ellis grinned. "You may have found your calling."

"Maybe," I said, giddy at the prospect of trying. There was so much more to learn, an entire world to discover. "It's exciting and scary at the same time."

"All the good things are," he said. And I had a feeling he was talking about us as well.

I smiled up at him. "We'll figure it out," I promised. "Together."

He planted a sweet kiss on my forehead. "Together."

No doubt it would be a wild ride.

Author's Note

Thanks a bunch for dropping in on Verity, Ellis, and the rest of their friends in Sugarland. I'm humbled and grateful for the wonderful reader response this series is receiving. In her next adventure, Verity will be "out" as a ghost hunter with the whole town watching. With Ellis's help, she takes on her first big assignment and it's like nothing they've ever encountered before. Meanwhile, Frankie and Suds are starting their own gang...with interesting results.

The next book is slated for release in fall 2016. If you'd like an email when it releases, sign up for my new release update newsletter at www.angiefox.com. You'll see the signup at the top right corner of the page. I keep all information private and emails only go out when a new book hits stores.

I also give out ten free advanced reading copies of my next book in each email. So if you do sign up, be sure to check for your name on the winner's list, published in every newsletter!

Happy reading,

Angie

Available now!
A LITTLE NIGHT MAGIC

A fabulously fun collection of six tales of love, laughter and friendship...under a full moon. All stories are by Angie Fox and the collection includes two Southern Ghost Hunter shorts.

Here's a sneak peek at the first story, GHOST OF A CHANCE, which takes place between The Skeleton in the Closet and The Haunted Heist

Chapter One

The smell of fresh-baked sugar cookies filled my kitchen, and the tinny sound of Frank Sinatra singing "White Christmas" echoed from my outdated iPhone. Behind me, the ghost of a 1920s gangster hovered while I pulled the last hot tray from the oven.

"Move. I don't want to burn you," I said automatically, realizing only afterward how ridiculous it sounded. Any object—hot or otherwise—would pass straight through the specter.

Frankie appeared in black and white, his image transparent enough that I could just make out the cooling trays on the kitchen island behind him. He wore a pin-striped suit coat with matching cuffed trousers and a fat tie.

He inhaled as if he could smell the crisp, warm cookies. "That's a killer batch, right there," he observed while I jockeyed around him, "but I gotta tell you, most of the gun barrels are crooked."

I winked, surprising him. "Everybody's a critic."

I'd given in to holiday cheer and let him tell me how to shape the last of the dough, and he'd chosen the things he loved most. Which meant I had a baking sheet full of revolvers, cigarettes, and booze bottles — all oddly shaped because, truly, who has cookie cutters for that sort of thing?

I placed the tray on a rack to start cooling, glad I'd included the surly gangster in my holiday festivities. He was technically a houseguest until I could find a way to free him. Although I had no clue what I was going to do with his contraband cookies.

I couldn't eat them all or explain them away to guests.

"What's next?" he asked before I'd even transferred one cookie off the baking tray, never mind the dough-flecked countertops or the dishes. The man obviously hadn't spent much time in the kitchen before.

"Why don't you go outside and look at the holiday lights?" I suggested. Perhaps that would get him into the spirit of the season.

My sister, Melody, had lent me a few strands of white ones in the shape of magnolia flowers. I'd foraged some lovely greenery from the woods and done up the front and back porches with pine garlands and homemade balsam wreaths. I'd been too broke to buy ready-made decorations, but these looked nicer anyway.

He snarled at the suggestion that he might be entertained by pretty decorations. "I'm Frankie the German," he clipped out, as if his words themselves should command respect. "Men fear me. Women want me."

"I'm very happy for you," I said, trying to straighten out a revolver barrel as I gently transferred the cookies to the cooling rack. "But this is the holiday season. It's the perfect time to take a break from inspiring fear. Try to live a little," I suggested, ignoring his scowl. "How about I finish cleaning the kitchen, and afterward you can challenge me to a game of chess."

Otherwise, he'd get bored and start making cold spots all over my kitchen. It felt nice in the summer, but right now, it would ruin the yeast bread I had rising.

He clenched and unclenched his hands a few times. "All right," he said, eyeing me as he glided through the stove and out to the back porch. His voice lingered in the air behind him. "You know I won't go far."

"Do I ever," I murmured. It was my fault he couldn't leave.

I'd tied him to my land when I accidentally emptied his funeral urn out onto my rosebushes. At the time, I'd believed my ex-fiancé had given me a dirty old vase in need of a good scrubbing or at least a rinse with the hose. But as it turns out, there's a reason why ashes are customarily scattered to the wind or at least spread out a bit. When I poured the entirety of Frankie's remains in one spot and then hosed him into the ground, the poor gangster had become my unwilling permanent housemate — at least until I could figure out how to set him free.

Only two people knew I had a ghost for a houseguest: my sister, Melody, and my sweet, strong almost-boyfriend, Ellis. I planned to keep it that way.

I transferred a cookie shaped like a bundle of dynamite that could have almost passed for a nice grouping of holiday candles, except for the "TnT" Frankie
had made me etch into the side.

Frankie had opened up a whole new ghostly world
to me, and let's just say things had gotten a little crazy
after that.

I left the tray on the stove to cool and brushed off
the well-worn green and white checked gingham
apron that had belonged to my grandmother. I tried
not to sigh. I missed having a house full of people for
the holidays. Of course, Melody had stopped by just
this morning, and my mom was coming in town next
week.

I began sudsing up the sink and placing my mixing
bowls into the warm, soapy water.

If I were honest with myself, I missed Ellis. We'd
become close enough that I felt his absence when
we couldn't spend time together. He'd been booked
solid with family events, and it's not like I could have
joined him. Not after I'd broken my engagement to
his brother and barely defended my livelihood and
home from his vengeful mother.

He'd come by when he could.

And as if I'd summoned him out of thin air, I heard
a knock at the door. It couldn't be. I dried my hands
on my apron. Melody liked to knock and immediately
walk inside. My friend Lauralee, too. I had an open-
door policy at the cozy antebellum home I'd inherited
from my grandmother. But when no one sauntered in,
it made my heart skip a beat.

"Ellis?" I called, making sure I'd turned the oven
off. And that my messy ponytail wasn't completely
covered in flour. Oh, who cared if it was?

I hurried down the hallway to the foyer and
dragged open my heavy front door.

"Matthew," I said, surprised.

The ghost of Major Matthew Jackson of the Union Army stood on my front porch, with his hands clasped in front of him, appearing almost shy. His image wavered and came into sharper focus. I could see the crisp lines of his uniform jacket, along with his high forehead and prominent cheekbones.

I'd met Matthew on my last adventure. Most of the time, I could only see ghosts when Frankie showed me the other side. But Matthew was one of the most powerful spirits I'd ever met, and he could appear to me on his own. He was also one of the more shy ones.

"Is everything all right?" I asked.

Major Jackson didn't get out much and I couldn't imagine what would bring him to my home.

He dipped his chin and glided straight through the glass storm door I'd neglected to open, his mind clearly elsewhere. I stepped back as he entered the foyer.

He stopped when he'd made it barely a few feet inside. "My sincerest apologies for intruding on your afternoon." He gave a formal bow, appearing somewhat awkward in his social skills, but clearly trying his best.

"It's quite all right," I assured him, gesturing him further inside as I closed the door. "My friends are always welcome. What can I do for you?" I didn't know the formalities involved in a late-nineteenth-century house call, and it's not like I could offer him a sherry, so we might as well cut to the chase. Still, I couldn't quite help myself from asking, "Would you like to sit in the back parlor?" just as my mother would have, and my grandmother before her.

Perhaps it was genetic.

He nodded and seemed more at ease with my formal response. I led him through my empty front room to the once-elegant sitting area in the back. The pink-papered walls and polished wood accents appeared so strange without the heirloom rugs and furniture the room had once held. Unfortunately, there wasn't much left besides a second-hand chessboard, a lopsided futon, and a purple couch I'd brought home after solving a ghost-related issue for a local merchant.

Matthew opted for a place on the couch while I tried to sit elegantly on the edge of the futon.

"I've come to ask a favor," he began earnestly.

Oh my. I crossed my legs at the ankles and sincerely hoped his favor didn't involve me opening myself to the spirit world. Yes, I'd been able to do a lot of good in the few times I'd ventured forth, but it had been scary and dangerous. Besides, I was a graphic designer, not a ghost whisperer.

As much as it pained me, I had to learn to start saying no.

Matthew cleared his throat. "I would like to locate a Christmas gift for Josephine."

"How sweet of you." I felt my shoulders relax. That didn't sound frightening or dangerous, and I was glad to see a relationship developing between the two ghosts. They'd reconnected during my last adventure. He'd been hurt and so very alone. She'd been shy and had suffered terrible luck with men—until that fateful night in the haunted woods. It had been rather romantic. "I'm sure Josephine would love anything you decide to give her, as long as it's from the heart."

Josephine cared about him for who he was, which was a rarity in Matthew's life. His own family had disowned him for joining the Union Army, and the local ghosts hadn't made him feel welcome in the afterlife for the same reason.

He glanced away before his gaze found mine. "She means everything to me," he said, with an urgency

most women only dreamed about. "That's why I
want to give her my mother's opal necklace. Before
the war — " he cleared his throat" — my mother said I
could have the necklace when I found the girl I wish
to marry."

"Oh, Matthew." I drew a hand to my chest. "You're
going to propose?"

"At Christmas," he said simply.

I felt myself go a little teary eyed for them, for that
perfect connection where you just knew. How wonderful for Josephine. She'd waited a hundred and fifty
years to be loved like that.

"I just need you to get me the necklace," Matthew
said.

I blinked back my tears. "What?"

He leaned forward, resting his elbows on his knees.
"It's at my family estate, now occupied by the seventh
generation of Jacksons."

Oh, I was familiar with the Jackson compound on
the edge of the county, with its twenty sprawling
acres and huge main house, occupied by his real, live
descendants, none of whom would be pleased if I
showed up and explained that the spirit of their great-
great-great-uncle needed a family heirloom, a jeweled
necklace for that matter, and I'd just be taking it...

"Why don't you go get it?" I suggested perkily.
Most spirits couldn't interact with the living world,
but Matthew's unusual strength made him an exception.

Like he hadn't thought of that.

Matthew's gaze dropped. "I can't," he said simply.
"My mother told me I could never go home. Not after
I signed my enlistment papers."

I wished I could hug him. "Oh, sweetie," I began.
"Are you sure that's not all in your mind?" It had to
be. I knew it was. But if he hadn't been able to get

over it for more than one hundred and fifty years, I didn't see how I could make it happen tonight in my parlor.

He stood abruptly. "I'm not part of the family anymore." His shoulders heaved. "She said so." He took two paces away from me, as if he couldn't even face me as he added, "She'd never let me in the front door and I don't think I could handle even trying."

"I understand," I said, coming to my feet. I wanted to help. I did. But, "I don't know what I can do."

"We could steal it," Frankie said from above my left shoulder. I jumped as the ghost shimmered into view next to me. Sometimes I think he did it for fun. "I can have us in and out of there in two minutes," he reasoned. "Five if they try to foil us with a cannonball safe."

"I can't steal an antique necklace," I balked.

"Don't worry," Frankie said, opening his hands, as if this were old hat. "I'll teach you how."

Learning how was not the issue. "You don't even know why we're doing this," I pointed out.

"Fun?" the gangster guessed.

Matthew turned to face us, clearly vexed by Frankie's questionable morals.

He'd better get used to it.

"There's no need for stealing," the late soldier insisted. "The necklace is rightfully mine. And it's on the ghostly plane, so none of my living relatives would even know."

That meant someone had died with it. "Does your mother have it?" I asked, taking a wild guess.

Matthew gave a slow, sad nod.

Frankie crossed his arms over his chest, frowning. "That's a lot less fun," he said, eyeing the other ghost, as if he'd let Frankie down. "I see where this is going."

So did I. Matthew wanted me to borrow Frankie's powers to see the other side, something I'd promised I wouldn't do again.

It wasn't only that I put myself in danger every time I opened myself to the ghostly plane, but I had to use Frankie's spirit energy to do it. The unnatural energy flow temporarily weakened him to the point of making parts of him disappear. Plus I used the opportunity to do nice things for other people.

Let's just say Frankie wasn't a fan.

"I don't believe my mother is a vengeful ghost," Matthew assured me. "Although I haven't spoken to her since I left to enlist. Even though she's angry with me, I don't think she'd go back on her word," he added hopefully.

Frankie eyed him up and down. "Anything else in her stash? Something to make it worth our while?"

"Frankie!" I protested. "We don't blackmail our guests."

"Technically," he said, holding up a finger, "it's extortion."

Hmm. "What if Matthew lends me his powers?" I asked. Then Frankie would be off the hook.

My guest drew back. "Oh, I most definitely could not," he said, as if I'd shocked him. "Josephine would be so very jealous."

Frankie huffed. "So this guy gets to have both a girlfriend and his powers."

He needed our help. I turned to Matthew. "How can we be sure your mother is still in her home?" She might have concluded her earthly business and gone to the light. And if that happened, she would have taken everything she'd died wearing with her, including the necklace.

Matthew strode to the old marble fireplace and rested a hand on the mantel next to Frankie's urn. "I still go home every Sunday. I watch my family from the yard. My mother still lives in that house."

Today was Sunday. "Did you check today?" Frankie pressed. He and I both knew ghosts weren't great at marking time.

Matthew turned to us. "I saw her through the window right before I came to you. She was upset. There were loud people pulling up in cars and vans. A party supply truck ran straight through me."

"That's right," I murmured. This was the last Sunday before Christmas. The Jackson family had been hosting their annual Christmas party on that same day every year for seven generations. "It's the day of the big party."

"It is." He lowered his eyes. "She was so busy with everyone else she didn't see me. She never sees me."

"I'll talk to her," I said quickly, and over Frankie's most inappropriate cursing. "Maybe I can get her to speak with you."

"No," Matthew said, clenching his hands at his sides, "I did the right thing. I'm not going to pretend otherwise or beg for her forgiveness. But I won't let her go back on her word about the necklace, either. Ask her for that. Please," he added, softening. "I have a new life now. That's all I want."

"Okay," I assured him. "I'll slip in tonight, during the party." Lord knew how, but I would.

"You think about asking me?" Frankie frowned.

"Yes, I did." I planted a hand on my hip. "Frankie, would you like to go to a legendary holiday party?" I could take him out of my house if I had his urn with me.

The gangster frowned. "It'll probably be full of stuffy society types."

"And ghostly ladies," I added cheerily. "I hear they love gangsters."

"I would be hard for them to resist," he agreed grudgingly.

"Then it's settled," I told him. We'd figure out a way into the Jackson's holiday party. We'd speak with the spirit of Matthew's mother.

I'd get the necklace for him and more. Somehow, I'd find a way to give the soldier an even better Christmas than he could imagine.

Chapter Two

It turned out our way onto the Jackson property was through my best friend, Lauralee.

She shot me a grin as we rattled through the tall front gates in her husband's beater truck. "I always said you'd be a great server given the right opportunity." The cranked-up heater tousled her wild auburn hair. "I'm so glad you decided to try it again."

I drew my bag closer to me, the one with Frankie's urn inside. "I promise I won't be too friendly," I told her, only half kidding. She knew full well how I'd been fired from the steakhouse in college for talking to the customers too much.

"I just can't believe I got this job," Lauralee gushed. "The Jacksons have always used the big catering service from their country club for the annual holiday party. Lucky for me, the club backed out at the last minute." She appeared positively giddy at the idea of proving herself. "I'm so relieved you were available to help."

Me too. "I'll do good," I told her. "I promise."

I couldn't let Lauralee down. This job meant too much to her. Plus, she didn't know a thing about my ghost-hunting abilities. It wasn't the sort of thing I could easily explain—or count on her to believe. Besides, I'd promised myself I wouldn't do it again.

Except for tonight.

She'd managed to slip me into a front-room server position, the kind I'd need if I were going to go looking for Matthew's long-dead mother. The money would be welcome as well. The least I could do was return the favor by being a bang-up worker bee when I wasn't ghost hunting.

"It'll be easy," she assured me. "I prep the appetizers in the back. You and the other servers put them on trays and give them out in the front."

I bit my lip. Before I started serving, I'd have to find a place to stash Frankie's urn. It's not like I could carry it on my appetizer tray.

Lauralee laughed. "Relax. You look almost scared."

"Concerned," I admitted as we traveled up the long driveway flanked by oak trees that had grown for generations. Their branches stretched over us, forming a canopy of naked, gnarled wood.

It must have been heartbreaking for Matthew to grow up in such a rustic, beautiful place and not be allowed back. If I'd lost my home like he did, I'd do anything for a chance to go home again. Especially for Christmas.

The house loomed ahead, a stately red brick manor with an elegant black iron two-story porch and a sharply curved circle drive clearly built for carriages instead of cars. This was nothing like the brand-new, faux-historic home of the Wydells, the other leading family in the county. I found it refreshing, if a bit dark and broody. If I recalled correctly, it had been built in the early 1800s, when the Jacksons began their iron-smelting dynasty. They'd added onto it over the years until it became this big, sprawling hulk of a building.

No telling how many ghosts lingered from seven-plus generations living and dying on the property. It would have been nice if Matthew had offered some guidance on where to look for his mother.

Frankie remained quiet and out of sight, hopefully saving his energy for our big night.

I reached down into my bag and rattled Frankie's urn a bit.

"Stop it," he groused. I turned and found him in the backseat of the cab. The corner of his mouth tipped up as he looked past me toward the house. "Get a load of that," he said, straightening. "Hot little number at five o'clock, rising up out of the ground and ready to party." He flashed me a grin. "This is her lucky night."

I raised my brows at him. Focus.

"Don't give me that look," he admonished, straightening his tie. "It has been far too long since I so much as danced with a dame." He pulled a flask out of his jacket pocket and gave it a small shake, as if to test how much booze he had left. Must have been enough because he grinned and took a long swig.

That was all fine and dandy, but, "I need to see the other side," I mouthed to him, twisting my features so he'd know I meant business.

"Relax," he snarled. "Geez-o-Pete. You got that same bug-eyed, grindy-mouth thing going that Suds's old lady used to give him when she'd catch us brewing gin in her washing machine. And you ain't my old lady." He slicked his hands through his hair, which never moved anyway. "You owe me this night out. And before you have puppies, I'll let you see my side of the fence. But that's all you get. After that, you're on your own. I'm going to party like it's 1929."

"Knock yourself out," I told him. Heaven knew Frankie wouldn't help if he didn't want to, so it wasn't a big loss to let him have an evening to himself.

Lauralee turned to me, her brow scrunched.

"What?"

"Just psyching myself up," I told her, ignoring the ghost spit-shining his shoes in the backseat as she pulled the truck around the side drive.

Several cars lined the parking area to the rear of the house. Lauralee ground the truck to a stop and shoved it into park. "You'll do great, as long as you stay focused."

She had no idea.

I stepped out of the cab as an unearthly energy settled over me. It prickled against my skin. I closed the truck door and tried not to fight the dull throb that worked its way through my muscles and bones. Frankie's power felt forbidden, unsettling. Other ghosts had told us we shouldn't be bending natural laws like this. But at the moment, I didn't have a choice — not if I wanted to help Matthew.

A gray, shadowy form took shape directly in front of us, on the stairs leading to the back entrance of the house. It was too small to be Matthew.

I watched as the shadow formed into the figure of a corseted woman in black. She appeared to be in her early twenties and wore a Civil War-era dress with a lace veil, which floated behind her. She gave us a long look before she walked straight through the red brick wall of the mansion.

"You see her eyeing me?" Frankie asked, straightening his tie. "I think I need to give her daddy something to worry about." He didn't wait for my answer. Instead, the ghost of the gangster simply disappeared. Well, that solved one problem.

I headed to the back of the truck to help Lauralee unload the food. We carried it up the back steps and into the kitchen from the staff entrance.

"Wow." I whistled as we entered the large, modern kitchen. It was done in whites and grays with sleek granite countertops and appliances. The space bustled with activity and smelled like a high-end restaurant. "Nice office."

"I know, right?" Lauralee said as we unloaded our food trays on the huge kitchen island. "I could get used to this."

Tall polished wood cabinets stretched up to the high ceilings and into the narrow butler's pantry sandwiched between the kitchen and the dining room. A counter ran down the right side of the room, with cabinets above and below to store dishes and entertaining supplies. Living, breathing, black-clad bartenders counted glassware under the watchful eye of a ghostly butler who stood directly behind them.

At least they had no idea they were being judged.

One of Lauralee's friends from the diner stacked trays of savory meat pastry puffs beside a tall double oven while another made shrimp cocktails in mini martini glasses garnished with fresh dill.

"What took you so long?" asked the redhead making desserts. "We're almost done with our assignments."

"That's how I planned it." Lauralee winked. "You both remember Verity."

We did a round of friendly greetings as the two women focused on their tasks. "Kim and Jen are serving after they finish with prep," Lauralee explained. "Mike and Steve work construction with my hubby, but both of them bartended in college."

The men in the butler's pantry grunted their hellos while hefting a large tub of ice out the swinging door and into the party area.

"You can put your purse under the table," Lauralee said, pointing to the personal items crowded underneath a dining table stacked with food service containers and serving trays. "And then help me unload the cold appetizers."

I left my purse with the heap of personal belongings under the table, but first I withdrew Frankie's urn. It was the only valuable thing in my simple hemp sack. If I lost it, well, I'd lose him. After a moment of consideration, I snuck it behind the trays on the table so no one would accidentally drop it.

One of the bartenders leaned in the door that separated the butler's pantry from the party. "Showtime," he said, rapping a hand on the edge of the door. The greetings and laughter of partygoers echoed behind him. "We've got guests arriving early."

"I got this," the redhead said, finished with her shrimp cocktail martini glasses. She grabbed a tray and began loading them up.

I took a tray from the table and moved to the center island to load deviled eggs with truffles, while the blonde handling the meat puff pastries took her hot-and-ready goodies over to the table and arranged her tray there.

All the while, I could hear the sounds from the party growing louder. We were suddenly behind and we hadn't even started yet.

"I get why you didn't worry about me talking," I said to Lauralee, who slid a platter of bacon-wrapped shrimp out of the bottom oven. "There's no time."

My friend grinned. "It's like a dance," she said, watching her two friends bustle toward the door while I worked harder on my half-loaded tray.

I glanced at them enviously, my admiration ending when I saw what the blonde carried on the center of her tray. Frankie's squat, copper urn perched in the middle of a grouping of mini beef Wellingtons.

"Why did she take that?" I thrust out a finger, pointing as the door swung closed behind her.

Lauralee glanced over her shoulder too late to get a

good look. "Centerpiece?" She was almost done with her tray. "Sometimes, clients leave things out for us to use."

"Not that." I gaped.

"Why?" Lauralee grinned. "Was it ugly?"

Not exactly. The green stones that circled the top were sort of pretty, but that wasn't the point. Although I couldn't quite figure out how to explain my shanghaied gangster and the dented copper urn to Lauralee.

"Keep moving," she reminded me gently.

"Right," I said. I needed to get out there before Frankie got a look at the blonde with the tray.

How did these people work so fast?

I loaded my deviled eggs as quickly as I could. I had to get out there and get Frankie's urn back. The last of his ashes — the only ones I hadn't rinsed away — were inside that urn. If they were spilled or lost, I'd never be able to take him out of my house again.

We'd both go bonkers.

When I had filled my tray, I plastered on my best, most waitress-worthy smile and hefted my holiday appetizers. "I'm going in."

With any luck, I'd locate Frankie's urn, speak to Matthew's mother, retrieve the necklace, and please all the party guests in one trip. Stranger things had happened, right?

Just then, a tray crashed to the floor outside and I heard something shatter.

The ringing echo made us cringe.

Oh no.

Frankie! I rushed for the door, and when I reached it, I nearly ran smack into the redhead coming the other way.

The door swung closed behind her. "It's not my fault."

"You dropped your tray?" I demanded.

"Yes." The redhead touched a shaking hand to her forehead. "Some joker in the parlor hit me between the shoulder blades with an ice cube. Shocked the heck out of me."

At least it wasn't the blonde. I swung the door open with my hand and searched the dining room for the wayward waitress with the urn amid her appetizers, but I didn't spot her among the glittering society folk.

Meanwhile Lauralee took the ruined tray and placed an arm around her friend's shoulder. "What a jerk. Are you okay, Jen?"

"Yes," the redhead said, rallying. "I'm a pro. I'm fine." She reached for a tray of bacon-wrapped shrimp. "Mike is cleaning up," she said, heading past me out the door.

At least Frankie was okay for now.

As if he knew I was thinking about him, the gangster shimmered into view directly in front of me, blocking my path. He held his flask in one hand and a cigarette in the other. I would have hugged him if I could, even though he stood frowning. "This ain't no party. It's a funeral." He pointed the end of his cigarette at me. "You owe me the real McCoy."

Ah, he must have struck out with the young woman we'd seen earlier. I scooted around him and peered out through the swinging door. Only a few ghostly guests stood in the dining room, speaking in hushed tones. They did seem a bit older and stuffy, but that wasn't my fault. "I'm sorry this isn't your sort of crowd. But try to make the most of it, okay?" You could bring a gangster to a party, but you couldn't make him enjoy it.

Frankie followed me and my deviled eggs out into the large, ornate dining room. When I had Frankie's power, I could see things as the dominant ghost residing on the property did. This dining room appeared Victorian, with a fire blazing in the hearth, and the current generation of Sugarland's upper crust conversing in groups. An antique table stood at the center of the room, and over it hung a ghostly chandelier with dozens of blazing candles. It made the jewels worn by the real guests glitter.

These were the types of parties I used to attend with my ex, before the scandal that had left me an outsider in my own town.

I paused as an older man in a reindeer bowtie winked at me and took a deviled egg from my tray.

Frankie stood next to him. "I tried to work that cute skirt we saw before. Found her in the parlor," he said, as if I wasn't busy working. "She's got that whole Southern belle thing going on. But she only had eyes for some dead guy."

I hesitated to point out the obvious.

"Have you seen Matthew's mother?" I murmured, advancing through the crowd.

Frankie took a drag from his cigarette. "Yeah, and I knew it was her because she's wearing a name tag."

I heard another crash, this time from the direction of the front hall. I tried to keep my own tray balanced as I rushed to see what happened.

The redhead knelt at the entrance to the parlor, frantically scooping up bacon-wrapped shrimp. I hurried to help her.

The guests had shrunk back from the mess, but make no mistake, our fumbled trays were the talk of the party. At this point, I feared more food had ended up on the floor than with the guests.

"Somebody tripped me," she whispered frantically as I knelt down beside her. "I swear!"

Her friend walked out of the parlor, with Frankie's urn teetering at the center of her half-filled tray. The gangster glared at his last resting place, then at me as if I were responsible for him becoming a centerpiece. "That dame lifted my urn!"

"What do you expect me to do?" I hissed.

Frankie didn't hesitate. "Shoot her."

Luckily, the redhead and the blonde were too worried about the mess to notice me and my not-so-friendly ghost.

"I'll help you two in a second," Frankie's urn-napper said, maneuvering around the mess. She leaned down. "They're complaining that the food is cold," she said in a harsh whisper before heading for the kitchen.

"I'm on you like a tick, lady!" Frankie gnashed, following her.

Oh, heavens. He'd better not appear to her.

Quickly, I gave the redhead my deviled eggs and took the ruined shrimp tray. I hurried after the blonde and Frankie and the urn.

Excerpt from
GHOST OF A CHANCE
Part of the A LITTLE NIGHT MAGIC anthology
by Angie Fox
Available Now!

About the Author

New York Times bestselling author Angie Fox writes sweet, fun, action-packed mysteries. Her characters are clever and fearless, but in real life, Angie is afraid of basements, bees, going up stairs when it's dark behind her.

Angie earned a Journalism degree from the University of Missouri. During that time, she also skipped class for an entire week so she could read Anne Rice's vampire series straight through. Angie has always loved books and is shocked, honored and tickled pink that she now gets to write books for a living. Although, she did skip writing for a week this past fall so she could read Victoria Laurie's Abby Cooper psychic eye mysteries straight through.

Angie makes her home in St. Louis, Missouri with a football-addicted husband, two kids, and Moxie the dog.

If you are interested in receiving an email each time Angie releases a new book, just go to www.angiefox.com. Sign up is in the upper right corner of the page.

Emails only go out for new releases and your information is kept safe by a specially trained guard skunk.

Made in the USA
Middletown, DE
12 October 2017